HBIC:
Head Bitch In Charge
A SERIES

Volume I
(Parts 1 & 2)

A Caroline McGill Exclusive

Synergy ✚ Publications

P.O. Box 210-987
Brooklyn, NY 11221

www.SynergyPublications.com

Synergy ✚ Publications
Books you can't put down!

HBIC: Head Bitch In Charge
© 2012 by Caroline McGill

ISBN: 978-0-9752980-9-1
Library of Congress Control Number: 2012939167

Cover by: Davida Baldwin

Edited by: Laurie Vaceannie

www.SynergyPublications.com

Printed in Canada

This is for my sisters,

Keya, Connie, and Ki

We did it big, girls.

And we did it hard... Our way.

Time can't erase where we been.

Author's Note

Giving honor to God above all else, I humbly thank Him first. My destiny is in your hands, God, but thanks for giving me the mindset to accomplish my dreams. I know it's been quite a journey, Lord, but thank you for loving me patiently and unconditionally.

Mommy, you are truly a class act. Your love is the overwhelming kind. It's indescribable. Pop, I remember those proverbs and bible scriptures you taught us well. They got me through some really dark places in life.

To all my friends and family, if you're reading this, you already know by now... To my baby brother, Carnell AKA Khalid AKA Casino, I told you once that you were my hero. You still are.

To my diehard readers, there are too many of you to thank individually but just know that you are the reason I do this book thing. It's been a long road from day one in this game until now, but you have stood with me through it all and supported my movement. I'm oftentimes choked up by your phone calls and messages demanding new books. You guys give me reason.

Justin "Amen" Floyd, I know you got my back. Mack Mama, much success, sis. K'wan, Treasure Blue, and JaQuavis, thanks for the black cover blurbs. (((HUGS))) Thanks Seriously Sensual Radio. HUGE SHOUT OUT to my peoples in the penitentiary. I see y'all and I got y'all.

Now I gotta shout out some of my favorite teams who have been supporting me and holding me down throughout my journey. Book clubs, I SEE Y'ALL. Much love to O.O.S.A. and ARC, Coast to Coast, Readers R Us, Black Faithful Sisters and Brothers, My Urban Books Club,

Diamond Eyes Book Club, my Nookies in Nook Lovers, Nook and Kindle Readers, DSP (Diamond Studded Publications), We Read Urban Fiction, and so many more!

What up, Facebook family?!?! Hey Twitter-heads!!! To ALL my very good friends who have been interacting with me throughout social media, there are thousands of you so we'll be here all day if I start naming y'all individually, but I certainly appreciate the love. I stay up all night long reading your posts and comments, and I look forward to it more than y'all know. Thanks for reppin' Caroline McGill.

That being said, I'm excited to be here again to debut another blazing series featuring characters I am confident you will all fall in love with, just as you fell in love with the cast from my phenomenal "A Dollar Outta Fifteen Cent" series. The interesting thing about this one is that the colorful "HBIC" series is based on my actual experiences. I look forward to discussing the details once you're done reading. I'm sure there will be lots of questions. (LOL) But my life is an open book so I don't mind.

Ladies, there is an HBIC in each of us. It's that super woman inside of us that just won't quit. From the single mom on a shoestring budget but handling her business and taking care of hers, to the entrepreneurs and corporate sisters on the rise - we're ALL bosses in our own right. Independent sisters around the globe, after reading this, HBIC will be our new anthem. HBICs, stand up and pump your fists in the air! And then put your big girl panties on because this series gets serious. Look out for the new HBIC tee-shirts too, girls. They're a must-have!

I sincerely love each and every person reading this right now. If you feel like I forgot you, I apologize, darling. Just write your name across my heart.

Happy reading, family! (((HUGS))) & Smooches!

"For what shall it profit a man,

if he shall gain the whole world,

and lose his own soul?"

Mark 8:36

Prologue

1981
Brooklyn, NY

In a crowded Brooklyn church in the heart of Bedford-Stuyvesant, a young woman sat at a piano pounding on the keys and directing three little girls with the voices of angels. The young woman was especially proud because the singing cherubs belonged to her. Her daughters, Etta, Elaine, and Elle were just ten, eight, and five years old. "The Mitchell Sisters" were singing their little hearts out and making a joyful noise unto the Lord. They had the church rocking to their rendition of the old gospel favorite, "Trouble In My Way."

"Trouble in my way (trouble in my way) I have to cry sometimes (I have to cry sometimes) So much trouble (trouble in my way) I have to cry sometimes (I have to cry sometimes) I lay awake at night - but that's alright (That's alright) Because I know my Jesus (Jesus, he will fix it) I know my Jesus (Jesus he will fix it) After while ..."

The little girls' father, Elliot Mitchell, was proud and choked up by his big voiced babies. He sat in the third pew clapping along with the rest of the congregation. Elliot was a goodhearted gentleman who was a big dreamer. He had huge ideas of making his daughters stars. God had blessed him with those girls, so he had the makings of a successful gospel group. He wanted his girls to sing for God. He also wanted

to capitalize off their talent. He didn't see anything wrong with wanting to make a better way for his family.

Elliot glanced over at his wife, Ellen, who was signaling their daughters to cut the song. Their big voiced eight-year-old, little Miss Elaine Twyla, was singing lead. When she got into the groove she hated to turn the microphone loose. Elliot caught his wife's eye, and they smiled at each other. Their girls were born to sing.

Elliot was the type of man who was driven by his ideas and unafraid to put them into effect. That was why his family had something. At just twenty-eight years of age, he owned the 4-story building his family resided in, as well as a business on the same street.

He and Ellen were in love and they were a match made in heaven. Both were from the same small town in North Carolina. Elliot courted Ellen at age fourteen, and they remained high school sweethearts who later got married the year they turned eighteen. Ellen was a southern bell who had the class and style of Jackie Onassis. She believed in her man and followed him to New York City, where he promised to take care of her like she was the First Lady. They purchased their first house at nineteen, and she gave birth to their first daughter, Etta, at twenty.

Elliot adored Ellen. He owed her his life because to some extent, she had saved him. He was from a family of hustlers. They were about money so education wasn't necessarily a priority. His mother, Sadie, sold bootleg liquor all night to support them when his father went out and got drunk and spent all the money earned from their puck wood business on other women. So she slept late some mornings. If he and his brothers hadn't gotten themselves up for school some days, they would have never gotten there on time.

As Elliot got older, he got wrapped up in the nightlife and hustle and bustle of his family's activities. There were juke joints and liquor houses along the roadside in his community. They were owned by his aunts and uncles, who had reputations so feared folks dubbed their community Little Korea, comparing it to The Korean War fought in the early 1950's. But they couldn't get enough of it. Folks came

from afar to indulge in the mischief Little Korea had to offer, so there was action going on all night.

Elliot often kept late hours and had the luxury of deciding whether or not he wanted to attend school. But Ellen was so pretty and sweet, he went as much as he could. He'd been smitten with her ever since seventh grade. She was the main reason he went to school everyday. And his fear of being rejected by her and labeled a dummy made him study hard to impress her with his intelligence. She was smart and seemed to get good grades effortlessly. Trying to impress her had motivated him to finish school.

They graduated from high school in May, 1968 and got married that December on Christmas Eve. A few months later, they picked up and moved to New York City. They tried living in Queens, but later settled in the borough of Brooklyn.

After Dr. King was assassinated in 1968, angry Blacks were determined to tear down the establishment so they vandalized, looted, and burned cities across the country. Brooklyn was no exception. Some of its neighborhoods suffered vastly. As a result, Whites began to relocate. Property values declined drastically, allowing Elliot to purchase his first house for a little more than a dollar and a dream.

Now all these years later, he and his wife were well respected pillars in their community. Ellen played the piano in church and directed the choir. She was his better half and she was a great mom to his daughters.

They had three girls but Elliot vowed that they would all be like him. He grew up with six brothers so he didn't really know how to be gentle. He often made his girls wrestle and tussle like boys. And he had big plans for them. He envisioned that they would all be women of power and head their own empires one day. They would be in charge, no matter what society said about women being unequal. The year was 1981, and times were changing.

Chapter 1

1991
Ten years later…

As Twyla dipped through the Manhattan bound traffic on the FDR Drive, she glimpsed over at the hundreds of cars in the oncoming traffic on the southbound side. Relieved that her side was flowing well, she looked over at her younger sister in the passenger seat. Elle's barely sixteen-year-old eyes were lit up with excitement. She thought she was pretty hot shit right about then.

She was on her way to do her very first run. Acting as a traveling student, Elle would be boarding an Amtrak train from New York City to Baltimore with a suitcase filled with heroin and everything necessary to prepare it for street distribution. The drug paraphernalia she carried ranged from bags to cutting agents. Elle was what the law would call a "drug mule" in the making.

Drug trafficking was commonplace for Elle and Twyla's demographic. It was quite a popular occupation. Lots of young African American women in their neighborhood made a living carrying work out of town for drug dealers who were aspiring for wealth and power. The reason the job paid so well was because the police usually suspected that inner-city, young, Black men were up to no good. They were frequently harassed and subjected to random searches. So using females to transport the product was the safest way for those migrating to rural parts of America attempting to lock down townships with high demand for New York City narcotics. A lot of dudes got

jammed up trying to move shit. It was just easier to pay a girl to take it on the bus or train.

Full of big sisterly concern, Twyla sighed, "Girl, I hope you know what you doing. Yo' ass better be careful. You playing some real big girl games now, baby sis. That nigga Knight got you doing all this crazy shit all of a sudden. Lady and Pop gon' kick yo' ass."

Elle grinned at her sister, who was almost three years her senior. If the two were the same shade of brown they would have probably been mirror images. Elle's milk chocolate complexion was a few shades darker than Twyla's caramel, and she was a few inches taller and a little thicker. But their facial features were almost identical. Their oldest sister Etta was light skinned, taller, and slimmer, but she looked just like them too. They all had paisley shaped eyes and perfect noses with full luscious lips and shoulder length hair. They were pretty young ladies who were often the target of envy from other neighborhood girls. The fact that their family owned a house and a business didn't help. The sisters had to fight a lot growing up.

Elle knew their parents would be upset about her endeavors. They had split up about three years before but they still shared the parenting process equally. "Elaine Twyla Mitchell, will you please quit?"

Twyla frowned at Elle. She hated to be called by her whole name.

Elle laughed, and continued. "Sis, I can only get in trouble if Pop and Lady find out. I'm okay! Don't worry, I'll be back in like two days. Just cover for me. I lied and said I was staying the weekend at Madison's."

Twyla nodded slowly. Her baby sister was growing up. She thought about forbidding Elle to go but she didn't want to be a hypocrite. Her respect for the game wouldn't allow her to. She was Elle's age when she started doing runs for her daughter's father, Bilal. Back then, Elle used to see her coming home from out of town with expensive designer gear and money. Twyla used to take her and their baby brother, Junior, shopping with that money. She had spoiled

Elle, so it was partially her fault. She wanted to be like her. Her little sister looked up to her.

The crazy part of it was that Elle was an honor student. She was enrolled in a specialized high school you had to pass a citywide test to get into. When it came to books, she was the smartest sister of the three of them. Twyla and Etta both proudly acknowledged that. Their baby sister had been a bookworm most of her life but she was hot in the ass now. Girlfriend was having sex and you couldn't tell her anything. She had hooked up with Knight, this gangsta ass nigga who was everything she should've avoided. He was a well known hustler who Twyla knew for a fact was a murderer. And Elle was smitten with him.

Knight's right-hand man was a guy named Rude. Rude was another bad boy boss who Twyla happened to have a little history with. He grew up across the street from them, so they played together when they were small. He asked her to be his girlfriend when they were eleven. It didn't stand the test of time but she still cared about him. She also knew how ruthless he was. Knight was the same way, so Twyla wasn't thrilled that he had hooked up with her little sister. She didn't really approve, but what could she say? Her boyfriends were cut from the same cloth. She had always dated drug dealers and killers. She guessed her baby sister had looked up to that too.

Elle was a good girl so she knew better than to associate with the likes. So did Twyla. They had been raised in the church by devout Christian parents. Their mother played the piano and directed the choir they were brought up singing in.

Twyla sighed again. Elle had grown up too fast. It seemed like just yesterday she was running behind her threatening to tell that she was sneaking out of the house. Twyla had been kind of fast when she was younger. She had a baby at sixteen and grew up quick.

When they got to Penn Station, Twyla thought about forbidding Elle to go again. In actuality, she could pull rank if she wanted to. She was older, and had always had the leverage of their parents' permission to discipline Elle when

she got out of line. Twyla could be a bitch when she wanted to, but she held her tongue.

Elle kissed her on the cheek and grabbed her bags. Twyla ignored the little voice in her head and prayed she wasn't making a mistake. Elle promised her she'd be careful, and stuck the paperback she'd been reading in the side of her tote. She hopped out and hurried inside Penn Station. Twyla whispered another prayer for her safety and pulled off.

Elle already had her ticket so she headed straight for her train. On her way, she saw two cops ahead of her. Her heart rate tripled at first. They didn't seem to be paying her any mind so she kept on going. Elle had her hair pulled back in a bun and she was wearing black spectacles. In the blazer and high heels she donned, she looked like a young college woman.

She boarded the train just in time. In the process she almost tripped over the foot of a handsome, long legged passenger. He sat up and apologized like a gentleman. Their eyes locked for a moment. Elle just blushed and kept it moving. The brother had nice sideburns and a memorable face.

After she settled in a seat, she relaxed and thought about her boo, Knight. At 21, he was almost six years older than she was. He was intelligent, handsome, and hardcore. The combination of those elements was the sexiest thing she had ever encountered. She was completely gone over him.

One of the things she loved about him the most was the way he was always encouraging her to get an education. He said he wanted her to become a lawyer so she could defend him if he ever got into trouble. Elle took that as his way of saying he was in it for the long run. She was young at the time so she figured it didn't get any better. He was thorough and he had money and brains. And she knew he was authentic because she had seen him at work. She thought back to an incident that happened when she was just twelve years old.

One lovely day in late spring, Elle was sitting out in front of her house talking to her friend Monifah. They were

*just coming from downtown Brooklyn, where they had gone
to purchase the new Polo sandals everyone was raving about
that season. The girls were feeling themselves and discussing
what outfits they would wear to school the following day.*

*A shiny brand new black Mercedes turned the corner
of their block thumping loud music. The visibly expensive car
was trimmed in gold; its hood ornament, door handles, rims
and all. The driver of the black and gold Benz slowed down
and stopped across the street in front of Monifah's building.*

*This dude named Malcolm, better known as Rude,
lived in that building too. Rude was a young hustler on the
come up. The driver of the Benz was clearly an acquaintance
of his because he came downstairs to have a word with him.
Rude was dressed in an Italian smoker's jacket over a pair of
designer jeans and expensive slippers. He had a cigar in his
mouth, and looked like a real mafia gangster.*

*He and the driver, a Puerto Rican dude named Tito,
exchanged daps and smiled at one another. Jovially shaking
hands, they appeared to be comrades to the naked eye. As
Elle and Monifah watched the young men conversing, they
whispered to each other about the rumors they had heard.
Monifah knew a lot of stuff because her family lived right
next door to Rude's. She said she could even hear his
telephone conversations through the walls sometimes.*

*Just then, these two cute guys turned the corner and
started walking down the block towards them. Elle
recognized one of them. He was a guy who went to school
with her older sister Etta. He winked at Elle when they
passed them, indicating that he recognized her too. She
grinned from ear to ear, overwhelmed at the notion of an
older guy noticing her. She was only twelve, and he had to
be like seventeen. That made Elle's day. It even topped
getting those Polo sandals. He was so cute! And he and his
friend were wearing these big gold chains just like the ones
rappers sported in their videos. Elle was awestruck. Her
underage curiosity peaked.*

*Monifah had seen that wink he gave Elle so they
giggled together about it. Then they noticed the guys stopped
about four houses down from them. They appeared to be*

engrossed in a conversation with one another. Elle was naïve and under the impression that they had stopped because they were contemplating coming back to talk to them. She got nervous because her father was across the street inside their family business, which was a supper club. If her father saw her talking to a boy that age, Elle knew she would get in trouble.

Meanwhile, Rude was still across the street talking to Tito with the Benz, who had stepped out of his car to speak with him. Laughing like old buddies, the young men said goodbye to each other and parted ways. Rude headed back inside his building and Tito opened his car door to get in.

Before he could get inside the car, the two rope chain wearing cuties crossed the street and approached him. The three of them exchanged a few words. Elle and Monifah stared on, under the impression that they were all cronies as well. They had to be because Tito smiled when he saw them. Suddenly, the men appeared to be scuffling. The next thing the girls knew, shots rang out.

The neighborhood had recently become a drug warzone, so crime was at its peak. There had been lots of random shootings lately. It seemed like they had to run from gunshots every other day, so they already knew the protocol. Elle and Monifah saw Tito fall to the ground, and quickly dipped inside her hallway. They slammed the door closed and ran up the stairs.

They ran up to Elle's third floor bedroom and peeked out the window. The big chain wearing cuties were gone and Tito was sprawled on the ground bleeding in the street. They had robbed him and shot him.

The girls heard sirens, and then it seemed like everybody on the block was outside. Elle's father, Elliot, was one of the first people out there. He was joined by lots of their neighbors. Seconds later, the ambulance got there, followed by a fleet of police cars.

Elle saw her sister Twyla's boyfriend at the time, Bilal, pull up out there in his Audi. He shook his head and looked real sad when he learned what had happened. Puerto

Rican Tito was a good dude who happened to be a friend of his. Tito was good-natured and cool with everybody.

Bilal was in the money taking game. He was in the streets heavy, so he knew what was up. Elle later learned from Twyla that Bilal told her Rude had set Tito up. He had called him over so they could conduct a business exchange, and then he called his friends and told them when he was coming. They had pretty much taken it from there.

Sadly, Tito later succumbed to his injuries. There were two detectives on the case who were disturbed by the violence and determined to make an arrest. They went from house to house knocking on doors trying to get someone to talk. The day they came over Elle's house, no one was at home but her and her older sister Etta. They were good girls who were somewhat sheltered since they had grown up in the church. So not knowing any better, they let them in.

The detectives told Elle and Etta the truth. They were looking for the men that killed George "Tito" Ruiz. They had three thick books full of mug shots of young men; mostly Black. They patiently thumbed through the pages with the girls and tried to get them to finger someone involved. Etta wasn't there when it happened but Elle knew exactly who the killers were.

She and Etta looked through the pictures, more amused than anything. It was exciting to them. Elle saw one of the guys' mug shots and Etta recognized a few of her classmates and some other boys her age from the neighborhood, but neither of them told the detectives anything.

The detectives left but they came back again another day and went through the same process. Still, the girls told them nothing. The detectives knew Elle was outside that day so they were convinced she could help them.

They returned a third time with more books full of mug shots. That time their father, Elliot, was at home. When the cops showed up at their door he went downstairs and started screaming on them, purposely making a huge public display. He yelled at the police so all the neighbors could hear. He told them to get the hell away from his damn door

and quit bothering his children. He lied and said he sent the girls down south, and warned them to never come back to his house again.

Elle stood at the top of the stairs listening, and was pretty confused. Her father was a church going man who she knew believed murder was wrong. He had drilled the Ten Commandments in her and her sisters' heads when they were small. So why had he chased off the police with all those lies? She hadn't planned on telling them anything anyway. For some reason she was just fascinated by thumbing through those mug shots. She had gotten a little peek at crime, and her young eyes were excited by its premise.

When their father came back upstairs, she asked him why he had chased the police off like that. Elliot looked at his inquisitive bright-eyed little girl who he was so proud of. Elle was a smart girl, and always asked questions. She was a Virgo like him, and had a lot of his ways. That day he was forced to tell her how things worked in the streets. He told her that even though killing was bad, a person living in their neighborhood couldn't tell the police about the things they witnessed because the people you told on knew where you and your family lived, and would more often than not come back and retaliate. He said he ran off the police because he wanted to keep her and the rest of their family safe and out of harm's way.

They had a neighbor, an African lady name Mazelle, who had been talking to the police too. The day before, her apartment door was shot up by some thugs. She got the message and shut her mouth after that. She also started looking for a new place. Elliot reminded Elle that he was a businessman and homeowner, and said he wasn't prepared to pick up his family and relocate. He told her he also didn't want to get into a street war with any of those knucklehead little drug dealers. He said he would kill one of those crazy ass young boys if he had to, so it was best they just mind their business. He had seen most of those punks grow up, and knew lots of their parents. Elle told her father she understood, and promised him she would never talk to the

police again.

Elliot was saddened by the reality of the situation but proud of her for understanding nonetheless. He hugged her and told her he loved her. That was Elle's first lesson on the street code. Talking to the police could get your whole family killed.

Elle snapped out of her daydream and pulled out her paperback so she could read a little bit. She thumbed through the pages of the Terry McMillan novel to find the place she'd stopped at. She got through about two chapters before her mind drifted back to Knight. She thought about their second encounter. It was three years after that incident happened when she was twelve. She closed her eyes and replayed it in her mind.

She was walking home from the train station after a day at high school when she spotted him just a few feet ahead of her. It was the guy with the big gold chain, who'd winked at her when she was twelve; just minutes before he'd crossed the street and murdered a man in cold blood. Her plan was to walk pass him nonchalantly but their eyes locked momentarily. Elle tried not to blush. He gave her an interested look and beckoned her over.

She approached him with her around-the-way-girl coolness, which was natural for a Brooklyn girl like her. He grinned, revealing the cutest dimples she had ever seen. His hair was freshly cut in a fade with a part on the side, and he wore a denim Polo jacket over a Polo sweater, some jeans, and 40 Below Timberlands. He was the epitome of the "it" guy at the time.

He introduced himself as Knight, and told her he liked her hairstyle. He said it looked cute on her. Elle blushed and thanked him. She told him her sister had done it.

Knight scratched his chin. "I know you, shorty. You Etta and Twyla lil' sister, right?"

Elle placed her hand on her hip and got sassy with him. "I'm their sister, but I ain't little. In case you haven't noticed."

He gave her a surprised look. "Oh, word? You a big girl, huh?"

She gave him the flirty eyes. "Yes, I am. And my name is Elle."

"So what that "L" stand for?"

Elle smiled because she got that all the time. "Not the letter L, the word. Elle, like the fashion magazine." She spelled it for him. "E-l-l-e."

He nodded his head. "Elle."

"That's what I said, boo."

He grinned. "I like that."

"Yeah? You like saying my name?"

He fought back a smile. "Yeah."

"So say it again," she dared.

She had his hardcore ass smiling after that. "Elle."

She grinned back at him, and then they both laughed together. She was easygoing, and he liked that. She was just as easy on the eyes. He thought about pressing her for the digits, but opted to give her his pager number instead.

Knight was from the projects around the corner from Elle's house, Lafayette Gardens, also known as L.G. The reason she hadn't seen him around lately was because he had been incarcerated for a few years. They chatted briefly and then agreed to keep in touch. When Elle walked away she switched her ass extra hard to impress him.

It worked. He called her back as soon as she paged him that evening. Her mother wasn't home, so he stopped by. Her parents had split up a few years ago, so her dad now lived around the corner. They just talked outside in front of her house for a little while. After that, Knight told her to go upstairs and make sure her homework was done. She didn't know what to think after that. He was treating her like a little kid.

They continued like that for about three weeks. Then he started coming inside. Almost every night, whenever he was in town. Her mother worked second shift and didn't get home until after midnight, and Elle's older sisters were hardly ever home. Knight won her little brother, Junior, over by always giving him money, so nobody told on her.

Elle thought they were evolving into something but

Knight was treating her more like a little sister than a girl he wanted to get with. And on top of that, she was hearing things in the street about him dealing with this Puerto Rican girl named Michelle, who went to school with Twyla. She was older but Elle figured she could love him better.

One day she got fed up and decided to approach the issue. She paged Knight and told him she needed to talk to him. He told her he had to take care of something but he would see her later.

For the next two hours, Elle practiced exactly what she would say to him. But when he came through she forgot all that hot shit. Instead, she approached him with child-like honesty. She told him how much she liked him, and said she didn't understand why he acted like he didn't like her back. She asked him why he was always talking about homework and shit.

He laughed, and told her he liked her too. He said she was his little girlfriend but he was waiting until she was legal. He earnestly said he was the wrong type of guy for her, and wanted her to focus on finishing school. Elle told him she could do two things at once. She could be his girl and go to school too.

He laughed and asked her if she was sure she was ready for that. She looked at him like she was. She was pretty bold for a fifteen-year-old. He smacked her on the butt and sent her back upstairs.

Elle asked him for a hug before he left. He held her close and kissed her lips gently. After that, she was on fire. She wanted to give it to that nigga bad as hell. Contrary to what he seemed to believe, she wasn't a virgin. She had been with two guys before, but she was smart enough to use protection.

Two days later, it was Friday. That night Knight picked her up in his BMW and they went on their first date. He took her to this seafood restaurant called Sizzler. Elle was elated. Afterwards, they got a hotel room. That night they made love for the first time. She couldn't just say they had sex because it was really beautiful. He kissed her from head to toe, and nibbled her in places she had never

imagined. Elle had already experienced having her pussy eaten by boyfriend number two, but no one had ever made her feel the way Knight did. He loved her like a grown ass man. She was open.

Elle stayed out with him all night, and then she went home the next morning floating on cloud nine. She told her sisters and her homegirls that she and Knight were now an item.

Her new relationship had a few of her friends looking real sour faced. Knight was a well-known baller so they were sick. The envy was evident because every time he came around, one of those tramps would start flirting with him. Elle didn't like it at all but she just looked at it as friendly competition. She had him already so they could kick rocks.

She started getting so attached to Knight. All she wanted to do was ride for him. But he kept her in her lane as much as he could. He stressed that she maintain good grades and stay in school. A few times she overheard him talking to other girls on the phone, but he always told her it was business related. Elle hated the fact that he dealt with other bitches that he said handled certain business for him. She quietly resented this because she didn't want to nag.

So now she had finally convinced him that she was ready. She was Baltimore bound on that Amtrak train because she wanted to hold her man down. Elle was excited about the idea of getting to see what Knight did out of town. He was always out of town, so if she took him the stuff he needed, she could see him more.

When she got there, she winded up being very disappointed because he didn't stay with her for more than two hours during the two whole days she was there. He told her he was really busy taking care of business. When she pouted, he reminded her that he was out of town working, not vacationing.

Knight gave her five hundred dollars for the run, plus money for her train ticket and cab fare, and then he told her he would see her back in New York. Elle was so hurt she

actually shed a few tears. She didn't let him see her cry but she returned home heavy hearted.

Chapter 2

"Good morning, sunshine!!!" Etta opened the curtains and let the light shine in her baby sister's face.

Elle threw up her arm to shield the unwelcome sunlight. She growled, "Close that damn curtain and get out!" Etta got on her nerves with that perky shit. She was a morning person like their mother. Elle was definitely not.

Her older sister was only amused by her cranky disposition. Etta laughed, "Girl, get your ass up!" She placed her hand on her hip and got stern with Elle. "Twyla told me you went outta town for Knight, with your *hot ass*! Did I give you permission to be running to some damn Baltimore? I ought to tear your grown behind up!"

Elle came to terms with the fact that she wasn't going to be able to go back to sleep, and sighed. "Oh boy, here we go ..." Damn, Twyla had loose lips. She couldn't keep her mouth shut for nothing.

Etta was the tall redbone version of Elle. At twenty-one, she was the oldest sister of the three. She stood over Elle frowning at her. "Did you ask me if you could go, Fast Ass?"

Elle sighed, "No, Etta, I didn't. 'Cause I knew you would say no."

"I sure would've. I *should* tell Mommy."

"Don't tell Lady that, sis."

Just then, Elle's little nieces came running in the room and jumped up on her bed.

"Hey Auntie!" they said in unison. They were both adorable. She hugged them and tickled them a bit. They giggled uncontrollably and loved it.

Janae, Twyla's baby, was almost three-years-old.

Micha, Etta's daughter, had just turned two. They were nine months apart and their nicknames were Nay-Nay and Mimi. They were both adorable and spoiled by the whole family.

Etta was in a relationship with her daughter's father so she was the homebody of the three. She kept Nay-Nay for Twyla most of the time because their daughters were like sisters. Their babies looked alike too. And a lot of times they dressed them alike, so the resemblance was sometimes startling. People often assumed they were both Etta's.

Elle and Etta's eight-year-old little brother, Elliot Jr. came walking in Elle's bedroom next. He had a stern look on his face and was brandishing a thick leather belt. Junior demanded answers immediately.

"Where the heck were you the last few days, Elle? You think you grown? I should tear your behind up with this belt!"

Elle stared at her kid brother in disbelief. She had to laugh. Etta started cracking up too. Junior really thought he was their father sometimes. He was the only boy, and he had been a bossy natured kid who demanded respect ever since he came in the world.

"Boy, *I'm* older than *you*," Elle reminded him. "You better go put that belt down somewhere. Come gimme a hug, with your big head self."

Junior smiled mischievously and walked over open-armed for a hug. When he got to Elle he hugged her tight, and then threw her in a headlock. Laughing, the siblings began tussling. Junior was like a Pit Bull that wouldn't let up. That little devil loved to fight. Out of breath, Elle gave in and declared him the winner.

Their little nieces tried to help her by attacking their young uncle with blows across his back. Junior knocked them off of him and chased them out of the room with the belt. The pretty little toddlers ran off hollering and squealing in fright and delight. Elle and Etta were both laughing out tears. Their little brother was a mess. He thought he was the boss of everybody.

After the kids were gone, Etta got back to the lecture at hand. She sat on the foot of Elle's bed and looked in her sister's eyes like she was trying to read her mind.

"Elle, what is with you lately? What you doing taking some mess outta town for some Knight? That is a *grown man*, so you ain't even got no business messing with him!"

Elle rolled her eyes. "I got paid to do it. If you shut up, I'll give you some money."

Etta made a face at her and narrowed her eyes. "How much?"

Elle shrugged. "Twenty dollars."

Etta rolled her eyes. "Since you think I can be bought, you gon' pay more. Gimme forty, heifer!"

Elle laughed. "Okay, but that's it! I gotta buy some stuff. And I wanna get the kids some sneakers."

Etta held her hand out expectantly. "Give it here now!"

Elle groaned, and got up and found her purse. She pulled out two twenties and handed them to her sister. She didn't appreciate the shake down but that hush money was a necessary investment. Her mother would be pretty upset if she knew what she had done. And her father would kill her.

Etta tucked the money in her bra and looked at Elle. She was growing up. What could she do? She was a little wild at her age too. Etta just wanted her little sister to be careful. She knew Knight. He was a drug dealer, a murderer, and a player as well. He was far too advanced for Elle. Knight was dangerous, and Elle just came out the house. Etta just shook her head and sighed.

Elle sucked her teeth. "Stop looking at me like that. I'm not as young and dumb as you think."

"Girl, you wouldn't know shit if you fell in it face first. You *are* young and dumb. Young, dumb, and try'na get some. And that nigga Knight gon' be the one to give it to you. Just make sure you can handle it. You in the big leagues now, little girl."

Elle nodded sarcastically and laughed.

"Keep laughing, with your lil' fast ass! Knight got

way more experience than you. And he got mad girls too. I keep on telling you, Elle. You better be using condoms with that nigga. Just 'cause you on the pill don't mean let him be running up in you raw! We only put you on birth control as a back up. Think smart, little sistah! Don't be nobody fool! I done told you, these niggas out here ain't about shit. Especially Knight!"

Elle didn't bother to tell her she'd stopped taking those birth control pills because they made her nauseous. "I know, Etta. I know."

Etta just stared at her for a minute. "Be smart, baby sis. Don't mess up your life and go down for no nigga."

Elle nodded. She knew her sister was right. "I got you. I won't."

Elle didn't know but Etta had a little talk with Knight too. She told him she didn't play when it came to her little sisters, and warned him that she would step to him if something happened to Elle. Etta was the protective type but she was a cool big sis. All she could do is give her sisters advice and pray they took it.

She didn't condone Elle having sex. In fact, she had literally jumped on her ass when she found out. But after she beat her up, what could she do? She warned her about STDs and took her to the doctor and got her on birth control. She'd just taken precautionary measures. Elle was smart so Etta wanted her to go to college after high school. Unlike her and Twyla did.

Etta exhaled and changed the subject. "You know Sunday is Mommy's church program, so we gotta go sing."

"I know, Lady told me like forty times. She wanna practice the songs tonight and tomorrow."

"Okay, glad you know. Oh yeah, we're going out this weekend, Elle! Poochie's party is Saturday!"

Elle's face lit up. "I know. You going?" Etta never hung out with them anymore. She was on her grown woman family shit lately.

Etta grinned. "Yup, Saturday we hanging!"

The sisters hit high five and shared a hearty hug. Their moods were oftentimes unpredictable but the

camaraderie between them was always evident. They were very close. If you fucked with one of them, you fucked with them all.

$$$

Saturday rolled around, and it was time for the party. That evening the sisters were all gathered in Etta's bedroom getting ready. They were joined by their cousin Needra, who was like a sister to them as well. As Twyla, the new cosmetology school attendee, put the finishing touches on their hair and makeup, the aroma of marijuana smoke blended with incense wafted through the air.

Etta was the only one in the group who didn't smoke. Sometimes she took a little toke on special occasions, but you could probably count them on one hand. She started coughing dramatically and heisted the window. Elle, Twyla, and Needra just laughed and rudely blew smoke at her.

Etta gave them the middle finger. "Man, hurry up and put that shit out. Y'all pothead asses got my whole damn room smoked out!"

"Sorry, boo," Needra apologized, frowning at herself in the mirror. "Y'all, I don't look right in this, do I?"

The three sisters just rolled their eyes. They knew it was coming. Needra was neurotic about her appearance. And there was no need to be because she was just as attractive as they were. Her complexion was darker than Twyla's but lighter than Elle's, and she could go for their sister. She was between Elle and Twyla in height and age too. That night Needra looked just as good as everyone else, but as usual, she found something wrong with her outfit.

They were first cousins; the children of two brothers, so they all grew up close. The sisters knew Needra like a book. She was just getting started.

She rubbed her chest disapprovingly and made a face. "I should stuff some damn socks in my bra. Etta and Elle got them big ass cannonballs. Ain't nobody gon' want these little bee stings."

She never failed. Twyla said, "Here we go. Every time it's time to go somewhere you start this insecure, low self-esteem bullshit."

Needra said, "Shut up, Twyla. You just as bad. You ain't got no tities either."

"Well, I ain't like you, bitch. I works what I *got*. And not to mention the fact that I got all this here *ass*!" She dropped it low right quick and came back up and smacked herself on the behind.

They all laughed but no one could dispute that. Twyla did have a big old funky butt.

Elle poured Needra a shot of Hennessy and Coca Cola on the rocks. She handed it to her, and said, "Needra, this gon' make you forget about your hang-ups. Relax! You look beautiful, boo. Let's go out and have a good time."

Needra tossed the drink back in seconds. She slammed the cup down and did a little two-step booty shake. "Okay, let's go, bitches. I'm ready now!"

The sisters laughed and everybody started spraying on different scents of perfume. The young ladies grabbed their purses. It was party time.

When they got to their friend Poochie's party there was good music playing. It was pretty crowded in there too. It looked like everyone was in their groove so the night seemed to be going well.

Etta, Twyla, Needra, and Elle were all dressed in similar outfits by Ellen Tracy. They each wore designer boots and had perfect hairdos and manicured nails. They were some of the best dressed girls at the party and started turning heads as soon as they got there. They spotted their homegirl Poochie and went over to wish her a happy birthday.

Afterwards, Elle bumped into some girls she went to junior high school with; Portia, Fatima, and Simone. Excited to see each other, they all exchanged smiles and hugs. In school Elle wasn't in their circle, which had consisted of them plus another girl named Laila, but they were all pretty cool back then. They had a mutual respect for each other

because they were all cute, and all on the list of best dressed girls in school.

Elle stood there chatting with her old friends until this dude from around her way they called Blaze grabbed her hand to get her attention. Just then, a popular reggae song came on. When Elle realized who Blaze was, she grinned and started dancing with him flirtingly. Blaze looked pleased by her reaction. He pulled her over in a corner where they could talk. Elle followed him willingly. It was no secret that they'd had a little crush on each other when they were small. They'd gone to elementary school together.

Blaze had a fresh haircut and looked really good. When he pulled her close Elle discovered he smelled good too. He was wearing Polo cologne. Elle loved the reggae song that was playing so she danced with him closely.

"Murder she wrote... Murder she wrote..."

Winding her hips slowly, she turned around and grinded her booty on him. He held onto her waist and got up on it. They stood there dancing intimately for some time.

Blaze was a young cat but he got respect on the streets because he had heart. Dudes knew he would bust his gun, so nobody slept on him because he was just sixteen. He was known for having an itchy trigger finger and feared by grown ass men.

Blaze leaned close and spoke in her ear. "Elle, lemme ask you something. What's a good girl like you doing fuckin' with a grimy ass prick like that nigga Knight?"

Caught off guard, Elle paused before answering. "I'm saying, Blaze... He ain't like that. He's cool."

Blaze ran his hands along her hips while she winded on him. Damn, she smelled good. "You know, dudes on our side, we don't like them niggas from the projects. You know that, right?"

"I know... But I don't got nothing to do with that."

"Don't be so sure about that, Elle. I hear dudes talking, so just be careful. You fuckin' with a dirty ass nigga. A lotta dudes wanna take his head off. I'm just saying..."

Elle was a little alarmed. She would have probably

taken that as a threat, had she not known Blaze so well. But they held hands in third grade. She wasn't afraid of him. She turned around and faced him for the remainder of the record.

"Blaze, look... I didn't come out tonight to hear about all *that*. I just came to have a good time. Okay? So be quiet and let's dance." She wrapped her arms around his neck and moved in closer.

Damn, she made him hard. Elle was sexy as hell. His hands started wandering like they had a mind of their own.

When Blaze squeezed her ass, Elle laughed to herself and didn't protest. She couldn't blame him for trying. She knew she was looking good that night. And he had liked her since the third grade.

Etta was looking pretty sexy that night too. She had an admirer who was pressing her like a Sunday shirt. He was about 6'5" and very aggressive. He kept grabbing Etta and insisting that she dance with him. She didn't know him and she wasn't attracted to him so she kept refusing.

Around half past midnight, Etta stepped outside with their homegirl Monifah. The touchy feely guy saw her leave out and took it upon himself to follow her. He spotted her talking to another dude she was actually sort of interested in. That must've really been a blow to his ego because when the dude stepped off he approached her on some "what the fuck are you doing" type shit. He grabbed Etta by the arm and started wilding. He called her a bitch and the whole nine.

Etta was a pretty girl but she fought a lot growing up. She knew how to defend herself. She pushed that nigga in the chest hard. *Bam!*

The guy stumbled. He was so startled by her strength he retaliated with an openhanded slap that sent her careening to the ground. Etta jumped up at the speed of light. In total shock, she grabbed her face and went off.

"Mothafucka, no the fuck you didn't just slap me in my face! Hold up, you punk ass nigga!" She started digging in her purse for her blade. That was a big nigga. She knew she couldn't beat him but she could surely cut his ass.

He saw her going in her purse so he ran over and scooped her up. Etta screamed, "Put me down, mothafucka!"

She pummeled his back and shoulders with her fists and clawed at his face.

This girl named Georgia saw what was happening and ran inside to inform her sisters. Twyla got the news first and let Elle know. Elle was dancing with Blaze when she heard her sister's big mouth yelling over the music. Twyla was always loud.

"Yo, Elle! Needra! Etta outside fighting some dude!"

When Elle heard that she ran out behind her sister without explaining anything. She just left Blaze standing there with a stiff one. But he heard Twyla screaming as well, so he knew what the deal was. He hurried out the door behind them to make sure they were okay.

Twyla was probably the boldest of the three sisters. She stood just 5'2" so she was short, but even shorter tempered. She was usually the quickest to fight and always carried a .45 in her Fendi purse. She thought she was pretty tough. So when she saw her sister tussling with that mammoth mothafucka her first instinct was to run over and punch him in the face. *Pow!* She caught that nigga good but he caught her right back. He punched her in the eye so hard she saw stars, moons, and little green men. Twyla grabbed her eye in pain but she didn't falter.

When Elle, Etta, and Needra saw that gargantuan nigga punch her in the face they all jumped on his ass. It was on. They were out there straight scrapping with that punk. The girls stuck together and they were holding their own. Needra had him in a headlock while they threw heavy haymakers at him, but Goliath was eating those blows and manhandling them.

Some guys intervened and tried to break it up. One of them was Blaze. The asshole they were fighting was so angry he didn't want to quit. He started wilding on the dudes too. He shoved Blaze, who in turn got angry and snuffed that nigga. He caught him square in the jaw. Goliath swung back wildly and missed. Not in a fighting mood, Blaze backed up and reached under his shirt for his burner.

By then, Twyla already had her shit out. She cocked

it and some dude yelled, "Oh shit, that bitch got a gun!" When people heard that they scattered. Twyla fired a warning shot in the air. *BOOM!!!*

That gunfire put some fear in Goliath. That bastard forgot about fighting Blaze and got the hell up outta there.

After he ran off, Monifah came over there acting like she was concerned. "Oh my goodness, are y'all alright?"

Etta smirked at her. "Yeah, no thanks to you. What happened, girl? We came outside together but when that nigga came up in my face, I looked around and you was gone."

Monifah lied, "No, I wasn't. I was out here try'na help you. You ain't see me, Etta?"

Twyla was angered by her phony ass display of concern. She screwed her face up at Monifah. "Bitch, get the fuck outta here with that fake shit! When that nigga was try'na fuck us up, yo' ass was hiding in the corner! So now you wanna come asking if we alright! As a matter of fact, bitch, hold this!" Twyla hauled off and punched her in the face. *Pow!*

Monifah's glasses flew to the left and she was completely dumbstruck. She just gasped in horror and scurried to find her eyeglasses.

Twyla said, "Bitch, that's for not helping my sister!"

Monifah just stared at her with her mouth hanging open. She wasn't the fighting type but she knew Twyla was. They had lived across the street from each other their whole lives so she knew Twyla didn't have it all. She didn't want to fight her. With no plans to retaliate, she kept looking on the ground for her missing eyeglass lens.

Everyone out there was staring at Twyla but those who knew her weren't really surprised. They already knew she was a firecracker.

Twyla looked at her family, and said, "These damn people looking at me like I'm crazy. Let's go, y'all. That nigga done hit me in my damn eye! My shit gon' be black as Elle's ass. "

Elle just shook her head and didn't even comment. Twyla was so stupid. The girls all laughed about the fight after that and compared battle scars.

Blaze looked around at them chuckling and was very amused. He said, "Y'all girls are somethin' else."

They all laughed again and thanked him for helping them. Twyla said, "Blaze, you got more heart than most of these grown men, with they bitch asses. Thanks a lot, baby!"

Blaze humbly told them it was nothing. They all said goodnight, and the girls started to the corner to get a cab. Elle smiled at Blaze and waved, and then followed her sisters.

He grabbed her hand and stopped her before she could get away. "Look, Elle, I would never sit back and let anything happen to you or your family. But it seemed like Twyla pretty much had things under control. Your sister crazy with that hammer."

They both grinned. Elle said, "I know, right? My sister was born crazy. Well, thanks again, boo. Bye, Blaze." She batted her eyelids at him flirtatiously.

He caught that and held onto her hand for a few seconds. Blaze realized he couldn't let her leave. He was compelled to offer her a ride home. He forgot about his plans to smash this other chick he messed with sometimes. If nothing else, he wanted to talk more with Elle. "Wait, lemme take y'all home."

To his delight, she agreed.

"Okay, thanks, boo. Lemme tell my sisters." She called the others back and they accepted the ride.

After she and Blaze dropped the others off at home, Elle stayed out with him all night. But all they did was talk and go for breakfast at this diner. There was no funny business whatsoever. They just had a great time connecting. It was almost eight AM when Elle walked in the house.

Chapter 3

"It's a small world after all" had to be the realest song lyric ever. Whoever wrote that was on point. After Elle left the party with Blaze that night, Knight heard about it all the way down in Baltimore. He came up two days later and he was pretty heated. He disguised it well but he made it a point to confront her about it.

Knight didn't mention it on the phone. He waited until they were face to face. That night they were alone in a luxury hotel room he had rented. Elle was suited up in a lacy French teddy he had bought her and sexy high heels.

Knight was kissing her neck and nibbling on her ear. Elle was breathing heavily and moaning softly. Things were really heating up. She wanted him inside of her.

Suddenly, he turned ice cold and grabbed her by the neck. His words dripping with contempt, he hissed, "You think you so fuckin' slick! I know about you fuckin' the shit outta that lil' nigga Blaze last Saturday night! You left a party with that nigga, and then let him dig you out all night! 'Til the sun came up!"

Shocked, she attempted to pry his hand off her neck. "Wait a minute, what are you talking about? Knight, that's a lie!"

"So you *weren't* with him? Lie to me, and watch what I do," he threatened.

"No, he just gave me a ride home, that's all. From this little get-together my homegirl had."

"I know *exactly* where you were. Your friend Poochie had a birthday party on Willoughby."

Alarmed and surprised that he knew her whereabouts, Elle said, "Well, whoever told you that need to get their facts

straight. What I look like, some kinda hoe? All we did was *talk*, Knight. And we went to go get somethin' to eat. That's it!"

He was so mad steam was shooting out of his ears. He demanded that she tell him exactly what they talked about. Before Elle could answer him, he bellowed, "Matter of fact, I don't wanna hear *shit*! Just know you put a nail in that little nigga coffin!"

Elle couldn't believe him. "Knight, don't say that!"

He looked at her like she was a real fucking traitor. "Oh, so you *care* about that nigga now, huh? Sound like you got *feelings* for him."

"No, I don't. I'm just saying … Kill him for what? Nothing happened."

He just looked at her suspiciously. "If you say so. But if I ever hear about you fuckin' with that lil' bastard Blaze, or any more of my fuckin' foes, I won't be responsible for what happens next."

Knight paused for a minute and exhaled like he was literally letting off steam. Elle stood there still and afraid.

Next time he spoke he was much calmer. "Baby girl, lemme tell you somethin'. Don't get that dispensable lil' nigga killed. There's a war going on out here in these streets, and you better know what side you on. You already chose, so don't be fuckin' with the enemy. It's important that you understand how very few people I can trust. How the fuck I'ma trust you when you ridin' around with this nigga?!"

Elle understood where he was coming from so she surrendered peacefully. "I'm sorry, baby. It won't happen again. Okay?"

Knight said he forgave her but he took it out on her during their sex. He hit it like he was punishing her and made her scream "I'm sorry" over and over. That night Elle learned the meaning of a grudge fuck. The crazy part about it was that now she loved him even more. The fact that he was jealous turned her on. She was young, inexperienced, and just really loved that thug shit.

$$$

About two weeks later, Elle was scheduled to take that Baltimore trip again. She left on a Friday evening so she wouldn't miss any days from school. Knight was still very strict about that. He even insisted that she bring her homework with her.

When Elle got down there this time she didn't stay at a hotel. She stayed at an apartment that Knight and his partner in crime, Rude, had recently rented. Elle got to stay with Knight for three days. She was delighted and felt like the wife without a doubt.

The first night she was down there, he came in late and didn't touch her. She had deliberately gone to bed clad in a sexy nightie to tempt him, but she went to sleep that night totally unsexed. It was nice sleeping in his arms but she wanted to make love to him. To a susceptible sixteen-year-old there was no greater connection.

The second day Elle was there, she was cleaning up in the kitchen when she came across a wad of money. It was just lying on the kitchen floor like somebody had dropped it. She started to pick it up but decided to leave it where it was and notify Rude, who was in his bedroom at the time. She knocked on his door and waited for a response.

"Yo, who is it?" he called out.

"It's Elle. Sorry to bother you, but I found some money on the floor that I think you dropped in the kitchen."

He got up and came to the door. Stretching, he said, "I probably dropped it when I came in. Thanks." He held out his hand expectantly.

She smiled. "No, I didn't wanna mess with it, so it's still in there. I don't fuck with nobody money."

He laughed and asked her to go get it for him. Elle agreed, and went to retrieve the bread. When she handed it to him, he smiled at her and gave her this approving look. Elle didn't know what that was about but she grinned and told him to get some more rest.

He asked her if she needed anything. She said no but he handed her a c-note and told her to order a pizza or

something, and keep the change. Elle thanked him and told him she wouldn't disturb him again. She wished him sweet dreams. He laughed and thanked her, and then shut his door and went back to bed.

Rude didn't tell her the real truth. He had planted that money in the kitchen on purpose. That was a test to see if she could be trusted. Unbeknownst to Elle, Knight had approved that little honesty assessment. It was actually his idea.

Later on around midnight, Elle was rereading one of her favorite Maya Angelou novels and half-listening to some videos on BET when Knight came walking in. She broke out in a huge grin and hopped up and hugged him. He palmed her ass and held her close for a moment. She could feel his erection growing through his pants. Satisfied, she pressed against him closer.

Knight backed up a step and took off his shirt. Elle gazed at his chiseled chest. She was almost drooling with dilating hearts in her pupils. He was so sexy. She was in love.

He unbuckled his belt and then stepped out of his boots and pants. Knight usually kept a serious expression. During intimacy there was no exception. "Take that off so we can get in the shower," he commanded.

Dumbfounded, Elle said, "Huh?" She had just got in the shower before he got there. And she had never showered with a man before. She was sort of shy because she had a little complex about her weight. She was 5'5" and 168 pounds, which was a little on the thick side.

Knight repeated himself, slowly that time. "Take your clothes off *now*, and come in the shower with me."

Eager to please him, Elle swallowed and took a deep breath, and then she disrobed. She was shaking like a leaf because he had the light on. The way she loved him, she couldn't disappoint him. His facial expression said he approved of her body so she relaxed a tad.

"Go 'head in the bathroom," he commanded.

Nervous and praying her booty wasn't ashy, Elle mustered up her confidence and headed for the private

bathroom inside the master bedroom they occupied. Knight followed behind her with this lust-filled gaze. She looked down at his penis and realized he was hard. He clearly appreciated the ampleness of her form. She smiled to herself, and her hang-ups about her body slowly disappeared. The fact that he seemed to find her sexy made her feel like a woman.

When they got in the shower he washed himself first, and then he slowly bathed her with a sponge, spending extra time on her private parts. After that, he massaged her nipples into tiny erect gumdrops and licked and sucked them like they were fruit flavored. She caressed the back of his head and gasped. It felt so good she didn't want him to stop.

Knight worked his way down and kissed and licked her belly. He stopped at her bikini line and spread her legs. Gazing at her womanhood, he parted her lips. Elle almost choked from excitement. When he placed his mouth on her he took her to another place. She spread her legs as far as she could and arched her back so he could get it good. And he did. She threw her head back and moaned.

Elle had received the star treatment before but their oral skills couldn't compare to Knight's. He had her hearing symphonies and shit. She exploded and begged him to stop but he kept on until she literally couldn't take it anymore. When he finished she was panting like she'd just run a marathon.

Knight may have been a hardcore killer in the streets but he was seductive and romantic in the sheets. When he stood up, he ran his fingers through her hair amorously and tongued her down. Elle was already dizzy with lust and desire but that kiss pushed her overboard. She was head over heels. At that point all she wanted to do was show him how much. She sank to her knees and swallowed as much of him as she could. That was the biggest form of adoration she could think of at sixteen.

Elle had sworn she'd never put a dick in her mouth but now she didn't care about that. She didn't care about the hairdo she was ruining either. Or the fact that he could lose respect for her. At the time all she cared about was pleasing

him. Knight was a grown man who she aspired to keep. Elle's young naïve heart believed that now they were exclusive. Oral sex in the shower solidified that.

Knight stared down at her in disbelief wondering where she'd learned to give head like that. She wasn't exactly a pro but she knew what she was doing. He was turned on by the sexy faces she was making. It looked like she was enjoying it as much as he was. The water cascading down on her was also an arousing effect. Elle was exotic-looking. And she looked a hell of a lot older than sixteen. Damn, she had him kind of open.

She did something with the back of her throat that almost made Knight cum. He stopped her and pulled her to her feet because he wanted to prolong it. He wasn't done with her yet.

When he stopped her, Elle looked at him awkwardly, and asked, "Did I do something wrong?"

Knight fought back a smile. She had these big, pretty, doe eyes. They made him think of that new song "Pretty Brown Eyes" by Mint Condition. Elle's eyes were so innocent and unsure. When she looked at him he could see the genuine love she felt for him. She wasn't corrupted, and that purity shit really turned him on. The look in her eyes was so different from that of the money hungry, gold digging scavengers he usually bedded. He was moved to taste her again. It was all good because that pussy was his. He went head-first once again in the shower.

That time he really made her kitty cat purr. Elle's vaginal walls were on fire. She was in ecstasy, trembling and crying out his name. After she came again, he rose and picked her up and backed her up against the wall. Sucking on her neck, he forced himself inside of her.

They went raw dog for the first time. Elle clawed his back and screamed in pleasure as he deep stroked her. She couldn't believe he was fucking the shit out of her raw. She didn't protest because she was ridiculously, unpretentiously and euphorically in love.

It was so beautiful. It was everything she had

imagined being in love to be. Knight stroked her with emotion. He was caressing her, kissing her, and staring at her like he was in love too. Elle was so caught up in the moment she closed her eyes and wrapped her legs around him tight.

That pussy was stupendous. Knight felt himself about to cum and warned her. "Damn, baby girl, I'm 'bout to bust! Aaaaggghhh!" He shot off right inside of her.

When he ejaculated Elle was delighted. Him cumming in her was synonymous to them being monogamous. He may as well have put a ring on her finger. They were that engaged. As he caught his breath, she held him close and murmured tiny declarations of her undying love for him. It was settled. Knight was her man.

They showered again, and then dried off and got in bed naked. They were both spent from all the glorious shower sex. Knight held Elle from behind and cupped her breasts. Caressing the left one, he told her how proud he was that she had stood up. He was referring to her finding that money earlier and returning it to Rude. He said they had purposely left the money out to test her, and she had passed with flying colors. He told her he was glad he found a girl he could trust.

Elle just laid there shocked for a second. She honestly had no idea. She was just an honest person when it came to stuff like that. She never had a reason to steal from anyone. She had boosted a few clothes from department stores like Lord & Taylor and Bloomingdale's in the past, but she never stole from anybody she knew. Let alone someone she cared about.

Knight told her that was the second test she had passed. Elle was a little puzzled by that comment. He laughed and told her he knew she was one of the little girls outside that day who had witnessed him and his man stickup Puerto Rican Tito with the black and gold Mercedes. He said he knew the police came to her house a few times but she didn't rat them out.

Elle couldn't believe he brought that up. The notion that they shared such a deep dark secret was almost overwhelming. She knew he was wrong for the things he did

but it felt so right. She turned around and faced him, drawn by the mystery and danger he eluded. She had never felt closer to Knight than at that moment.

He kissed her on the forehead and made a strange request. He asked her to sing to him. Thinking he was kidding, Elle just laughed.

"Elle, I'm serious. I love to hear you sing."

She smiled in the dark and cleared her throat, and then she commenced to sing him a lullaby she used to sing to her little brother and nieces when they were babies.

"Hush little baby, don't say a word. Elle's gonna buy you a mocking bird. If that mocking bird don't sing, Elle's gonna buy you a diamond ring. If that diamond ring turn brass, Elle's gonna buy you a looking glass..."

It must've sounded pretty soothing because he fell asleep holding her within minutes. Elle was elated.

She spent the next two days playing wife. During the day when Knight went out to handle business, she cooked and cleaned the apartment. When he came home in the evenings she fed him well and then sexed him all night.

She learned a lot from him that weekend too. Besides his weak spots and preferred sexual pleasures, he taught her how to bag up. She stayed up with him until the wee hours of the morning getting the product she brought down from New York ready for the workers.

Elle got to see heroin in its purest form. Knight told her it was China White – the best. He took small amounts at a time and diluted it with a cutting agent called quinine. The purpose of that was to stretch it and bring back more money. He said the concoction was so powerful that a person could overdose off the quinine alone. He warned her to never mess with that shit. Elle assured him that he didn't have to worry about her using nothing like that.

After he cut the dope, they spooned it into little wax bags for distribution. The goal was to place the same amount into each bag. To be concise, they used these little coffee stirrers with a tiny spoon-like end. One level scoop went in each bag. The bags then had to be folded and taped shut.

Each would sell on the street for twenty bucks. Sitting there they bagged up over $20,000 worth of product.

Elle left Baltimore fifteen hundred bucks richer, and armed with the sexual prowess to make a married man leave home. She also knew how to cut and bag up heroin. She didn't know it at the time, but in the years to come both of her new skills would prove to be financially beneficial.

Chapter 4

When Elle returned home she was on cloud 69. She was so happy everyone noticed a change in her. And some didn't like it one bit. One night she was chilling with Twyla, Needra, and three of their homegirls named Pringles, Mena, and Cherry. They were all bugging out, smoking weed, and drinking a little bit.

Everybody was laughing at the bickering that was escalating between Elle and Pringles. Pringles was a dark-skinned girl around 5'7" and sort of broad in stature. She had a decent face, a huge ass, and knock knees. At the time she was wearing neon pink spandex leggings and a long ponytail that came down to the middle of her back.

Pringles had been a "friend" of theirs for years. They hung together at times but her mouth was slick and she was a hater on the low. And sometimes she played too much. That night she kept grabbing at Elle's breasts and teasing her about their size. Pringles called herself playing but she was getting on her nerves.

"Ooh, you got some big ass tities, Elle! I just wanna milk these shits!"

Elle didn't find her funny. "That liquor got you bugging, bitch! I'm telling you, Pringles. Quit fuckin' playing with me!"

Pringles just laughed and did it again. Elle cursed her out and called her every type of lesbian and dyke there was, but she just did it again. After she squeezed her breast that time, Elle got fed up and backhanded that bitch.

Even after Pringles got popped in her lips, she still kept on. The others were laughing so she must've thought

she was a real comedienne. Sick of her, Elle got fed up and spazzed out.

"Bitch, you like my tities so much 'cause you wish you had them. Pick up them droopy shits you got! Your long ass tities! Them shits look like flapjacks! Or those flippers you swim in. I bet you can float on top of the water with them shits! Bitch, them ain't tities - you got four arms!"

Everybody was tipsy and doubled over in laughter, including Pringles. She knew what Elle said was true so she couldn't deny it. She had three kids and gravity had taken its toll.

Pringles finally quit heckling Elle and they were all chilling. Everybody in the crew was cool. Cherry approached Elle and told her she had to talk to her about something. Wondering what it was about, Elle followed her into the bathroom.

Cherry was a slim, brown-skinned girl around 5'6" who had a thing for hair gel. She was a cute girl but every hairstyle she wore was plastered to her head. Cherry had these huge tities but she was shaped just like a boy. She had no ass and no hips.

Inside the john, she began an Oscar-worthy performance. Elle sat there listening as her so-called friend tearfully confessed to a late night sexual romp with Knight. The bitch was acting like she was all choked up and even cried crocodile tears. She told Elle how he had followed her home the other night and tried to talk to her. She claimed he came on to her and begged her "just let me taste it." She said they didn't have sex but she allowed him to eat her out.

She paused to let that sink in for a minute. Then she told Elle she was too nice for Knight, and didn't deserve to be hurt that way. She suggested she leave him alone because he was just no good. She said she was sorry she was so weak and then she broke down in tears, blubbering what a horrible friend she was.

Elle was appalled. She was dumbfounded for a minute but she was no dimwit. She knew men cheated all the time, but she didn't believe a word Cherry said. First of all, everybody knew her twat smelled like fish and sewer trash.

Elle doubted Knight would put his mouth on some shit like that. She gave him more credit than that. It took him a long time to sex her, so she knew he wasn't the thirsty type.

Cherry had been hating ever since Elle first got with Knight. She was just jealous. The Brooklyn spirit in Elle told her to hook off on that bitch. But that would make her think she believed her. For that reason alone, she didn't even give that hoe a reaction. She would never give Cherry the satisfaction of getting the best of her. Elle just looked at her like she was stupid.

She wrinkled her nose like she smelled something, and then calmly fired on that trick. "My man is real big on hygiene so I'ma just assume that you lying. But I will certainly ask him about that."

From the look on Cherry's face she didn't like that one bit. She was the epitome of a frenemy – a friend and enemy. She was one of those treacherous, smiling faced mothafuckas who acted like they were rooting for you, but really wanted to see you lose. That bitch deliberately tried to hurt her. Elle would never forget that. She would never trust her trifling ass again.

Elle said, "Cherry, if *anything* happened between y'all, you ain't the first and you won't be the last. But y'all bitches just hoes. Knight loves me to death. Ask him, he'll tell you. Now, do you have anything else to say to me?" She smiled at her frenemy sweetly.

Cherry wanted to slap that smile off Elle's face but she didn't have the heart. "Nah. I already told you what it is, so it's on you. We ain't gon' let no nigga come between us anyway."

"You finished?"

Cherry nodded, and fake-smiled back. "Yeah. You know you my bitch."

$$$

Knight was out of town for a few days but he made sure he called Elle twice a day. Every time she spoke to him

on the phone it killed her not say anything about Cherry's little "confession." She planned to ask him about it but she wanted to do it in person. She wanted to see his reaction.

Two days later, she got the opportunity to confront him about it. Elle waited until they were alone and came right out with it.

"Cherry told me she saw you in the projects on her way home the other night. She said y'all two crept off and had a little *fun*, and the guilt was eating her up so bad she just *had* to tell me."

"*What*? Why would I do that? That's your so-called friend. And don't nobody want no rotten ass Cherry! You crazy? *Hell no*, I ain't hit that!"

So far so good. Elle almost breathed a sigh of relief but she kept a poker face. "No, Cherry didn't say y'all screwed." She paused and looked in his eyes to see his reaction. "She said y'all *didn't* have sex, but you begged her to let you eat her out. And she let you."

"*What*?! Is you out your mo'fuckin' *mind*? You must be *crazy*!" Knight frowned at the thought. He looked like he was disgusted and shook his head in disbelief.

"Elle, are you honestly crazy enough to believe I would put my mouth on a stank ass smut like Cherry? Niggas call her Mary Jane Rotten Crotch."

Knight wasn't lying to Elle. He would never go down on Cherry. But he didn't tell the part about Cherry going down on him. She had given him some head in his car the other night. He had spotted her walking home late and scooped her up because he was bored. And he only let her suck him off because he knew she would. He skeeted all down her throat and then she got upset because he didn't want to fuck her. So now she was mad.

Knight looked at Elle sincerely. "Elle, I don't even know why you fuck with Cherry. That dumb, dropout bitch ain't no type of friend to you whatsoever. She's just a little slut who smells like piss and fish, and will give her rotten twat up to anybody with two pennies. That bitch is jealous of you. She can't stand the fact that you got it so together, and

you *know* it. That confidence is what attracted me to you in the first place."

Elle couldn't help but crack a little smile. He sounded so genuine.

Knight kept on. "Listen, baby girl, you the *HBIC* so don't let them wannabe ass hoes change that. You HBIC, so *you* in charge. And always remember that. Some of them hoes you hang with are beneath you. You smart, Elle, and you going places. I *see* somethin' in you. Them bitches ain't gon' be shit."

Elle knew Knight was right about a lot of the things he said. Cherry definitely envied her. She wanted almost everything she had. Cherry wanted her man and her family as well. Elle was annoyed by the way she constantly referred to Twyla and Etta as her big sisters.

Everybody felt sorry for her because her mother was on drugs and her father had been in jail all her life. The aunts she lived with mistreated her so badly they wouldn't even allow her to use a bar of soap in their house. That was why she had a reputation for smelling bad. Nobody ever taught her anything, so Elle's sisters tried to teach her about feminine hygiene. They put her up on Summer's Eve feminine wash and taught her how to douche. Elle knew she didn't have anybody, but enough was enough.

She refused to break up with Knight behind that nonsense. Elle let it go but she made it a point to rub all the gifts and money he gave her in Cherry's face. That actually hurt her more than that ass whipping she should've given her.

$$$

Knight didn't let it go. In fact, he was so deeply disturbed by Cherry's accusations that he had in mind to do something to her. He didn't express this to Elle, of course. She was his PYT so she never really saw that side of him. But he could be cold when he wanted to be.

About a week later, he caught Cherry walking home

late again. When she saw him, she got nervous and put some serious pep in her step. Riding alongside her, he rolled down the window and "suggested" she get in for a minute. She said she had a curfew and refused.

Apparently she didn't get it. He demanded, "Get in the car *now*. Lemme talk to you for a minute."

He didn't raise his voice but his tone told her how serious he was. Cherry was so frightened she thought about just taking off and running. But she knew better. Knight was not playing with a full deck. Everyone knew that. She stopped walking and obediently opened the car door.

After she got in, he drove down Classon Avenue to a dark street in Williamsburg. Aside from the sounds of a fire engine's siren in the distance and the car hitting an occasional bump, there was silence the entire ride.

He parked on a side street and shut off the engine, and then he reached under his seat for his ratchet. Still silent, he began wiping the gun down with a hanky. Knight was a master at manipulation so he knew the intimidation factor never failed. Without even looking at Cherry, he calmly commanded her to undress.

He never once pointed the weapon at her but she was persuaded by the mere presence of that pistol. She didn't protest. She just obediently stripped down to her panties. Knight didn't want her funking up his car seat so he stopped her there.

Sitting there in her underwear, Cherry was afraid Knight was going to kill her and leave her body in some dark alley for the rats to gnaw away at. She knew how he got down. He was a stone cold murderer.

She pled for her life. "I am *so* sorry, Knight! Please don't shoot me!"

He wanted to laugh but he kept it icy. "Why shouldn't I? You been telling some serious lies on me. You told Elle I ate you out, right? You lying ass bitch, you gon' pay for that. Now get ready to suck on this tip."

When Cherry heard that she was surprised and also a little turned on. She licked her lips and assumed Knight wanted some more head. She actually didn't mind. She

figured if she did it well enough she would get out of whatever cruel punishment he had in store for her. And maybe she could even manage to get him away from Elle's black ass.

The tip Knight wanted her to suck on wasn't on his dick. Not that time. He reached over and grabbed the back of Cherry's head and rubbed the tip of his gun across her lips. After a few seconds of this, he shoved it in her mouth, almost chipping her tooth in the process. He coldly commanded, "Suck it, bitch!"

Terrified, she started sucking on the tip of that gun like it was a chocolate penis. She was frightened to tears. She'd never been that scared in her life.

Taking great pleasure from her fear, Knight laughed quietly. Then he simply unlocked the car doors and told her to get out. He didn't let her take any clothes and he promised he would kill her family if she told anybody. He drove off the minute she shut the car door. Knight traveled a few blocks south and then tossed her clothes out the car window.

Cherry was so relieved to get out of that car alive she started running fast as hell. The whole time she was praying Knight didn't shoot her in her back. Everyone knew how ruthless he was. He was responsible for the deaths of a whole family in their projects. He had run up in this apartment and killed three generations, from grandparents to grandkids. He had finished them all with headshots and then doused them with gasoline and torched the apartment. By the time the firemen put out the blaze the family was burned to a crisp. Naked and barefoot, cold, and scared shitless, Cherry made tracks toward home.

$$$

Elle woke up the following Saturday morning to the smell of pancakes and smiled to herself. Her mother was cooking in the kitchen. She remembered that was Lady's day off.

Elle had fallen asleep while she was reading so she

removed the copy of Toni Morrison's "The Bluest Eye" from her chest, and got up to go urinate and brush her teeth. Reading was an old habit of hers.

After she peed, she got the stuff she needed to slay the dragon. Toothpaste covered toothbrush in hand, she walked down the hall to the kitchen.

Brushing, Elle greeted her mother with a grin. "Hey Lady!"

Ellen Mitchell, affectionately known to her children as Lady, was a beautiful woman with a personality that matched. She smiled brightly at the younger version of herself. Elle resembled her more than any of her other kids. They were the same milk chocolate complexion, the same height, and same shoe size.

She had given her the name Elle because she had been her prettiest baby. Ellen loved all her children and they were all beautiful, but Elle had these huge brown eyes and a mass of curly black hair. She looked just like a little doll. Ellen named her Elle because she was picture perfect like the photos in Elle, a high-end fashion magazine she loved to thumb through.

Ellen said, "Well, good morning, little me. What are you doing up so early?"

Elle grinned. "Good morning, my queen." People constantly told her she looked just like her mother but she secretly wished she was that pretty. She knew she was cute but Lady was beautiful. Even after birthing four children, she had a youthful appearance and tiny waist that often got her mistakenly referred to as her daughters' sister. She was flawless.

Elle looked at the stove clock and saw that it was half past noon. She laughed at her mother's sarcasm and then she spit toothpaste in the sink and proceeded to rinse her mouth.

Her mother hurried over and popped her on her backside. "You ol' nasty cow! You know better than to spit in my kitchen sink!"

Elle laughed, "My mouth was burning, Lady. This Colgate is strong!"

Just then the babies, Nay-Nay and Mimi, burst in the kitchen running for their lives. They were screaming hysterically.

"Uncle's chasin' us with the facuum monster! Help! Help!"

The little tykes were so upset they were trembling. They both took cover behind their grandmother. Junior came casually strolling in the kitchen a few seconds later. He tried to look innocent but he had a little smirk on his face.

Ellen shushed the little ones and addressed her devilish son. "Elliot Mitchell Jr. what in the world did you do to these babies?"

"I didn't do nothing, Lady," he lied.

Elle knew her nieces were scared of the vacuum cleaner, which they referred to as the "facuum monster" because of the noise it made. Junior told them there was a monster inside of it, and that made it worse. Whenever they didn't listen to him, or whenever he felt like torturing them so he could get a good laugh, he powered on the vacuum and chased them through the house.

Elle had tortured him similarly when he was small so she had to laugh. Children learned what they lived. She knelt down and hugged her little nieces until they stopped crying.

She rubbed their backs, and cooed, "Awww... Its okay, Auntie's angels. Don't cry. I'ma beat him up for y'all, okay?"

In unison, the cherubs chirped, "Yes! He's mean!"

Junior laughed and dipped his finger in the pancake batter. He smeared it on Elle's nose and stuck his tongue out at their nieces. Elle didn't feel like wrestling with him because she just woke up. She wiped the batter off her nose and gave his little bad ass a pass.

Chapter 5

A few weeks later, the season had changed again. Spring was in the air. The weather was lovely but the clear skies belied Elle's gray temperament. She was depressed and in a serious funk.

One day after school, Elle walked in the house and saw that her sister had a guest she wasn't fond of. Mena's trifling ass was there. She was smoking a blunt with Twyla, and had her feet kicked up on the coffee table.

Mena was originally Twyla's friend. Elle tolerated her but didn't really like her. She didn't trust that bitch, and she had her reasons. Mena was an outright thief. Elle didn't understand why her sister was still fucking with her.

A few weeks before, Twyla was looking for her bankcard so she could get some money she needed from an ATM. She couldn't find it anywhere so Elle and Etta helped her search the whole house. After they were unsuccessful at finding it, Mena was the first person Twyla suspected.

A few people said Mena and Twyla resembled each other, probably because they were around the same height and complexion. Twyla knew how greasy Mena was because Mena had done so much dirt around her. She stole from her own mother so Twyla didn't put it pass her.

Always bold and upfront, Twyla called her and flat out asked her if she had her bankcard. That fake bitch Mena tried to play it off. She rushed over there to act like she was helping them look for it. The sisters had searched that house inside out, and she walked right in and "found" it immediately. She literally came in the door and looked under the sofa, and then she was like "Here it is, girl! Y'all asses ain't look under here."

They had picked that couch up and looked under it three times. She was hilarious. With friends like that who needed enemies? Elle wanted to beat Mena's ass after that incident but Twyla gave her a pass.

Mena got a pass on another occasion too. They all used to go out boosting from high-end department stores like Saks Fifth Avenue. Twyla had this bad ass Escada outfit she'd stolen, and planned to wear on her birthday. But when her birthday came she couldn't find her outfit.

Twyla had a bad temper and was going off like she really paid the four hundred dollars it cost. Olan, their first cousin from down south, had been staying with them for a couple of weeks. He swore he saw their homegirl, Monique, steal the outfit a few days before. Twyla stepped to Monique but she vehemently denied stealing from her. The poor girl was scared and did not want to fight. But Twyla took her cousin's word and beat her ass.

The crazy part was that it turned out that Olan lied on Monique. He was just mad that she wouldn't give him some ass. He was a real creep for that, and Twyla felt horrible. When the truth came out, she sincerely apologized to Monique. But Monique still kept her distance after that.

About a week later, Mena's dumb ass slipped up and wore the outfit around them. When Twyla saw her stolen merchandise, she was like "Bitch, is that my shit you got on?" Mena laughed and swore it wasn't. She claimed she went and got her own but everyone knew she was lying. And Twyla was still fucking with that conniving bitch. Elle couldn't understand why but she gave Mena hell every chance she got.

Annoyed by the sight of her, Elle walked over and kicked Mena's legs off the coffee table. "Bitch, get your feet off my fuckin' table! Do I come over your house puttin' my feet up on *your* shit? These fuckin' hoes ain't got no damn home training!"

Twyla just laughed and offered Elle the blunt. Mena rolled her eyes but she moved her feet. She knew Elle had it in for her so she didn't even bother responding. Elle just

wanted to fight and she wasn't in the mood.

Elle told Twyla she didn't feel like smoking. More and more irked by Mena's appearance, she went to her room. She was already in a bad mood when she got home. Mena just made it worse.

Elle had heard another rumor in the streets about Knight cheating. Brooding over their future, she sat down on her bed and cried. She was putting everything she had into her relationship and it felt like it was all for nothing.

She felt herself slipping. Despite all the preaching Knight did about her getting good grades, she had put school on a backburner the past few weeks. Her once praiseworthy grades were now barely passing. She was losing herself more each day. Loving him was draining her. She was literally losing weight and more self-esteem everyday. All because there was always some drama with some bitch.

$$\$\$\$$$

A couple of weeks later, Knight managed to make a fool of her again. This time it was with Mena's dirty ass. The bitch actually went out of town with Knight. Unbeknownst to Elle, she had passed him her number right underneath her nose, and they had been communicating. Elle couldn't stand Mena. She was older than her and was always fronting like she was so sophisticated, but that bitch was just a chicken head.

Elle was still young but she was learning how low a man could sink. Knight was a creep for going behind her back like that. He claimed it was just business but she was still hurt.

Mena was a foul bitch who leapt at the opportunity to stick a knife in her back. She knew about the way Elle, Twyla, and even Etta sometimes carried work out of town, and she wanted to be down with their hustle. And Elle knew that bitch well enough to know she wanted her man as well.

Knight claimed he only called that bitch to set up a run because Elle and Twyla were traveling too frequently. He said he didn't want them to get too hot. He swore he

didn't have sex with Mena, and it was just business. Elle didn't know what to believe, but she knew Mena wouldn't be going on any more runs for him.

Out of town, Mena was put to the same test Elle was put to. Knight and Rude left a wad of money around her as bait as well. But Mena's stupid ass found the money and stuffed it in her bra. She made that dumb mistake because she was uninformed and used to fucking with a bunch of lames. She didn't realize she was in the presence of some live niggas who would pop her top, then cut it off, and mail it to her mother.

They asked her about the money and she denied having it, so they made her strip butt naked and searched all her belongings. They got that money back and also confiscated everything she had of value. Her gold earrings, gold chain and bracelets, and all the cash she possessed. Then she was not paid the $500 she was promised for the delivery she made, and sent home penniless. And only on the strength of her being Twyla's homegirl was her life spared. Those dudes had both killed for less.

Elle knew what happened because Rude actually called Twyla and told her he was contemplating offing her foul friend. Twyla had no idea Mena was even in Baltimore but she begged him to spare that fool's life and send her home. She said she would've told him Mena was no-good and saved them the trouble of finding out. Rude had lots of love and respect for Twyla because she used to be his little girlfriend. He granted her that solid, so Mena owed Twyla her life.

Elle and Twyla never said a word about knowing to Mena. She lied to them and said she had gone to Atlantic City that weekend. She didn't know they knew she went to Baltimore and got caught stealing. She made up some mumbo jumbo story about getting robbed for her jewelry when she was walking home from her man's house one night.

Knight gave Elle the gold bangle earrings and she spitefully flaunted them in Mena's face. She smiled at her

and said, "Look, Mena, my boo Knight bought me some earrings just like the ones you had. I always liked these, girl. Too bad yours got stolen."

Mena's face looked like she tasted giraffe shit but she dared not comment. She knew there was nothing she could say.

Chapter 6

Ellen woke up early on Sunday morning. The first thing she did was smile and thank God for life and for her family. He had been so good to her. God was good all the time.

Ellen got up and had some coffee before she showered. After she was done she went down the hall to wake up the troops. She made a mental note to make sure her girls had everything they needed to attend church that day. She was willing to bet that at least one of them needed pantyhose or something. Excited about the Easter program they were participating in that afternoon, she decided to get her children up one at a time so they wouldn't bump heads in the bathroom. Being a mom of four, she had formulated little strategies to keep the peace.

Cherubic and virtuous, Ellen was a Godly woman with a heart of pure gold. There was nothing more important to her than her family. Smiling, she opened the door to Elle's bedroom. That one was the slowest when it came to getting ready so she usually got her up first.

Ellen tapped on the door loudly. "Elle, wake up, honey! Time to get the day started. Rise and shine, and give God your glory! Happy Easter!"

Stretching, Elle greeted her mom. "Good morning, Lady. Happy Easter." She peaked on the side of her bed to make sure no one had tampered with the Easter baskets she got for the kids. Satisfied, she trudged to the bathroom.

Easter was a happy time so Elle got in the grove. They were all going to church with their mother. Even her father was going. Then they were taking the kids to Coney

Island to the amusement park. As Elle brushed her teeth she hummed the tune of one of the gospel selections they were singing at church that day. They had practiced them the night before. When she got in the shower she belted the song out at the top of her lungs.

"...An empty grave is there to prove my Saviour lives. Because He lives, I can face tomorrow. Because He lives... all fear is gone. Because I know- He holds the future. And life is worth the living just because He lives..."

Elle was out there in the world doing some ungodly things at times but the fact that she was raised in church always helped circumvent the backlash of the negativity. She knew how to call on God. She didn't proclaim to be perfect by any means but she knew God heard sinners' prayers too. Every single day she prayed to be washed of her sins. And she prayed God would keep her safe in the life she couldn't seem to stay away from.

That day Elle prayed a slightly different prayer too. She prayed for God to show her a sign. Tired of all the rumors, she was starting to lose faith in her and Knight's relationship. But she kept giving him the benefit of a doubt. She needed a sign. Then she'd have something concrete to base her decision on.

$$$

Elle had been raised to treat her body like a temple. She was brought up to believe that cleanliness was next to Godliness. She was a very clean girl, and saying so wasn't exaggerated. So imagine her shock when she sat on the toilet and discovered a weird discharge in the crotch of her panties.

Horrified, she bent down and smelled the gross looking paste. Elle wrinkled her nose. Wow! That didn't smell great at all. Damn, what the fuck was wrong with her twat?! Hardly used to foul-smelling discharge running out of her, she began to panic. Her instinct told her Knight had given her an STD. But she prayed she was wrong.

Too embarrassed to share her misfortune with her mom, sisters, or anyone else, Elle cut school the following

day and made tracks to Planned Parenthood. A gynecological exam and pap smear confirmed her fears. She was infected with Chlamydia. To make matters worse, they also discovered that she was pregnant.

Elle sat there shameful with her head hung low listening to the lecture the doctor gave her about safe sex. Afterwards, she hurried to fill the prescriptions she got and started her treatment.

Elle was devastated. She didn't want a baby anymore than she wanted an STD. She rehearsed in her head what she would say to Knight. He had knocked her up and burned her at the same time. She couldn't believe he put her in that position.

Elle put some of the blame on herself. She was playing the victim when the fact was that her intuition told her Knight was sleeping around, even when he denied it. She knew but chose to ignore it. Ignorance was bliss but ignoring the facts felt even better sometimes. Elle couldn't count on two hands the issues she chose to ignore in her relationship. Now she sat there with teardrops and regrets. She felt like a fool.

She hated to admit it but she had associated having unprotected sex with love and commitment. So as long as Knight was fucking her raw she had assumed she was special. Now she saw that she was the only dedicated one in their relationship. He was older than her but she was no dummy.

When she approached Knight about the STD he audaciously asked her if she got rid of it. He was completely unapologetic, like that was some everyday shit. If he felt any remorse he sure didn't show it.

Unsatisfied with his reaction, Elle pulled out what she thought to be the big guns. "And I'm also pregnant, asshole! So our baby could be born blind from this!"

She just knew he would feel horrible about endangering their baby's welfare with his whorish and unsafe ways, but the words he spoke were nothing like the sorrow-filled sentiments she expected.

"What? You *pregnant*? Elle, I don't want no *kids*! Nah, you gettin' rid of that! As soon as possible! Call somewhere and find out how much it cost. You really making my fuckin' head hurt with this shit!"

His verbal ambush cut through her spirit like a spray of buckshot. After that he just turned his back and walked out on her.

The apathetic prick offered no empathy about the situation whatsoever. Elle was floored. She stood there for a second dumbfounded. She felt numb but the pain gradually seeped through her veins to her heart. And then it penetrated her soul. At her breaking point, she sank to the floor and wept.

About twenty minutes later, the doorbell rang. Elle assumed Knight had come back to apologize and declare his undying love for her. She wiped her eyes and did a quick mirror check, and then hurried to the door.

When she looked through the peephole and saw Needra, her heart fell. Disappointed, she opened the door and greeted her cousin with a forced smile.

Needra was grinning from ear to ear but her smile faded at first glance. "Girl, you look horrible. What's wrong, boo?"

That statement just triggered more tears. "I'm pregnant, Neej! And when I told Knight, h-h-he just walked out on me!"

Needra frowned and shook her head. She had a sensitive heart and hated seeing people cry. She hugged Elle and attempted to comfort her. "Don't cry, ma-ma. Don't cry. It's gon' be alright, girl. Trust me, boo."

Elle tried to shut off the waterworks while they headed inside the kitchen. No one else was home at the time so they could speak freely. Elle poured her heart out for about ten minutes and Needra just let her vent. She told her cousin about the STD she had and the whole nine.

When she was done spilling the beans, she said, "Please don't say nothin' to nobody about this, Needra."

Needra just made a face at her. She didn't bother to respond because Elle knew she could keep a secret. Needra

had dirt on Elle and her sisters that wild horses couldn't drag from her. She was a "take it to the grave" type of bitch.

"Do you want this baby, Elle?"

That was the million dollar question. Elle shook her head. "Honestly, I'm not ready yet."

"So maybe he did you a favor by walking out. Think about it like that."

Elle thought about it. Needra was right. She didn't want to have it. But it still hurt to know he didn't care. Damn, Knight was cold.

The following day, Elle researched the going rate for abortions. When she found out she paged Knight. When he called her back, she let him know the price. He said he had left town that morning but would wire her the money soon. Then he just hung up. Elle didn't like his tone. He really sounded distant.

He sent the money through Western Union that evening and insisted that she "go handle that" before the week was out. Then he cut the conversation short like there was nothing else to say.

The following Thursday, Needra accompanied Elle to an abortion clinic. She pocketed the money Knight sent her and used Needra's Medicaid card to pay for it. She went through with the abortion, but afterwards she prayed to God for forgiveness.

That incident changed Elle's feelings for Knight indefinitely. His nonchalant reaction to the situation made her see he definitely didn't love her the way she loved him.

$$$

That Monday, Ellen took the day off from work because she needed to see about her child. That afternoon she sat there at the kitchen table sorting out bills and worrying. She had been putting away some sock laundry that belonged to Elle when she stumbled across a pill bottle in her drawer. It was prescribed antibiotics. Ellen was no fool. She got alarmed and researched the medication. When she

learned that her daughter was being treated for an STD she knew an intervention was in order.

Ellen blamed herself more than anything. She worked all the time so she wasn't at home like she wanted to be. The kids had a lot of leeway but she trusted them to do the right thing. Her oldest, Etta, had been an easy going child. But number two, Twyla, was terrible. That one had really taken her through it. She was by far the most defiant one of the bunch. Her rebellion had contributed to Ellen and Elliot's separation. Elliot had blamed Ellen when Twyla got pregnant at fifteen.

And now Ellen's baby girl, Elle, was running astray in the world. Elle had always been the smartest of the litter book-wise, but she was really dumbing down lately. Elle was following in her older sister, Twyla's footsteps. She was trying to date drug dealers and run up and down the road doing mess she had no business involved with. Ellen loved Twyla just as much as she loved Elle but she didn't like that part one bit. Elle's recent off-track behavior was so out of character, Ellen wondered for the trillionth time if it was her fault.

About an hour later, Elle found her way home. She had high hopes of creeping in the crib unnoticed since she'd cut her afternoon classes to come home early for a nap. She was surprised to see her mother sitting at the kitchen table when she came in. She smiled to herself. Damn, she was busted. She knew there was a talking to in store for her.

No one was home but the two of them. Lady told her to have a seat. When she finally got Elle to stop tap-dancing around the issues she brought up and open up to her, they had a pretty good talk. At first Elle was so ashamed of the fact that her mother had found her antibiotics, she didn't want to talk about it. But she knew no one cared about her wellbeing more than Lady so she started acting more mature and told the truth. She broke down and tearfully told her about the STD and the pregnancy she had terminated.

Ellen was surprised and saddened that Elle had been forced to make such a grownup decision but she didn't judge her daughter. She just hugged her and told her she was

putting herself in the wrong situations. Making the wrong choices was causing her to grow up too fast. She said she should be enjoying her youth and molding her future instead of running around behind some old ass, unfaithful, diseased, manipulative fool that meant her no good.

Elle had no response for those words. She knew her mother was right. All she could do was cry.

Chapter 7

Elle probably could've gotten Knight out of her system if they had some time apart. She told him she hated him and wanted him to stay out of her life. But he wouldn't let off. He backed off for a few days, but he came back sincere, apologetic and bearing gifts. He told Elle he was sorry about the way he'd handled the news of her pregnancy. He said he didn't want any kids because he didn't believe he was going to be around long enough to raise them. Having children required making long term plans but the life he lived wouldn't allow him the luxury.

Elle was hurt by his words and told him to quit saying stuff like that. But she gave in and accepted his apology and also the new earrings and bracelet he gave her. She couldn't resist him.

He insisted that he'd been treated and cured of the Chlamydia so she dropped her guards. They showered together and then he licked her from head to toe and sexed her silly. Despite all the promises she made to herself, her mother, and to God, they had unprotected sex. Elle was a fool in love.

$$$

Olan, also known as O, was Elle's cousin from North Carolina. He was her father's sister, Aunt Audrey's son. So he was a first cousin just like Needra was. His mom and their dads were siblings so they were all very closely related.

O and his mother had a rocky relationship. She had a drug habit that was largely influenced by her husband, who

O didn't get along with at all. So he was raised by their grandparents.

Their grandmother had passed away three years ago so Olan was supposed to be living with their grandfather, who had since remarried. But Granddaddy's wife was strict and she despised Olan's love for the streets. So he winded up in Brooklyn staying with Elle and them. He was a fifteen year-old kid at the time with no where else to go so Ellen opened up her heart and took him in. Olan was her estranged husband's sister's child, but he was still her nephew.

He was a year younger than Elle, and the problem was that he didn't want to go to school or do anything positive. It was no secret that he desired to be a big time dope boy. He was so fascinated with Knight he had sort of developed some type of boy-crush on him. He admired Knight's swagger and wanted to get money with him bad as hell.

O managed to talk Knight into taking him out of town with him. He left Brooklyn with visions of big gold chains and drug dealing aspirations. He called home ever so often, but it was months before they saw him again. On the phone O always sounded like he was doing well so everyone figured he was living the good life he had predicted.

Then one day he just returned without any notice. He was acting real nervous and told Elle to tell Knight that she hadn't seen or heard from him. She and Knight were still dealing but O was family so she didn't ask any questions.

The following day, Knight called her and nonchalantly inquired about Olan's whereabouts. Elle told him she hadn't heard from her cousin, and asked how he was. Knight said O was good and changed the subject. She played it cool and chatted with him about the usual, and then they got off the phone.

Later that night, O confessed to Elle that he had run away from B-more after Knight beat him with a bicycle chain because some work and money came up missing. He was so hurt by that incident he had water coming out of his eyes as he was speaking. He had looked up to Knight on

some real "father" shit, so he couldn't believe he wouldn't take his word that he didn't steal from him. O said Knight was a lunatic. He told Elle some of the coldhearted things he had seen him do.

Some of the stuff he told her was hard to believe. Most of the time she was around Knight he was this thoughtful and intelligent creature who said positive and enlightening things. But she knew he had a flip side. That bastard could be cold. She thought about the murder she had witnessed him commit when she was twelve years old. Knight was ruthless. He had killed that guy in broad daylight, so he could be capable of anything.

O looked in Elle's eyes and told her he was afraid for his life. He said he knew too much. He had so much dirt on Knight and Rude they told him they would kill him if they ever came to a fork in the road. O said he thought he was tough but those niggas were beasts.

Out of town, everyone knew Knight as Corleone. And Rude went by the name Bugsy. He said they were on some real mafia shit. When you entered their "family" the only way out was death. Olan said he knew they would kill him because he had witnessed them kill two other young boys who wanted out. They had seen some gruesome stuff and discovered they weren't built for that lifestyle. They were killed simply because they wanted to go home.

O broke down and admitted he was the hit man on one of the jobs. He said he only killed the boy, who was around his age, because he wanted to show Corleone and Bugsy how gangsta he was. That was his way of proving his loyalty to the family.

He said they had celebrated afterwards with expensive champagne, and that night they gave him rank. He was in charge of two corners, which each had eight workers apiece. His job was to make sure the money was straight and keep the boys supplied with product. O said he was thrilled that he no longer had to hustle hand-to-hand, and started acting like a real boss. He admitted he started being a jerk to his underlings. He said he thought he was something, and started spending thousands of dollars on expensive Italian

suits and shoes, trying to dress like Rude and Knight, AKA Bugsy and Corleone.

But his bubble was burst the day that money and work came up missing. It happened at the hands of one of his subordinates, but O was in charge of them so as far as the bosses were concerned, it was his fault. And they took it out on his ass too. O said Bugsy just stood there smirking while Corleone beat him bloody. He said he was told if he didn't get that money back, he was a dead nigga. He promised them he would straighten face the following day, and hopped on the next thing smoking.

O said all he left with was the clothes on his back and the money in his pocket. So his stint as a high rolling, drug dealing boss was short-lived.

Olan was pacing back and forth so much he was about to walk a hole in Elle's bedroom carpet. He was exasperated. "Cuz, I done did enough shit where as I know I'm goin' to hell. I done sold my soul to the devil, and I ain't got *shit* to show for it. I ain't hafta kill that boy, so why the fuck I do that? I'm goin' to hell, cuz! My soul been claimed by Satan. I'm doomed! Cousin, I'ma fuckin' *burn*!"

Elle felt so sorry for him she almost cried. She was raised to fear God as well, so she was afraid for him too. They were brought up in the church so they both knew better. "Thou shall not kill" was one of the Ten Commandments. O was in so deep she regretted ever introducing him to Knight.

Forever the optimist, Elle hugged him and spoke positively. "Stop sayin' that, boy. God is a merciful and forgiving God. He'll give you another chance... If you repent."

Elle's parents had given each of them a bible when they were small. Elle kept hers on her nightstand. She retrieved it with the notion that her cousin should read some bible verses and pray.

When Olan saw that bible it was like he saw Jesus. He dropped to his knees and covered his head like he was shielding his eyes from blinding light.

Elle took that as a good sign. The presence of the bible moved something in him. He acknowledged God's power. She placed her hands on his shoulders. "O, calm down so we can pray."

At the mention of prayer, a ray of hope flickered in his eyes. O was raised by their grandmother, who was one of the hardest praying women on Earth. Grandma Ree used to pray so hard you could hear her five houses down. O knew the power of prayer. And he knew their grandma would've turned over in her grave if she knew the way he had sinned. Overwhelmed by the guilt, he broke down in tears.

Olan began begging God for forgiveness, morphing from a gangsta killer to the frightened fifteen year old kid he really was. "Oh God, please forgive me. I know I was wrong to do that stuff, but *please* don't turn your back on me, Lord! I don't wanna go to hell, Lord Jesus, please have mercy on my soul! I'm sorry, Lord. God forgive me, please!"

Elle prayed with her cousin and comforted him but she was more spooked by his stories than she let on. How could Knight do that to him? He was supposed to look out for Olan. He promised her he would. Elle was really hurt that he would do her family like that. She thought he loved her.

Where there is love there is pain. For the first time, Elle seriously rethought her position with Knight. Hearing about the bicycle chain beating he had given O was quite sobering. He wasn't the type of dude she could have a future with. Set aside the times she'd caught him cheating on her and the fact that he'd burned her. He was cruel.

In her heart, Elle knew she was ready for a change. She was also tired of living in fear. Knight and Rude had beef with all the corner boys around her way. They were troublemakers, and kept on sticking up spots. Dudes were angry and tired, and there was talk of retaliation.

One of the dudes they had beef with happened to be Twyla's new beau, Rome. Rome was also the father of the child Twyla just found out she was carrying. Rome was always going on about killing them niggas Knight and Rude. And Knight and Rude were always telling Twyla that her boyfriend was on the list. Twyla took their words serious,

especially because she used to mess with Rude. She knew he still cared about her, and that alone could be a reason to kill Rome. Rude had killed for less.

Elle was so scared of fueling the fire she had been avoiding Blaze. She spoke to him on the phone a few times but she didn't want to be spotted with him in public. She knew Knight had eyes everywhere so she couldn't take a chance like that. She didn't want to be the cause of them hurting each other.

Elle and Twyla were really worried about the guys bumping heads at their house. Shit could really get ugly because neither side was scared. They all sent threats to each other but neither sister desired the drama so they never relayed the messages.

It was getting so bad all the dudes around the way were calling Elle a traitor. They were saying she was running around with the enemy. She was constantly explaining that she was neutral. On several occasions she had been approached and warned in not so many words that there was a mark on her man's head. And Elle thought about what Blaze had told her at the party that night.

She was beginning to feel frightened. She didn't want to end up caught in the crossfire of bullets exchanged between rivals. It was real in the battlefield. A girl from their neighborhood named Eliza was recently killed when some dudes shot up her boyfriend's car. The fucked up part was that he saw them approaching and hopped out and ran without warning her. He just left her alone in the car to be ambushed. And she had a little two year-old girl.

When O got himself together, he also told Elle about the double life Knight was leading. He was messing with some girl who he was using to stash shit at her crib in Baltimore, and she was due to have a baby by him in a few months.

Elle was crushed by that news more than anything. She had been faithful to that bastard the whole time they were together. And he was having a baby with another girl

after he made her go get rid of hers. She thought about the way he had reacted to the news of her pregnancy.

Elle felt like somebody stabbed her in the chest and stomped on the wound. She fought back the tears starting to form. The news about that baby was the scissor that cut the string holding her to him. She decided she needed a break. Their relationship was over. She knew entirely too much now to love him the way she had. And there was no way she could be with a man who wanted to kill her cousin.

It was funny how she was so finessed by him at first, and now she was just depressed. Being with him was an emotional rollercoaster. It was literally draining her. She had lost sixteen pounds.

She wanted to break up with Knight yelling and screaming but she couldn't even let him know she knew about the baby. That would indicate that she had been talking to Olan. A part of her wanted to just ignore his calls but she had to act normal. Keeping quiet about things would protect her cousin.

God was the best of all planners. About a week later, Knight was picked up in Baltimore by the Feds. He was a known drug dealer from New York so they were trying to throw the book at him.

A small part of Elle was a little relieved but she was saddened by his arrest. What they had was special. Knight had taught her a lot. Depressed and in dire need of a change in her life, she thought about relocating. It was the end of the school year so she considered going to North Carolina in the fall. She only had one more year left in high school. Both of her older sisters had gone away for high school, and they told tales of how television-like school down there was. All the kids rode the school bus, and they actually had pep rallies and school dances.

More than anything, Elle wanted to go to a senior prom. Her older sister Etta's prom pictures were proudly displayed on the wall in their house. Elle wanted the whole storybook experience as well. She just wanted to be a normal kid for a while. She was wise beyond her sixteen years, and in too deep. It had been one hell of a year.

The following day, Lady told her she needed to talk to her when she got home from work. When her mother came in that night, she asked her what was going on with school. Elle looked baffled so she showed her a small stack of cut cards, which were these postcards the Board of Education sent out to your parents when you missed a class. Elle had cut a bunch of classes lately so she didn't even bother to lie. She just told her mother the truth. She was tired of school and wanted a change.

After talking with her mother, Elle decided to move down south and finish high school. She was feeling too weary at sixteen. She was so wrapped up in all the street shit around her she was missing out on all the things she should've been doing at her age. And she had let her grades slip so she had fallen behind like crazy. Elle just wanted to get her life back on track. She was unhappy with herself and wanted to do better.

Ellen knew what happened to Knight. She expressed sympathies but was secretly glad he was out of her daughter's life. He was always respectful around her but she heard things in the street. And her husband was always saying how dating drug dealers was going to get their daughters killed. She hated to hear him say such things but she knew he was worried and concerned just as she was. They both prayed every day for their kids' safety.

Ellen happily made arrangements for Elle to start school down south in September. She had sisters on that end that got her the information she needed. It was settled. Elle would be staying with Ellen's mother, her Grandma Susie.

Chapter 8

Elle spent her summer hanging with her girls and just having fun. She was a teenager again. Life without so much adult responsibility was good. She went to parties, hung out until the break of dawn doing nothing useful, and slept all day. She actually felt like a normal sixteen year-old. On Mondays and Wednesdays she volunteered at the public library in her neighborhood to support their literacy drive. It felt good because she was motivating kids to read. Hopefully they would fall in love with books like she had when she was small.

That summer Elle also played the flirt game with a couple of dudes just to see where it went. One of the dudes was a little more special than the others. She'd been chilling with Blaze quite a bit. They hadn't been intimate yet but they spent a lot of late nights talking. He was only seventeen but he had swag like he was destined to be a boss.

Blaze was a smart dude who wouldn't hesitate to bust his gun. Elle had a thing for street dudes who were also intelligent. She couldn't help it. And him being her age made them even more compatible. He was more her speed.

During her summer fling with Blaze, Elle realized that she really liked him. After they had sexual intercourse she found that she liked him even more. Much more. But he was young, and seeing other girls as well. Elle didn't approve of that but she was leaving soon so she didn't stress over it.

The summer vacation was over before you knew it. Elle's family threw a huge cookout on Labor Day weekend, and then she left for North Carolina. It was September of 1992, two weeks before her seventeenth birthday.

$$$

Elle expected down south to be lots of fun. She had always enjoyed herself when she visited before. She had cousins her age down there who could show her around, so she assumed it would be a blast. But when she got down there her grandmother was tripping. She was treating Elle like some bad girl from the city that had been sent away for imprisonment. Elle explained that she had made the decision to come down there and finish school herself. It wasn't a punishment.

Grandma wasn't trying to hear that. Her exact words were "Look'a here, girl. This ain't New York City! You don't come down here with all that street runnin' and mess y'all do up north."

Elle just shook her head. When she got enrolled in school she met some new acquaintances. A lot of them were actually related to her. Her mom and dad were from the same town so between the two of them, she had a lot of kinfolk. Her new friends boasted about the happening nightlife down there so she was anxious to check out the club scene. She wanted to see how they partied in the south.

Elle begged her grandmother to let her go out but she still wasn't trying to hear that. On weekends she was on 23-hour lockdown. The only place Elle was allowed to go was church for choir rehearsal on Saturday and service on Sunday. Her grandmother directed the church choir just like her mother did in New York, so Elle was forced to join.

Elle didn't mind going to church and singing in the choir. She learned some new gospel songs that were real nice. She loved to sing. But she needed other social outlets as well. She was used to partying all through the week whenever she felt like it. As long as she went to school, her mother cut her lots of slack. Lady let her rock so Grandma Susie was really blowing her buzz. She came down there to have a great senior year experience. She couldn't do that hiding in the woods.

Elle put up with being a prisoner for a couple of weeks but on her birthday weekend she decided she was going out - even if she had to sneak out. While she was in school on Friday she arranged for this girl she had befriended, Natalie, to pick her up that night. The trick was Natalie had to park down the road from her grandmother's house and shut off her car lights. She was to arrive at ten o'clock.

That night Elle cleaned up the kitchen for her grandmother and asked her if she needed her to do anything else before she went to bed. She faked a yawn and a stretch, and said she was beat. Grandma said she was good and told her to go on and lay down. Elle went and got in bed, where she pretended to fall asleep.

She knew her grandmother's schedule. She went to bed around nine o'clock at night and was up at dawn every morning. At 9:06 the lights went off in the front room. Seconds later Elle heard Grandma Susie's footsteps go pass her room down to her bedroom. Elle smiled in the dark.

She laid there until she no longer heard any movement. When she glimpsed at the clock it was a quarter to ten. She got up as quietly as she could and stuffed her bed pillows under the covers to make it look like she was still laying there. Then she used a nightlight to quickly get dressed. After she combed her hair Elle opened her bedroom window and broke out of prison.

Her heart was beating like she was a runaway slave. She carefully closed the window behind her and started down the long driveway to the road. It was so dark out there she was spooked. The crickets and frogs sound effects only made the atmosphere more eerie and Halloween-like. It was creepy. Elle broke into a little trot.

Grandma's house was sitting right next to a pond. As a child Elle had fished for tadpoles there with her cousins Abe and Keith. And she especially loved how the frogs used lily pads to maneuver across the water. That pond was like a gateway to another world during the summers of her childhood when she and her sisters were shuttled down south from the city.

But right about now that pond was as spooky as The Black Hole. Nighttime in her grandmother's community was the blackest night she'd ever seen. Fear of the unknown made the hairs on the back of Elle's neck stand up.

When she finally got to the road, she saw Natalie's car sitting there with the parking lights on. Elle hurried to the car and jumped inside. They laughed and hit high-five.

Natalie said, "I see you got out okay. Yo' ass lucky I was on time. It's dark as hell out here." She started up the car and pulled off.

Elle laughed, "It sure the fuck is. Girl, thanks for picking me up. It feels so good to get out that house! It's my mothafuckin' birthday! I'm ready to shake my ass!"

They partied until about two AM and had a ball. That night Elle met Randy, who was one of the most wanted dudes in town. While conversing with him she got quite a few dirty stares from some of the local girls. She discovered that he was just as cool as he was cute.

Either Randy was used to getting what he wanted, or he just thought city girls were easy. At the end of the night he boldly asked her to accompany him to "go get a room for a few hours." Elle laughed and told him he had the wrong chick. He grinned and said he liked a girl who didn't put out on the first night. They exchanged numbers and set up an informal date to "go see a movie or something."

Elle accepted Randy's offer to drive her home that night. He lived in the town's city limits but he knew those back roads pretty well. He said he had some kinfolk just down the road from her grandmother's house. She joked that they were probably related. He said he hoped they weren't but being cousins didn't count after third. They shared a good laugh at that one.

Right before they got to her grandma's house he pulled over and killed the engine. It was interesting to know he'd heard of her before he actually laid eyes on her. Allegedly, there was a rumor out that she was hustling weed. Elle thought about the five fat nicks she had brought down south with her. The other day she sold these boys at school a

bag for twenty dollars. They wanted more but Elle didn't want to part with her last shit. That hardly constituted being a weed dealer but word really spread fast down there.

She and Randy sat there talking for about thirty minutes before Elle finally said goodnight. She liked him so she kissed him on the cheek before she got out of the car.

Elle tiptoed across the lawn to the side of the house where her bedroom was. As quietly as she could, she attempted to lift the window so she could re-enter the house the same way she had exited. But for some reason it wouldn't open. Elle cursed under her breath and tried with all of her might. That shit wouldn't even budge.

Somehow the window was locked. Her heart sank. She knew her grandmother was behind that. She locked her out of the house. Just then Elle heard a dog howling in the distance. Another dog joined him, and her imagination ran wild. She envisioned a pack of wild wolves sniffing out her flesh and heading towards her scent.

The sounds of the frogs and crickets chirping were amplified like she was in the jungle. Elle imagined she heard ferocious hooves and paws pounding the pavement like untamed beasts were approaching! Lions and tigers and bears were coming!

Elle got so frightened she ran around the house to the front porch. She started hollering and banging on the door for her grandmother to let her inside. She was frantic. She just knew those beasts were coming.

Grandma Susie finally turned on the porch light and opened the door. She was wearing a blue floral print nightgown and stood there with her arms crossed. She was just as calm. "Well, look'a here …"

"Grandma, you ain't have to lock the window like that. It's dark out here!"

Granny just looked at her for a second, and then she closed the door in her face. Elle stood there in disbelief.

A minute later she came back to the door. Elle breathed a sigh of relief and got ready to go inside the house. Her grandmother handed her a blanket and a pillow. Elle

took the items and stared down at them like they were foreign objects.

Her words dripping with sarcasm, Grandma Susie laid it on her. "You wanted a long night out, child. Ain't that right? You wanted to get out the house. Now you out here, so enjoy yourself."

Grandma chuckled at her own wit, and continued. "And since you like to check in and out at your leisure… I'll act like this here the Motel 6 and leave the light on for you. Good night, darlin'." After that she closed the door.

When Elle heard that lock turn she wanted to scream and kick the door in. She imagined herself choke-slamming her granny. She knew she had no wins so she fixed her blanket and pillow up like a sleeping bag and laid on down. Ensconced in the bedcover, she laid there for a while feeling sorry for herself. She wanted her mama. Her grandmother was cruel. She should've never come down there in the first place. When Elle finally dozed off it was after 4:00 AM. She fell asleep with her blanket over her head like a frightened child.

She didn't know but her grandmother sat by the window with a shotgun the whole time she was out there. She wanted to teach her a lesson but she didn't leave her in harm's way.

At sunrise, Grandma Susie opened the door and shook her awake. She asked her if she enjoyed her night out. Elle just made a face. Grandma laughed and told her to go inside and get in the bed.

$$$

Elle was ready to go back home after that incident but her mom and her older sister encouraged her to stay down there and finish out the school year. When Elle told them how Grandma Susie had locked her out the house, Lady and Etta actually found it funny. After that, Elle had to laugh too. Grandma Susie was no joke. That old lady did not play.

To Elle's delight, her cousin, Keith, came back home in October. Keith was her mother's sister, Aunt Janet's son. He and Elle had been very close when they were younger. Keith had joined the Navy but was dishonorably discharged for smoking marijuana. He told Elle he didn't care because the military just wasn't for him. He said he'd just been trying to follow in his dad's footsteps.

Elle finally got a little freedom because her grandmother let her ride out with Keith on the weekends. He was a year older than Elle, and had graduated from the high school she was attending the year before. Keith was a pretty popular dude so it wasn't long before she knew just about everybody in the town.

Elle was still talking to Randy off and on but she had acquired other friends too. There was Big Fats, a very well-known local big timer who wooed her with gifts and money. She wasn't sexually attracted to him but fucked with him because he was so freehearted. Then there was Tango, who was a hustler on a smaller scale. He had a nice car and a nice face and body but he was known more for his short temper than long money. He got respect because he was feared. Fats and Tango had never been the best of friends, nor were they rivalries. But after Elle got in the picture they did a lot of face fighting and mean mugging each other.

Elle met some cool ass chicks down there too. Toni and Natalie were two she became rather close with. Toni was actually related to her on her mother's side. They got so cool Elle started staying overnight at her house sometimes. Toni's whole family was cool. Her mother treated Elle like she was one of hers.

Recognizing the high demand for good weed in the town, Elle got fed up with smoking that backyard boogie and decided to supply it. Toni was interested so they went half on a quarter pound. Elle sent the money to her sister in New York, who got what she needed and mailed it back to her. Then she and Toni officially became weed dealers.

Each time they needed to re-up, Elle wired Etta the money to cop for her. Twyla was her go-to girl at first but now she was wobbling around almost eight months pregnant.

She had her own place now too. Rome was living there with her and she was in her own little world. Elle called it "The Twyla Zone."

But her big sis Etta stepped up and came through for her. Etta would wrap the weed in saran wrap and hide it inside of a stuffed animal through a slit she made on the bottom. She would then package it as a gift with a card inside and send it through the post office. Elle had lots of "birthdays" and even more cake.

Another girl Elle had befriended down south was Theresa. Theresa was real heavy into her cousin Keith but she was cool. She insisted that she and Elle hang out sometimes. She had a car so Elle didn't have a problem with that. A friend with a car was a big plus down there. It was so rural you had to drive to the doggone store.

One Friday night Theresa drove them out to this club called Triple AAA. It was located two towns over so it was a thirty minute drive. Elle was riding shotgun and the back seat was occupied by this girl named Loretta and these bitches Elle didn't care for, Bianca and Wendy. Those two were some childish hoes.

Loretta was a nice looking girl with a nice personality. She seemed like she was really sweet. But every time she turned her head Bianca and Wendy kept making fun of her. They kept making ape-like gestures behind her back insinuating that she looked like a monkey. Stupid shit like scratching themselves and pretending they were peeling bananas.

Loretta didn't look anything like a monkey. They were clowning her because of her dark skin. Elle wasn't amused. She was a chocolate sister just a couple shades lighter. Loretta was cuter than both of those bitches, so they were just hating. Her flawless dark coffee colored skin put Bianca's pizza face and Wendy's huge open pores to shame. They were so ignorant, Elle hated being in the same car with them.

That whole night Theresa kept saying how much she was looking forward to Keith showing up. She loved him to

death and swore they were an item. Elle knew better but she didn't say anything. Keith had told her that Theresa was basically just a booty call sometimes. He had a main girl, Angel, who he loved and would likely marry one day.

Around midnight, Keith showed up with Angel. Theresa looked like she saw a ghost. She wanted to fight Angel but Elle pulled her out of the club. She told Theresa she was out of line because Angel didn't know anything about her. And she was playing herself by trying to fight over a dude.

Theresa then channeled her anger on Keith. She started going crazy and yelling how she would kill him for hurting her that way. Then she just took off and ran to her car. Elle followed her, assuming she had a weapon or something. She wanted to make sure that nutcase didn't try to hurt her cousin.

Theresa frantically popped her trunk. She pulled out two butcher knives and then she declared that she was about to end it all. Elle reasoned with her and got her to give her the knives. They got inside the car and she spent about twenty minutes talking to her and calming her down. She told her how dumb and desperate stabbing a dude for not loving you was. And she let her know she wasn't going to just stab her cousin without some serious repercussions.

Teary eyed and scorned, Theresa finally pulled it together. She swore she was done with Keith and would never let him hurt her again. Exhausted, Elle summoned the other girls from the club so they could head on home.

It was a long ride back, especially with those dumb bitches still clowning Loretta. Their little jokes were so annoying, Elle barked on them. She looked back there and said, "Word up, y'all bitches need to grow the fuck up!" She was hoping they would jump but neither one of those hoes said shit. Not to her face anyway.

Chapter 9

Time had gone by pretty fast because Elle was enjoying herself for the most part. Before you knew it the holidays rolled around. She was excited because she'd be spending the school break at home.

When she got back to New York she and her girls picked up right where they left off. They partied the whole Christmas vacation and had a great time. But the real joy of Elle's vacation was the fact that she had a new nephew. Twyla had just given birth to a fine son.

The women in their family outnumbered the males three to one so they were excited to finally have another boy. The whole Mitchell clan was overjoyed. Elle was down south during the first two weeks of his life but she had the privilege of naming her nephew the day Twyla had him. Xavier Malachi Mitchell was adorable.

$$$

Meanwhile, down in NC some serious foul play was underway. Theresa was still a bitter scorned woman, and leapt on the opportunity to turn on Keith. She had a cousin named Tyrell who used to be Keith's boy, but now envied him for driving a better car than he did. Theresa told Tyrell she overheard Keith saying he disliked him. Tyrell told all his boys, twisting the words to reflect Keith saying he had a problem with their whole crew.

To a pack of petty rebels without a cause, that was all the reason they needed. At the club on New Year's Eve a bunch of broke haters assembled and surrounded Keith in the

parking lot. Keith was a lover not a fighter, so he never really had much beef. He listened to the bogusness they approached him with and was unprepared for what happened next.

Keith had no idea what they were talking about. He opened his mouth to deny their accusations but barely got a word out when this knucklehead in the crowd sucker punched him. Keith was surprised but he delivered a counterpunch. He had no problem defending himself but he was grossly outnumbered so the odds were against him. There were around twenty of those assholes and they had one thing in common. All those bastards envied him.

The crowd got rowdy and moved in on him. He fought back but he was no match for the army of screaming madmen. Keith tried to make a run for it. He headed for the woods but didn't get far. Someone fired a shot at him and the bullet struck him in his lower back. He fell to the ground and those savage beasts beat him like a dog. He was mercilessly pummeled, kicked, and stomped. Two of the monsters had wooden baseball bats and hit him upside his head repeatedly.

When they were done beating him to a bloody pulp, one of those bastards pulled out his penis and pissed on him. Afterwards, they just left him lying in the woods alone. The excessive inhumane abuse he suffered left him unconscious and barely clinging to his life.

$$$

Early New Year's morning Ellen was in the kitchen. She had just put on a pot of greens and a pot of field peas to commemorate the occasion and bring forth New Year's blessings. Her daughters were sleeping late after celebrating with too many vodka shots the night before. Ellen was just happy they were all at home.

They had adhered to their family tradition and gone to church the night before. Ellen was from the old school. She believed it was best to bring the New Year in inside the house of the Lord. But after that her daughters were anxious to go partying.

The phone rang so she peaked at the caller ID. There was a number with a 910 area code so she knew it was family from down south. Ellen got that familiar knot in her stomach she got sometimes when she got a phone call. She whispered a quick prayer that everyone was okay and picked up the receiver. "Hello?"

"Ellen, this is Rhonda. I'm afraid I have some bad news, girl."

Ellen gripped the counter and braced herself for her younger sister's news. Praying their mother was okay, she asked, "What happened?"

Rhonda sighed like it hurt to say it. "Last night at some old hole-in-a-wall nightclub, Kitty's son Keith was shot and beat half to death. It's real bad, Ellen. He's in I.C.U. in… In a coma." Her voice cracked like she was on the verge of tears.

At the news of their baby sister, Kitty's son suffering a beating bad enough to leave him comatose, Ellen's eyes filled with tears. That was absolutely heartbreaking. "Oh Lord, no! Dear God, Rhonda, what happened?"

Her sister went into details as best she could. Their nephew had been brutally attacked by some boys he went to school with. Boys he used to be good friends with. They had jumped him and beat him in his head with bats and sticks. And then somebody shot him. She said they left him lying by the woods to die.

After she spoke to her sister Kitty and their mother, Ellen hung up and went to wake up her kids. She hated to but she had to give them the bad news. Their cousin Keith was a humble and respectful child. She fought back her tears and prayed for him.

When Lady woke them up and gave them the news about their cousin clinging to his life the sisters were all crushed. Elle gasped in horror. She was just with Keith. He drove her to the Greyhound station to catch the bus home for the holidays. And she just spoke to him the day before, on New Year's Eve, to confirm that he would pick her up when she got back down there. She literally pinched herself to

make sure she wasn't dreaming.

They all joined hands and prayed for Keith's recovery. After that, Elle called down south. Her homegirl Toni let her know what the word was. That crazy obsessed bitch Theresa was involved. Elle thanked Toni for the info and pulled her sisters' coats.

The family made preparations to head south to be with their loved ones. Their father, Elliot, was going down there with them. He was distraught by the news as well. Needra was going too. They were all leaving the following day. Everyone was going except for Twyla's four-week-old baby, little Xavier, who would stay at her crib with his father.

Before the family could make that trip they got a call saying Keith didn't make it. He had succumbed to his head injuries. Needless to say, there were tears spawned by that news. It was hard to believe he was gone. And the way he was killed was just senseless.

There was no way Theresa was going to get away with that. That psychotic bitch had caused Keith's demise. That was some dirty shit she did. He died because she was mad he didn't want her ass. And he died at the hands of his so-called friends. That was some bullshit.

Grief-stricken, Elle and her family journeyed down south for Keith's homegoing service. They got there in time for Ellen to help out with the arrangements. Everyone down there was taking it real hard so it was definitely a time for family to stick together.

When the day of the funeral came, the turnout was amazing. That bitch Theresa had the audacity to show up. Elle and her sisters viewed her coming there as blatant disrespect to their entire family. Especially to Keith's mother, Aunt Kitty.

At the end of the service Elle spotted Theresa walking towards the church doors. She quickly notified her sisters that the bitch was trying to bounce. Teary eyed and emotional, they walked out behind her. Needra knew what was up so she followed them too.

The girls all grew up in the church so they were God-fearing young ladies who acknowledged and respected the fact that church ground was sacred. But lucky for them, Theresa stepped off church ground and headed towards her car. There were so many people at the funeral the church parking lot was full, so she had been forced to park down the road.

The girls leapt on that opportunity like predators, each almost foaming at the mouth for a piece of her. The four of them ran up on Theresa and surrounded her like wolves. Etta put her hand in her face and demanded to know why she had done their cousin so dirty. Theresa tried to play like she was innocent, so Etta lost it. She hauled off and slapped fire out that bitch. Elle, Twyla, and Needra followed suit, and the four of them fucked her trifling ass up.

Theresa was scared to death. She was crying the whole time, and kept shouting, "Wait, I'm pregnant!"

A couple of her homegirls tried to help her but it was no use. They were no match for the rowdy New York girls. They scragged Theresa out there and then pushed her down in the ditch. Her dress was torn off in the process.

Theresa lay on the ground sobbing but Twyla was unsatisfied. She wanted blood. That busted nose wasn't enough. She reached in her bag for her blade, determined to cut that dirty bitch across the face. That way she would never forget that ass whipping.

Elle saw her sister going in her purse and stopped her. "Twyla, no! Not here!" She didn't know what Twyla was digging for but she knew her sister. There were too many witnesses out there.

Twyla knew Elle was right so she stopped and didn't pull out her razor. But she used her fist to sock Theresa in the face again. After that she spit on her.

Elle snatched that bitch's head back by her ponytail and snarled, "It's on every fuckin' time I see you, hoe!"

Throughout the melee people were hollering and speculating. Someone yelled "Somebody better call the police!" After hearing that the girls slid back to the church

where their family was.

Later on that day everyone was back at Grandma Susie's house when a sheriff's car pulled up in the yard. The sisters knew what it was before he got out and knocked on the door.

Just as they had feared, the police had an arrest warrant for Etta, Elle, and Elaine Mitchell. Needra was lucky. They didn't call her name. Theresa had so many people whipping on her she probably didn't know who was involved.

They were taken down to the county jailhouse and booked. Their mother and aunts followed the police cars so they were waiting to bail them out immediately. The sisters came out of it with assault charges but it was well worth it. And they would do it again if they had to.

The paperwork said that bitch Theresa was really pregnant. She was saying it was Keith's baby. The family didn't know if that was true or not but time would tell.

Their family would slowly regroup from their loss but Cousin Keith would forever be missed. His mother would never be the same because a part of her died too. And he was her only child.

Chapter 10

The past months had been difficult but amongst all the adversity Elle managed to stay in school and maintain her grades. It was March now so the semester was quickly coming to an end. She was so close to graduating she could taste it, so she kept her eyes on the prize, determined to be done with school.

One day Twyla called down south and put her up on the latest happenings up top. She started off by saying she had yet to go back to cosmetology school. Elle reminded her how close to finishing she was. That maternity leave was no longer an excuse. Silly as usual, she started singing "Beauty School Dropout" from the movie "Grease."

Twyla started cracking up, and said, "Elle, you so stupid." She proceeded to fill her comedienne wannabe sister in on all the latest dirt. She told her that Mena and Cherry got caught while taking some shit out of town for Cherry's cousin, Rich. Twyla said they were locked up and Rich was fronting on them. He had it, but he didn't want to up no bail money or lawyer bread. So they had no choice but to lay up in there until their $200,000 bond came down.

Cherry and Mena both had a lot of shit with them but the sisters prayed they would be alright. They wouldn't wish that trap on their worse enemy. They all got their hands dirty so that could be any one of them.

$$$

Easter came around a few weeks later. During her time off school Elle went home for a week. When she got

there she discovered she had mail from Knight. That was funny because he had been on her mind lately. She guessed they were on the same page.

She opened the letter and began reading the first page. Wow, he was apologizing for all he did to her. He said he really missed her and hoped she was doing well. He said he was sorry he wouldn't be able to make her high school graduation but he'd be out before she finished grad school. Elle smiled when she read the part where he said he would always love her, and still intended to make her his little wife one day.

Knight said he'd still been getting those headaches, even though he was getting all the rest he needed. Then he ended the letter with words Elle needed more than she knew:

Elle, I made you get rid of that baby because I loved you. I didn't want to mess up your life. You going places. (smile) Baby girl, I always knew my end was near. I didn't want to drag you down that road with me. You're special, and you were too good for me. I knew that from day one.

Love you forever,
Knight

Elle cried when she read that letter and cherished it. They hadn't been in touch but she had to write him back. She even thought about going to visit him. He was in federal prison in Kentucky. She couldn't go see him yet because she wasn't old enough. But she would be eighteen soon. Then maybe she would surprise him. Knight was out of her system but she would always love him. Regardless of what happened between them, she wished him well and would never forget him.

$$$

When May came, Elle got a chance to go to that prom she had always dreamed of. She went single with her homegirls and they did it way big too. She felt like a princess

that night, and took those prom photos she knew would adorn her mother's wall like Etta's.

A few weeks later, it was graduation time. The whole Mitchell clan came down south for the occasion. Her parents, sisters and brother, and nieces and nephew. Elle was thrilled. She walked across that stage proud. She hadn't quite decided what to do with her life yet but she knew one thing. She was going back home. NC had been fun but NYC was calling.

$$$

When Elle went back home, she and her sister started hanging real tight. Twyla still had her own crib so Elle started staying there most of the time. Twyla's daughter was usually with Etta so it was just her, Elle, and the baby. Little Xavier was six months old now.

Twyla's baby daddy, Rome, lived there too but he was quite the "outdoorsman." The nigga never came home. After she had the baby she wanted them to be a family but he couldn't stand still long enough. That saddened Twyla for a while but when Elle came back she quit moping around and they got moving. The two sisters started running the streets and that baby weight she was carrying fell right off. Before you knew it, she was back to her old self.

Twyla and her daughter's father, Bilal, were good friends. He always had something for them to do to make a lick. That summer she and Elle made the bulk of their living transporting drugs to Virginia. They were alternating trips every other week. Etta even did it sometimes.

Twyla was lucky because Etta kept her children most of the time. It was like Etta had three kids. She complained about babysitting but she did it because she loved her sister's kids to death. Before Twyla had the new baby, Etta swore she wouldn't be keeping that one. But now that he was getting a little older, she kept him all the time.

$$$

Winter rolled around, and Mena and Cherry finally got out of jail. What was funny was that they both had all these jail stories about each other being scared to death in there. One of Cherry's recollections was that bitches had Mena under so much pressure she was hand-washing their panties for them. Mena said these chicks in there got so tired of smelling Cherry's smelly ass they threw her in the shower and scrubbed her twat with a long handled brush. Neither could prove who was telling the truth but both of their stories were hilarious.

About a month after she came home, Mena came through to holler at Twyla and Elle about a new hustle she had. She knew a dude who was looking for girls who were willing to get married for money. The catch was they had to travel to Bangladesh to do it. She said there were lots of intelligent young men over there that needed green cards so they could get into the United States. They just wanted a chance to get a piece of the American dream.

Mena said the guy, Mohammed, paid for the passports required to travel abroad and also gave shopping money to the girls who agreed to go. She swore she knew it was safe because she had gone and done it herself. In disbelief, the sisters demanded details.

Mena laughed and told them all about her experience. She made it sound wonderful and exciting. When she told them how much it paid, and how they took her shopping over there and treated her like royalty, Twyla and Elle were pretty much sold. They told her to count them in so she said she would make it happen. They just had to give her a hundred dollars apiece, which was like a finder's fee.

Two days later, they met Mohammed. He was a tall and lanky dark-haired Bangladeshi gentleman who chained smoked these strong ass smelling cigarettes. He wasn't bad looking but his teeth were badly stained, obviously from those cigarettes.

He was a man of Muslim faith so he said he couldn't shake their hands when they extended them, but he greeted them cordially nonetheless. Mohammed asked them a few questions and then explained how things went. They were

going to get passports and then he would provide the plane tickets and any other expenses associated with the trip. And Mena was right, he told them he'd also give them a hundred dollars apiece so they could buy cigarettes and stuff for the trip. He said the stores in Bangladesh did not carry the brands they were accustomed to. Elle nor Twyla smoked cigarettes but they were cool with that.

They spent the following week gathering all the necessary documentation required to obtain their passports. The process was especially tedious for Elle, who had to get a corrected birth certificate issued first. Those people had her running back and forth like a chicken with its head cut off. Finally, after three weeks, the sisters had their passports and it was time to go. Their flight was leaving in five days.

They purposely didn't tell anyone where they were going. Especially Etta and their parents because they knew they would worry. Elle and Twyla lied and said they were going to Atlantic City for the weekend with some guys they met.

Three days before they left, Twyla got fed up with Rome fucking up and put him out of her house. She finally came to terms with the fact that their relationship wasn't working. He was cheating on her again and she was tired. She said she wanted him out before she left for Bangladesh because she was afraid he might bring a bitch in her crib or something. That was how little she trusted him.

It had gotten so bad between them it even got physical a few times. Elle and Etta had to break up some pretty bad fights between them. And their sister was usually the aggressor. Twyla's crazy ass broke plates across Rome's head and the whole nine. And it was always over him not respecting her enough to come home.

Twyla had a bad temper but Rome was a piece of work too. He had been since they hooked up. He wasn't Mr. Right but Twyla had a soft spot in her heart for him. She felt sorry for him because his mother died when he was small and he didn't really have anybody. But now she said it was over. She cried him out of her system for two days and then

she was good.

Chapter 11

The day finally came for them to leave for Bangladesh. Elle and Twyla took a taxi to Kennedy airport and boarded an American Airlines flight to London. When they got there they would catch a plane to Chittagong, Bangladesh.

They arrived at London's Heathrow Airport almost eight hours later. They had prayed their flight would be safe and thankfully it was. Over there they were in a different time zone. London was five hours ahead of New York. The girls realized they had a ten-hour layover until their connecting flight to Bangladesh departed. Ten hours was a long stretch so they had to kill some time.

They wanted to get out and see London but then decided against it because they were afraid they might get lost. There were stores right there inside the airport so they got some food and then did some shopping. They started out at this chic European boutique. In order to purchase the shoes they selected they had to exchange some of the American dollars they had for pounds. So they had a hands-on lesson in currency exchange. They were both surprised to learn that a pound was worth more than a dollar.

Elle and Twyla each copped two pairs of bad ass European shoes and then they looked in some souvenir shops. After that they went to a duty-free liquor store and purchased two bottles for their trip. There was still time to kill so they thought about leaving the airport again. Elle reminded Twyla that they also had luggage. And if they messed around and missed their flight they were in trouble.

The sisters didn't buy cigarettes with the shopping

money Mohammed gave them but they bought weed. They copped an ounce so they'd have enough to last them during the trip. They had smuggled it on the plane inside their panties. That was no big deal to Elle or Twyla because they had both smuggled worse and far greater.

Twyla had some White Owls in her carryon bag so they searched for a less busy section of the airport. Along the way they stopped and bought a pack of cigarettes. The girls found a bathroom in a quiet spot on the other side of the airport that seemed desolate enough, so they quickly twisted up an el. Twyla flushed the blunt guts down the toilet and they were done in no time.

Elle peeked outside to make sure the coast was clear and then Twyla sparked up. The sisters passed the blunt back and forth until they were both mellow. To combat the smell, Elle lit a stogie from the pack of Benson & Hedges they bought and just let it burn out to cover up the pungent weed smoke.

Seconds after Twyla flushed the blunt roach down the toilet, a woman walked in pushing a cart full of cleaning supplies. She was dressed in a uniform so they assumed she was an airport custodian. When the acrid smoke hit her she made a face and fanned under her nose. The girls were nervous but they played it off cool. They just washed their hands and then politely smiled at the woman on their way out. She gave them a knowing look and then spoke to them in a thick British accent.

"You girls are from the States, I know, and you better be careful out 'ere. If they catch you smoking that stuff, they'll 'ang you. Personally, I don't 'ave anything against it. My old man smokes it, but I can't stand the smell of it. Travel safe now, young ladies."

They thanked her for the heads up and headed back to the other side of the airport. They knew how lucky they were that the person who caught them was cool. They could've got locked up in London. They were crazy to be smoking weed in the airport but God looked out for fools.

Feeling groovy and relaxed, they went into this news store and thumbed through some magazines. Elle wanted to

get something to read on the plane. While making her selection, she noticed this chubby White guy in glasses just staring at her. It was creepy because he didn't even look away when she caught him. He made her uncomfortable so she walked over there where her sister was. He must've followed her because the next thing she knew, he was standing right across from them staring again.

Elle nudged her sister and put her on point. "Twyla," she whispered, "Don't look, but this creep over there keeps staring at me."

Twyla being Twyla, she looked. When she noticed the guy she agreed with Elle. He looked like a damn pervert the way he was just leering at her. Twyla was shorter than Elle and a little smaller in stature but she was still the big sister. Her automatic defense mechanism kicked in and she stepped to that mothafucka.

With lots of Brooklyn in her tone, she asked, "Mister, can we help you?"

It worked. The man gave them a little smirk and left out of the store. Relieved, the sisters continued making their selections. After they were done they found a seating area close to the gate where they would be boarding their flight. They were pretty tired so it wasn't long before both of them were sitting there dozing off.

Twyla woke up about an hour later. The first thing she saw was that same creepy dude's face. The fat perv was sitting directly across from them. She poked her sister and woke her up. "Elle! Look at this fuckin' *weirdo*!"

Elle sat up and saw him just gazing at them. He was probably watching them the whole time they were asleep.

The man smiled and stood up and tipped his hat at them. He said, "Good morning, girls." Then he folded his newspaper and winked at them and walked off. After that television-like occurrence the girls didn't close their eyes again until they got on the plane.

$$$

The airline they were flying next was Air India. When they boarded the plane Indian culture was reflected in every aspect. They were greeted by these pretty Indian flight attendants who were dressed in traditional Indian attire and the staff and pilot all spoke Hindi as well as English. There was soft Indian music playing during the flight and the food they later served was Indian cuisine. Its aromatic spices wafted throughout the atmosphere and made everything smell like curry. It was actually a rather soothing experience.

The only Black girls onboard, Elle and Twyla received strange looks from some of the other passengers. Even the White people were looking at them strange. But both sisters were social butterflies. They were barely on the plane an hour before they befriended some German drinking buddies named Amit and Hans.

The plane made several stops along the way; Germany, Dubai, India, and then finally Bangladesh. It was interesting to learn that India was Bangladesh's sister country. And China was just on the other side. That was a lesson in geography.

They landed in Chittagong, which was a very large city in Bangladesh. When the sisters got off the plane they were a bit unnerved by the airport. It was sort of old fashioned looking but extremely busy. Lots of the native people were staring at them like they were something in a zoo. Mena had warned them about that and she was right. Those people could tell they were not from there. And them being dressed in jeans and boots and holding winter coats in their arms didn't help. It was about a hundred degrees in the airport and the natives were wearing lightweight traditional garments.

Elle and Twyla felt really out of place. When they spotted two men holding up these paper signs with their names written on them, they were so relieved they almost shouted for joy. Praise God, the Calvary had come. The men were dressed in button-up dress shirts and dress pants and spotted the only two African American girls in the crowd effortlessly. Grateful they were being rescued, the sisters started towards them.

They were greeted respectfully and whisked out of the airport and ushered to a car outside. The car was tiny and colorful. It looked like a cross between a go-cart and a golf car. The sisters were so happy to get off that plane they would've rode on a magic carpet with those Aladdin looking bastards at that point. They got inside the little car with their new friends and the driver quickly pulled off.

The men apologized for hurrying them but said they were concerned about their safety because the common folk were extremely poor. Americans were assumed to be well off so they were targets for crime. The men introduced themselves as Moziq and Harum. They were both kind natured and gave off good vibes.

It was a bumpy ride in that car. If the airport was nerve-racking, the ride to the hotel was terrifying. The girls learned that there were very few traffic laws in Bangladesh. Elle was so thrown off by the dangerous weaving in and out of traffic she had to close her eyes for a minute.

Along the way to their hotel, she and Twyla looked around amazed. It was hard to believe they were all the way across the world in Bangladesh. They thought of their family back home and laughed to themselves. They had to call their mom the first opportunity they got.

As they rode along, the gentleman named Harum pointed out monuments, landmarks and other things of importance and told them the significance behind each one. Intrigued by some of the things he said, the girls listened intently.

After hearing about the country's history, the sisters were awed and enlightened. But they were horrified by something else they saw there. When they stopped at a streetlight they were approached by some children who looked like they were very poor. The eldest was a pretty little girl about five years old. She was barefoot and wearing a filthy, tattered, threadbare dress. The girl had a little boy with her about two, who was completely naked. The kids stared at them with big sad brown eyes.

"Takas, please?" the little girl asked, holding out her

soiled little hand.

The sisters didn't understand what she meant but they assumed she was asking for money. It was saddening. The poor children looked like they'd just been abandoned. And they were around the same size as Twyla's little cubs so that really broke their hearts. Elle and Twyla both almost cried.

Their first instinct was to grab those babies and put them in the car with them. They knew they couldn't but they did what they could. They dug in their purses to give them money. They were appalled when the men they were riding with protested.

They tried to shoo the kids away and yelled, "No! Do not give them currency! They are just beggars!" The sisters ignored them and slipped the little girl five singles. Her little eyes lit up like she had just received a million bucks. She stood there smiling and waving as they pulled off.

The men told Elle and Twyla that one American dollar was worth one thousand takas, so they had given those children a small fortune. The men said that was enough to make some crazed or famished adult harm them for it. After hearing that, the sisters prayed they would be okay. That was heartbreaking.

Shocked by their blatant disregard for starving naked children, Elle asked the men why they had a problem with them helping some kids. In not so great English, they explained that that was their way of life. In their culture they lived by a caste system. There was a social order; therefore, the poor were of little importance. It was taboo to associate with the likes of such. They said it didn't matter that they were children. That was just the way it was.

The men were wealthy and not so compassionate. They were actually surprised that the sisters disagreed with their ways. When Twyla told them she had two kids the same size they understood and softened up a little. And they couldn't deny that those children needed that money.

Bangladesh was a very poor country that was under British rule, but had no welfare system or assistance for their poor at the time. It wasn't hard to tell because even the animals they passed looked like they were starving. You

could actually see the cows' ribcages and the chickens were so frail they looked like they were on crack.

As the party neared their destination the sisters realized that what had started out as a simple ploy to hustle up some extra cash would turn out to be a humbling lesson in humanitarianism.

Along the way the men stopped and granted their wishes to call home. They wanted to call their family to inform them that they were safe. Harum gave them a calling card he said would allow them a two minute call to America. Then he ushered them to a payphone booth in a busy shopping center.

There was a lot of activity out there so he posted up outside the phone booth while the sisters squeezed inside and closed the door. Twyla dialed the number Elle read off the calling card to her. After a series of beeps and tones, she was connected to an international operator who then connected her to their mother.

When Lady answered in her sleepy voice Twyla was reminded of the 11-hour difference in the time. It was the middle of the night in New York. She hated to wake her mother but they had to call when they could.

"Hey Lady! Me and Elle took a little trip so we just calling to let you know we're okay."

Ellen wasn't that surprised. Not by those two. "Twyla, where are you? I told y'all 'bout not letting somebody know where you are."

Elle leaned in closer ear hustling every word.

Twyla took a deep breath. "We're in Bangladesh. It's in Asia, right next to India."

Ellen sat straight up in bed. "What?!"

"Don't worry, we're fine. We just came over here to handle something. We're gettin' married, Mama!"

"*What*?! Gettin' married to who? Where's Elle?"

"I'm right here, Lady," Elle yelled. "We okay, don't worry!"

Ellen didn't know what to say. "Y'all don't know them people! Have you lost your minds?"

"No, we just doing it for the money," Twyla explained as if it was no big deal. "We gettin' paid."

Her attempt to calm her mother only scared her more. Ellen imagined them being kidnapped and stripped of their U.S. citizenship and never returning home. Before she could ask the questions racing through her mind, Twyla started rushing her off the phone.

"Lady, please don't worry. We love you, and when we get back we're gon' do somethin' real nice for you. I love you! I know my babies are sleeping but please kiss them for me and tell them I love them, and I'll be back soon."

"I will. Twyla, be safe, look after your sister, and get home to these kids! I love you too, baby."

"Okay, Ma, talk to Elle right quick 'cause we gotta go. The phone gon' cut off."

Elle jumped on the phone real quick. "Hey Lady, I love you! Are you okay?"

"I'm fine, Elle. Just get back here safe. *Please.*"

Elle heard the urgency in her mother's tone and knew she was worried. "We'll be back in a few days, Lady. We'll call you again as soon as we get a chance. Give everyone our love! Smooches! I love you!"

Ellen said, "I love you too, baby." There was a click so she hung up the phone. She lay there for a minute thinking. Twyla and Elle were at it again. It was always something with those two. She prayed for her daughters and asked God to protect them.

$$\$\$\$$$

When they finally got to the hotel the sisters were pleased by the décor and amenities it had. It was so comfortable they spent the first day inside just resting up. But the second day was crazy busy. The men who picked them up from the airport were the bosses. They wanted to show them off to the others.

Elle and Twyla were greeted and treated like royalty by a multitude of gentle respectful Muslim creatures that flocked in to meet them two by two. They seemed like clean

and decent people who were visibly excited by their arrival. Elle and Twyla did a lot of smiling and head nodding but they didn't understand a word they were saying.

A gentleman they learned was a lawyer spoke English also, so he translated their sentiments. He said they were grateful they had come to give their families the opportunity to live the American Dream by way of their sons. In Bangladesh, a chance to go to America was a once in a lifetime thing. That move would change their families' lives for generations to come. After hearing that, the sisters felt like they had come to do a good deed.

Later that day they were scheduled for a photo shoot of sorts. They were introduced to the young men they were to marry and then it was time to take some of the pictures that would help convince immigration that their love was real. Elle's future husband's name was Sheikh Mosleh Uddin. Twyla's was Shanawahz Mahmud. Neither was bad looking and both had a sense of humor. They cracked some jokes the sisters couldn't comprehend but the camaraderie was so strong they laughed along too. The group was full of happy people. Smiling was universal.

Elle's hubby thought he was a real playboy. His friends called him Love-Loo and he had this perfect hair, which he seemed to fix with a comb every five minutes. Every time they got ready to take a picture he pulled out that damn comb. Then the whole room would just erupt in laughter. It was hilarious.

Elle's brother-in-law, Arif, was fond of her and Twyla. He was a comical fellow who showed them the latest dances over there and kept asking if they knew Michael Jackson or Madonna. Circa 1994 in Bangladesh, those were the only American artists he really knew.

$$$

Two days later, it was time for their wedding ceremonies. The nuptials were performed by a jolly and wise bearded Imam. Elle and Twyla wore long white dresses that

were nice but rather plain. But their wedding rings made up for it. They were actually quite pretty, and made of 24-Karat gold.

Twyla's in-laws showed up bearing gifts and anxious to welcome her into their family. Especially the women. They fussed over her like she was a princess. Her mother in-law and sister in-laws were all pretty and very friendly. They were excited about the pictures they all took.

After the weddings, more pictures were needed for proof of the validity of their marriages, so they spent the next days going out to restaurants and other forms of entertainment. They rode two cars deep accompanied by an entourage of six; their husbands, the two bosses, their lawyer friend and Elle's brother in-law, Arif. There wasn't any lovey dovey stuff going on but from the pictures they took hugging, smiling, and gazing into each others eyes, you would believe the young couples were in love. It was acting at its finest.

They went just about everywhere for photos. Even the zoo. At the zoo, Twyla's silly behind kept managing to find animals that looked like someone they knew. She looked at this hyena and was like, "Oh shit! Elle, look! This hyena look just like Ronette from Willoughby."

Elle studied the animal's face and then just started rolling. It did look like Ronette. Her and Twyla laughed so hard tears came to their eyes. Ronette was this girl from around their way who had these big ass lips. She wasn't ugly but that hyena's wide mouth was just like hers.

To Elle and Twyla's delight, the entire following day was dedicated to shopping at the outdoor marketplace. There were some good finds out there. They bought stuff like beautiful scarves and jewelry. The leather sandals over there were really nice too. The sisters picked out a pair for each member of their family. When they were done shopping they were exhausted, so they headed back to the hotel to order a quiet dinner from room service.

The following day their new families showed up with more gifts. They were so kind they even bought gifts for their mother and Twyla's children. When they presented

Twyla with the gifts for her children it was funny because they bought her son a pair of shiny red shoes with a big red and white polka dot bow on the toe. The sisters gave each other the eye and silly Elle choked back laughter. Twyla was gracious about it. She smiled and thanked them but she informed them that she believed there had been a mix-up because she had a son who wore that shoe size, not a little girl.

They talked amongst each other in Bengali, their native language, for a minute. When they were done, their English speaking buddy said, "Twyla, in our country this shoe is used for both boy and girl."

Twyla smiled politely. "Oh, I see. Well thank you so much."

She didn't want to offend them so she would just keep the shoes. Returning a gift would only insult them. She was raised better than that, but her son would never wear those shiny red shoes with the polka dot bow a day in his life.

Elle and Twyla liked the way the Bangladeshi women dressed, so they had each requested an outfit of their own. The native women's traditional garb was called a sari. When they received the lovely garments they were delighted. The women fussed around the sisters and assisted them with wrapping themselves in their saris properly.

Before Elle and Twyla knew it they were dressed just like them, complete with the parted down the middle and pulled back hair, and a decorative bindi between their eyes. They loved the way they looked. They took photographs for their memories as well.

The English speaking lawyer, Shimsui, had become their pal. In a conversation about the world and politics, he revealed the fact that his people identified with the struggle of Black people because they did not trust the White man either. They had been oppressed by them as well. He said "we are Black like you." The girls looked around at all the different shades of folks they were surrounded with and couldn't agree more. Their skin tones ranged from

cappuccino to black coffee. They were people of color too.

Shimsui also told them he misunderstood why Black women, who he found to be naturally beautiful, used chemicals to straighten their hair. Elle and Twyla were both guilty as charged so neither of them had a good answer for him. But he had definitely given them something to put into their pipes and smoke.

The sisters were awed by their experiences and would never forget. Visiting the continent of Asia was stirring and culturally enlightening but they were ready to get back to the U.S.A. Their mission was accomplished. The sisters called their family and told them they were coming home.

The time finally came to leave and the bosses arrived to drive them to the airport. Along the way they informed them that the tickets they had were for standby so there was a possibility that they may not get a flight out. This upset the girls but it prepared them for what was next.

As their luck would have it, when they got to the airport there were no seats available on any of the two flights departing that day. Disheartened, the sisters were ushered back to the hotel for another night. Twyla gave them the business about it but they had no choice but to just try again the following day.

That night the girls were depressed and homesick. Twyla missed her kids so much she actually started crying. Elle was bugging out too. They were sad and lonely so they started drinking and singing songs to make time pass.

After a couple of drinks and a few more tears, Elle bought up Mena and the fact that she really couldn't stand her. She still had a grudge about her sneaking down to Baltimore with her ex, Knight. She owed Mena one for that foul ass move. Elle reminded Twyla that Mena did her dirty too when she had stole from her. The tipsy sisters made a unanimous decision to withhold the bread they owed Mena for putting them on. She would never see that finder's fee. She was dead on that money and that was that.

Another drink later, they got a little happier. The sisters started bugging out and singing. They had pretty good

harmony so they got an idea. They decided to try their hands at song writing. Elle was a natural poet so she came up with most of the lyrics. Twyla was great at creating melodies. They actually collaborated on two songs.

The next day the girls were lucky and got a flight out. Set aside the scrutiny and looks they received from Customs when they returned, their arrival back in the States was drama-free.

Chapter 12

When Twyla and Elle got back they greeted their family with gleeful hugs and kisses. Everyone was ecstatic and loved the gifts they presented them with.

The next stop they made was Mohammed's crib to get their money. He paid them half of the five thousand dollars they stood to make and assured them that the other half would come as soon as the green cards were issued. Before they left he thanked them and encouraged them to recruit more girls for him. The sisters agreed and then made their way to Twyla's crib to chill out. They were still jet-lagged from their journey so they just needed to lay back.

Elle and Twyla stuck to their guns and did just as they had decided. They didn't give Mena a dime. She had the nerve to come over the same night they got back. Elle was looking forward to taking the confrontational approach to the situation so she was ready to pop off.

Mena came through with some trees and rolled up an el. She waited until they were all smoking before she casually brought it up. "Man, I just had to help my mother pay all this back rent and shit so my pockets is fucked up. I'm so glad y'all back. I'm broke as hell, so y'all bitches right on time."

Elle took another pull and passed the el to Twyla. Then she looked dead in Mena's eyes. "Right on time for what?"

Mena smiled. "Right on time with that money."

Elle just played dumb. "What money?"

"Y'all was supposed to gimme a hundred dollars apiece. The finder's fee, remember?"

Twyla looked at Mena like she was confused. "But Mohammed said he paid you."

Mena laughed nervously. "No, that ain't have nothin' to do with y'all. We had an agreement on the side, remember?"

Elle got irritated with the way she kept saying "remember" like she was checking them. Who did she think she was? Annoyed, Elle snapped, "Too late. We spent it."

"But y'all just got back…" Mena caught the look Elle gave her and trailed off her sentence. She knew what it was. They were deading her on her money. Wow.

Mena was disappointed as hell but she remained calm because she knew she didn't have any wins. She knew Twyla and Elle were sisters, and would have no problem jumping her ass. If she fought one of them, the other would turn on her like a rabid dog. And she was in their house so there was nothing she could do but chuck it up. Mena wasn't stupid. She had done them dirty in the past so she knew she had it coming.

A few days later, Elle and Twyla went to see Mohammed. Details of their vacation had motivated a few of their friends to want to go to Bangladesh too. When they met with him they told him they had a few girls who were interested. He was pleased and then surprised them by saying he liked the way they carried themselves. He said the bosses in Bangladesh had been impressed by them. He wanted their assistance in recruiting classy girls like them.

Mohammed went on to say that he despised Mena and her begging ways. He told them she was always asking him for cigarette money and then said something about her doing "the cocaine." He said he didn't trust Mena. They laughed and told him nobody with sense did. That was one trifling chick.

The sisters cut Mena out of the operation just like that. She was such a chicken head Mohammed preferred dealing with them. Especially Elle because she could understand his badly broken English.

Elle and Twyla's new hustle was sweet. They just

started recruiting girls and he paid them a finder's fee for each one. And they also cut side deals with the girls to earn money off them as well. The job was so easy it was literally passive income.

Twyla was with it for a while but she was gradually slipping back under Rome's spell. They had a young baby and she wanted them to be a family. While she was playing house, Elle went at it hard. She was recruiting bitches left and right. Before long, they were sending up to ten girls a week. All of their friends went and then all of their friends' friends went too. Elle did most of the work but she still hit her sister off. She felt like it was only right. They were loyal like that.

The money was good and really came in handy since they quit doing so many trafficking runs. Bilal, Twyla's first baby daddy, was locked up again at the time. He was the only dude they really fucked with on that tip lately but he was out of commission. Cherry and Mena's little prison experience taught them not to fuck with just anybody. Cherry's own flesh and blood left her for dead, so anything was possible.

After a few weeks Twyla woke up again and realized Rome still wasn't ready. He just couldn't do right so she turned their switch off again. She and Elle started hanging out and practicing the songs they wrote in Bangladesh. They impressed themselves so much they decided to form a duo. They just needed a name for their group.

They grew up singing in church all the time so they were pretty good. The sisters started rehearsing their material and taking it serious. With their family and friends' encouragement, they proceeded to try to get on.

They went to a bunch of clubs trying to network but nothing solid came about. Then one night they attended a Wu-Tang Clan concert at Trafalgar Square in Queens. After the concert was over they met this Hip-hop duo called Casualties of War. They had quite a few hits under their belts so Twyla let them know they could sing and were trying to get on. One of the dudes, Meningitis, told them to hit a note for him.

The sisters started singing the hook from a song they wrote and his face lit up. He called this other dude over to listen too. The girls received approving nods and when they were done singing they received some applause.

Elle and Twyla were all smiles. This dude out there named Cliff turned out to be someone who could actually help them. He told them he was impressed and passed them a card. Excited as hell, they took it and agreed to call him the following day.

They called him and he set up a meeting so his partner could see and hear them too. His partner turned out to be this retired rapper they knew named Big Joe. He was impressed by their voices too. Less than a week later, Elle and Twyla had a management contract in their hands. Their new group "Street Chic" was on their way.

Twyla and Elle were leery of anything that seemed too good to be true and they didn't trust anybody. They were smart and took the contract to an attorney to make sure it was on the up and up, and then they negotiated a better percentage.

Big Joe was more of the decision maker. He must've seen dollar signs because he agreed to fifteen percent instead of the twenty they'd asked for initially. Elle and Twyla signed the paperwork and then it was on to the studio.

Including Street Chic, Cliff and Big Joe managed six R&B and Hip-hop groups. Their plans were to record a collection of demos from new talented artists and then shop for a distribution deal for their new label, Hard Times Entertainment. At the time the majors were giving out big fat checks.

When the time came for their first studio session the sisters met the third partner in the Hard Times label venture, Barshawn. He was a kind and gentle creature who happened to be from Brooklyn like them. And he was a handsome fellow too. Barshawn was from Roosevelt projects, which was just a stone's throw away from the street they were from. They immediately clicked and set out to make some good music.

Barshawn was the music man. He was the one that produced all of the material for the artists. That brother was super talented. He could play twelve different instruments.

Needra accompanied Elle and Twyla to the studio most of the time and she and Barshawn kept eyeing each other on the low. As the days passed it became obvious that she had a thing for him. Needra was just coming out of a bad relationship with this dude named Bliss. He'd been staying with her but Elle and Twyla had encouraged her to put him out because he had her stressed all the time. So Barshawn had her smiling again.

To Elle and Twyla, Barshawn became more like a big brother figure. They spent a lot of time together and were making some good music. They worked well together and Barshawn got a kick out of them. They were always lively and down to earth, and they were Brooklyn girls. Over the next weeks they all became very close. After long grueling hours in the studio he would drive them all back home to Brooklyn. Needra always sat in the front with him.

In reality, the sexual tension was building up between her and Bar. Needra was fresh out of a bad relationship so she wasn't getting laid. She wanted to give it to him bad but Elle and Twyla warned her to wait until they got on. They were determined to look like professionals. Needra didn't want to be known as the label slut so she agreed. There were sparks shooting between her and Barshawn that Stevie Wonder could see but business didn't mix well with pleasure.

Barshawn's partners, Cliff and Big Joe, were always at the studio too. Cliff never had much to say. He was a man of few words until he got a drink in him. Big Joe was the complete opposite. A tall, fat dude with a loud ass mouth, he was a jerk in a sense. He was bossy and annoying so he and the girls argued quite a bit. But they had a common goal that made them put their differences aside and work together. The girls didn't have a great relationship with Big Joe or Cliff but they all wanted success.

Bar was the coolest one of the partners so they clung to him. They were from the same place and he was jovial and

good spirited. Every time one of the girls had to curse Big Joe out for being obnoxious and overzealous, Barshawn always laughed. He was always the one to try and keep the peace.

Another thing they had in common with Barshawn was the fact that they all had church roots. He was a church musician growing up, and could play just about every instrument there was. Barshawn was the truth. He was the brains of the operation. Big Joe had a little fame from the gold hit record he had a few years ago and Cliff knew a few important people, but Barshawn was the man behind the music.

All of the artists wrote their own songs and he produced all the tracks. The Hip-hop records, reggae, and R&B. He ran the entire studio operation and did everything. All his partners had to do was listen to the masterpieces he created and approve. Those fools didn't even know how to work any of the equipment. They were nothing without Barshawn.

Cliff had a brother who just came home from jail. His name was Buckshot and he was a seedy looking character who was supposed to be on the team too. He was supposed to be security but he never did shit but stand around ice grilling Barshawn. It was like he hated him. Bar would be playing something on the keyboard and bobbing his head to the groove, and Buckshot would just stare at his back with this nasty look on his face. The girls talked about it amongst themselves and wrote it off as that nigga just being plain jealous.

On the low, they let Bar know about the dirty looks and negative vibes. They told him to watch his back but he took it lightly and laughed it off. He was goodhearted so he saw some good in everybody.

Chapter 13

The girls were in the studio most nights but during the day they were still recruiting girls to go to Bangladesh. Their sister Etta gave in to the hype too. She and their homegirl Madison were scheduled to depart for Bangladesh in two days.

Etta was nervous and kept asking her younger sisters questions about the way things were over there. She had a few qualms and lots of doubt, but the money she stood to make was her motivating factor.

When Etta and Madison arrived there they called and said they were good. They actually sounded chipper and excited. They were only supposed to be there for about four days but after they got married they were unable to leave on time due to a religious holiday. It was Ramadan, a sacred Muslim holiday, so they got stuck over there for a few days.

At first it was all good. They loved the shopping and sight seeing. But it started to wear off. Etta and Maddy held up okay for the first week but then they started to crack. On day ten they were almost hallucinating. Maddy even came up with a conspiracy theory. She believed the Bangladeshi men were all in cahoots to kidnap them and keep them away from their children and families forever.

The girls spent a lot of time praying and comforting each other. The people there did what they could to make sure their stay was comfortable but they were very depressed.

After being in Bangladesh for twelve days, six hours, and thirty three minutes, they were told they were going home that day. You should've seen them hugging and crying like they were prisoners of war being rescued from

murderous torture chambers. Never mind the four-star hotel with room service and full amenities they'd inhabited during their stay. They were ready to get back to their own country. They both lived in the hood - hell, Madison straight lived in the projects - but there was no place like America the Beautiful.

Etta and Maddy had a few drinks along the way home. When they finally touched American soil they were still tipsy. And they had never felt so patriotic in their lives. When they got off the plane they actually kissed the ground. And then Etta put on an opera voice and started singing.

"My country 'tis of thee, sweet land of liberty, of thee I sing; Land where my fathers died, land of the pilgrims' pride, from every mountain side – let freedom ring!"

Laughing her ass off, Madison joined in. People were looking at them like they were crazy but they couldn't care less. They stood up and commenced to loudly singing "The Star Spangled Banner" and marched hand-in-hand to claim their luggage.

When they went through Customs they got the full business but Etta and Madison were so elated to be home those assholes couldn't take away their joy. After they were relentlessly grilled about the purpose of their trip, they grabbed their shit and boogied to a taxi.

Etta and Madison returned with reports that some of the other girls who went over there were having sex with the young Bangladeshi men, vaginal and oral. They said the girls were prostituting themselves and had even taken a few boys' virginity, and then joked and bragged about it.

Elle didn't approve so she planned to check them about their whorish ways. It was her fault because she had been sending any and everybody who would go. So a few of them who flew over there were birds. They were all adults but they were making it bad for the decent girls who went. According to her sister, no one had used rubbers either. Etta said she knew because she saw this boy running out of the girls' room across the hall hollering and holding his penis. She said the girls told them that that was his first ejaculation

ever and he didn't understand what was happening.

$$$

Elle and Twyla's dreams were finally within reach. Their demos were complete so their mission was almost accomplished. Hard Times Entertainment had stepped to Sony with a package of professional demos from all six of their groups, and Sony was interested. They had just signed a seven-figure distribution deal so there was reason to celebrate. The label partners were popping bottles and smoking cigars like they had the check already.

Big Joe blew out a cloud of Cuban smoke and smiled around at the team. "Congrats y'all. I'd like to propose a toast to our dope ass producer, Barshawn! We couldn't have done this without you, man!"

A naturally humble creature, Barshawn just beamed with pride. Big Joe grinned and slapped him on his back in a brotherly fashion. He announced that he, Cliff, and Barshawn planned on throwing a launch party for the label real soon. They were just looking for a nice venue that was large enough to hold all the people they anticipated attending the event. Elle and Twyla told them about the supper club their father had. He asked a few questions about the space and they agreed on a time when the partners could check it out.

Big Joe and Cliff were from the suburbs in Queens and tried to be snobbish about the location. But they were just trying to negotiate a better price. Elliot, Elle and Twyla's father, didn't like being haggled but he came down a little on the strength of his daughters. He shook hands with the three gentlemen and they set a date. They left a deposit with him before they parted; half the price up front.

Elliot and his daughters spent days getting the place cleaned up and ready. Meanwhile, the girls were also promoting hard and spreading the word. Elle and Twyla worked hard as hell preparing for their launch party. Their whole family did. And their efforts paid off. They did some renovations and the place was beautiful.

When the day finally came, the turnout was amazing. It looked like the night would truly be a success. The bar was open, drinks were flowing and love was in the air. At least for the Brooklyn attendees.

Some of those Queens mothafuckas were on some other shit. When the evening first began Big Joe's drunken girlfriend was starting trouble. She almost got into a fight with Elle and Twyla's cousin, Gina. Before the night was over that incident was grossly overshadowed. Barely midway through the party, somebody shut off the lights and then some ignorant ass nigga started shooting right inside the club. They fired three shots and people were so scared they almost trampled each other trying to run for safety. The party was ruined before any of the artists even got a chance to perform.

Most of the local neighborhood guys there were young gunners but that night they had all shown up with no heat. That was done out of respect for Pops' establishment and love for his daughters. They had all grown up together so they were proud to see the sisters get on. A lot of them were even looking forward to being in their first video.

Dudes tried to be on some peaceful shit that night but no one appreciated those Queens niggas violating their hood or Pops' establishment like that. So when those gunshots went off they quickly disbursed and got strapped up. Then they waited outside for them Queens niggas to come up out of there. They were posted all up on rooftops and shit. There was some heavy artillery out there.

Barshawn had a brother named Bo who had just come home from prison. That night he had showed up with some friends. Their crew was also pretty upset. They were armed and gunning for those stupid Queens niggas. Bo had just showed up to support his genius music producer little brother in his record label endeavors, so to be greeted by unfriendly fire was a big slap in the face. Bo and his peoples pulled out their toast and started searching for the shooter on the inside.

People were running for their lives and there was

total chaos and mass confusion. There were mothers, children, and even grandmothers there that night so that was really fucked up. Needless to say, the police were called. The night ended up being a complete disaster. But thank God nobody was seriously hurt.

$$$

Around a week later, it was Needra's turn to go to Bangladesh. Instead of waiting on a partner to accompany her like Elle and Twyla suggested, she boldly went over there all by herself. Mohammed didn't have a problem with her going solo and her experience over there wasn't half bad. Unlike some of them, she got out of there on time. Her trip was pretty good but the most fucked up thing happened while she was gone.

A day before Needra was scheduled to return, Twyla and Elle got a call from Big Joe. He said, "I got good news and bad news. Yo, we got the check from Sony so it's on! But Barshawn is no longer with us. Don't worry 'cause we gon' be all right. We gon' continue with the plans and we gon' all be successful."

Elle and Twyla figured Big Joe and those grimy ass Queens niggas finally did something to make Barshawn get fed up and quit the partnership. He probably decided to move on and do his own thing.

Elle rolled her eyes and said, "I know what an asshole you can be, Joe. Why did Bar leave? What you do to piss him off?"

Sounding surprised, Big Joe said, "Huh?" Then he realized she didn't get it. "Oh nah, that nigga Barshawn *dead*. He got shot five times. Early this morning when he was coming home from the studio. The cops said some nigga in his projects probably tried to rob him."

The sisters gasped in horror and stood there motionless. They couldn't believe it. When the news sank in both of them just started wailing. They were truly heartbroken. Barshawn was like their big brother. How could he have gotten shot five times? He didn't even live that kind

of lifestyle. Elle and Twyla were crying so hard they couldn't even talk. They were so upset Big Joe told them he was coming through to check on them.

An hour later, he stood in Twyla's living room doorway giving them a vivid description of the way Bar had been shot and killed. He told them how the assailant ran up on him and shot him in the side of his head twice and then blasted him in the chest. He said then as Barshawn lay dying on the street, the nigga shot him in both hands. As Big Joe spoke he acted out the crime like he actually witnessed it.

The purpose of his visit was to console them and assure them that plans would not change. But the girls were just spooked by his presence. After he left, Twyla locked the door and she and Elle just looked at each other.

In unison, they asked, "Now how the fuck that nigga know so much?"

The sisters smelled a rat. Big Joe was involved. That was a dirty mothafucka. They knew he was behind Barshawn's death. Look at the nonchalant way he had mentioned Bar was dead when he first called them. He was heartless. After he told them the killer shot Barshawn in his hands too, the girls were totally convinced.

Bar was a musical genius who used his hands to create; so those hand shots were an indication of pure envy. There was no doubt in their minds that Buckshot was the one who did the hit. He used to stare at Barshawn like he wanted to kill him. He probably couldn't wait. That nigga Buckshot hated Bar just because of his musical abilities so the bastard killed him and shot him in both hands. That was some cold spiteful shit.

Immediately, the girls decided they were no longer doing business with Big Joe and his cronies. Fuck that damn contract. They couldn't trust them niggas. Those filthy bastards waited until Bar had created and mastered all of the music that got them that multimillion dollar distribution deal with Sony, and then they killed him before he could get his share of the proceeds. That was the dirtiest shit they had ever heard of. The girls were from the streets and had seen lots of

folks die at the hands of larceny, but that shit took the cake.

They had to figure out a way to get out of that contract. Big Joe referred to their managerial agreement as a marriage but they wanted a divorce ASAP. And they had to figure out a way to tell Needra about Bar's passing. She was going to take it real hard.

When Needra came back and got the news, she flipped. She cried her heart out and told them she had spent time in Bangladesh rehearsing the words she would use to tell Barshawn how much she was feeling him. She said she cared about him so much she had fallen in love. Elle, Etta, and Twyla consoled her and they all cried together. It was truly a pitiful site.

The week after Barshawn's death, Elle and Twyla were approached by the detectives investigating his murder. They wanted to know what they knew but the sisters wouldn't cooperate. They wanted to but they couldn't. They couldn't violate the street code and snitch so they said they didn't know anything. Where they were from snitches got stitches.

The police were already on the right track anyhow. Contrary to what Big Joe said, the killer didn't rob Barshawn. He was still wearing his jewelry when he was found and had over seven hundred dollars in his pocket. So the robbery motive was out the window.

The cops suspected his death was related to some shady music industry business so they raided Big Joe's studio and confiscated the DATs that contained all the music Bar recorded. The detectives knew about the new Sony distribution deal the label had acquired but they made it clear that the music was off-limits until their investigation was complete.

Twyla and Elle were smart enough to know that meant that none of Big Joe's artists would be coming out anytime soon. So perhaps getting out of that contract would be easier than they thought.

Bar's funeral was the following weekend. Elle and Twyla's whole family went with them to see Barshawn laid to rest. It was really sad but they put him away beautifully.

The service was extremely emotional. Bar's family took it very hard. There were probably buckets of tears shed in that church.

Bar knew a lot of people. There were quite a few celebrities there amongst the grievers. Big Joe and Cliff showed up with suits on trying to look noble. They had a few other Queens cats with them as well. Those bastards had the nerve to stand there in the house of God and look Barshawn's mother in the face and offer their phony ass condolences. They were going to bust hell wide open.

The girls never told Big Joe about their plans to get out of their contract. They went about it the legal way. Two days after the funeral passed, they sent out certified mail notifying Big Joe and Cliff in writing that they were fired.

When Big Joe got the letter he was pissed. He called them and went off. He told them it wasn't that easy to get rid of him and said he owned them, so only over his dead body would their agreement end. That nigga turned out to be even crazier than they'd thought he was. The sisters got on their Brooklyn shit and told that mothafucka to go fuck himself. He said their music was his property and he wasn't releasing it. The girls didn't bother to tell him they knew the police had seized all of the music. They simply told him that they owned all the copyrights to their lyrics so he could eat a dick and rot in hell.

Joe made some idle threats but the sisters assured him that he would get an ass full of lead if he came to Brooklyn with that bullshit. They promised him that death would be right around the corner. Their "marriage" to Big Joe ended pretty ugly but they were free.

Chapter 14

As if things could get any sadder, two weeks later Elle was hit with more unfortunate news. She found out Blaze had been arrested for first-degree murder, and then she learned Knight had passed away in prison from a brain tumor they found in his head. The tumor had burst when he died two days before. When Elle heard she cried for three days.

She found out from his brother where the arrangements would be held and mustered up the strength to attend. Twyla and Etta agreed to go with her. When the day came it was really a somber occasion. The sisters sat together through the service and each of them was teary eyed.

When the funeral was over, the drama started. There was bickering and finger pointing between old and current girlfriends who wanted recognition for their status but Elle stayed out if it. She hadn't seen Knight in years. She was simply there to pay her respects to a person she once loved dearly. That dude had taught her a lot.

She viewed his body one last time and left the church weeping. When they got outside the sisters spotted Cherry out there running her mouth to a crowd of nosy girls from the projects who just showed up to see who was crying or not.

Cherry was saying, "That nigga Knight was a dirty nigga anyway. He killed a lotta people so he deserved to die, shit! I remember he used to try to get with me. He begged me to eat my shit …"

For some reason Elle just snapped. She felt so disrespected by Cherry's comments she went up in her face. "You out here running your mouth, bitch, but you need to shut the fuck up! You stupid ass hoe!"

Cherry didn't realize Elle heard what she said but she wasn't about to back down now. "What? Bitch, fuck you! I say what I wanna say!"

"Word, Cherry? You bad now? Huh, bitch?" Elle backed up and two-pieced that bitch in the face. Then she took all her frustrations out on her.

Surprised, Cherry swung back but she was blindsided by another blow to the jaw. The two began to rumble right in front of the church. Elle's sisters helped to break it up but they were both holding Cherry more so Elle could get the best of her. Not that she needed them to. She had scragged Cherry before anyone could break it up.

$$$

Loud Latin music blared from the speakers of a Brooklyn pool hall. In a small office in the back, two businessmen, Black and Hispanic, sat dining over a meal of stewed chicken and Spanish rice and beans. In between bites of food and sips of Malta, the men were negotiating a joint venture they were contemplating.

Bilal, the Black dude, was Twyla's first baby daddy. He was just coming home from serving a short prison sentence. He looked at Coco, the Puerto Rican owner of the establishment, and said, "C'mon man, you gotta show me more love than that! The quantity I'm coppin' deserves a way better discount than what you talkin'."

Easygoing and suave, Coco laughed. In a heavy Puerto Rican accent, he said, "My friend, I told you… Prices too high right now. But I gonna put you on to somethin'. I got some sweet shit lined up in South America. The best shit, I'm telling you. But I gotta get it over here. And that's where the problem comes in. Getting it from A to B. I got a lotta overhead, my friend. It cost me a whole lot to get that shit over here."

Coco and Bilal were friends. They went all the way back to when Bilal was a young teen. They had been doing business for the last twelve years, set aside a four-year-bid

Bilal did. The feds had caught up with him but he had done his time like a man and not mentioned any names. Coco was his connect but he remained anonymous. He was simply the man behind the heroin he supplied the streets with.

Coco made a face like he was deep in thought. He had a dilemma. The girl who was scheduled to make the Caracas trip was knocked up and second-guessing her occupation now. The bitch got cold feet. He decided to just level with Bilal.

"This fuckin' punta don't wanna do her job no more. The trick is pregnant, talking about her pussy too precious to fill with my shit. Bitch brand new now. I was so mad I thought about kickin' her in the fucking stomach, bro, but she'd probably go running to the police. Then I'd have to kill the bitch, you know?"

Knowing Coco was serious, Bilal nodded.

Coco continued. "My plans on hold for a lil' minute, until I find somebody trustworthy. So meanwhile, I gotta give it to you how I can. Prices are high, man."

Bilal only half heard him because he was still stuck on that "sweet shit in South America" he'd mentioned. "So what the person who go gotta do?"

"Why, you got somebody with the balls to pull it off? And the smarts to not get themselves fucked up and not fuck up my shit?"

Bilal shrugged. "I might. What you payin'?"

"Ten thousand. And I pay all the plane fare and expenses."

"I got somebody in mind. *Two* girls. They young and pretty but smart enough to do it."

"They do this before?"

"Plenty of times for me here in America."

"Any mishaps?"

"Never."

Coco scratched his chin. "When can I meet them?"

"As soon as we come to an agreement. And you gotta pay both of them."

"Okay, two girls can bring more. I'll pay fifteen apiece. You get the girls to bring the shit, I give you the best price of your life! Deal?"

Bilal nodded, and shook his outstretched hand. "Deal."

$$$

Elle was regrouping from all the tragedy surrounding her and praying death didn't really come in threes like they said it did. She was on edge because losing Barshawn and Knight so close together was really nerve-wracking. She was just trying to stay busy.

Elle and Twyla were still trying to get in the music industry. They didn't want Barshawn's efforts to die in vain so they were trying to shop their demos. Over the last two weeks they had tried everything in their power. They had exhausted their resources. They realized it was an uphill battle. The only offers they got were "opportunities" to have sex for a shot.

That was the one thing the sisters were not willing to do. Tired of being looked at like pieces of meat, they were determined to get to the top without screwing their way there. There was no doubt in their minds that they would get a chance to do their thing. They just needed the money. The industry was so male-dominated they decided they would rather enter the business with the means to executive produce their own shit. Being HBIC was the only way to survive in that game.

They decided they needed to step their fashion game up so they could look the part, so they splurged with the bread they'd been stacking from the marriage hustle they had going. They looked at the designer clothes as an investment, but it turned out to be bad timing for a shopping spree.

Mohammed went home to Bangladesh for a few weeks and was unable to return to the United States. His visa expired and the embassy wouldn't renew it. So basically, their hustle was at a total standstill. The cash cow had run

out of cream so the girls were back at square one. They were fly as hell in their newly acquired wardrobes but their pockets were almost empty. High fashion and low finances just didn't equate. That was tacky.

Their backs were against the wall but the sisters were determined to come up with a plan. The type of broads they were, they would not be broke for long. God had blessed them with enough common sense to always figure out how to make a way. With the exception of Elle's three day stint as a telemarketer and Twyla's little Summer Youth Employment gig that ended in just two days, neither of them had worked a legal job a day in their lives. They preferred to take destiny in their own hands and make it happen fast.

As luck would have it, Twyla's daughter's father Bilal called and said he was coming through to discuss a proposition he had for them. He knew those two were always down to catch a come-up. They had heart and they were classy, so he figured they would be good candidates for the plan he had.

Bilal was a leery cat who didn't like talking business over the phone. One of the prison bids he had done was due to some dude mentioning his name while carelessly yapping on the telephone. They hit him with a bunch of conspiracy charges and played the tapes in court. He did four years behind that.

When he got to the house he announced that he had some work for them. After he verified that they still had passports he let them know the location. It was Venezuela. Bilal laughed at the looks on their faces and asked if they were with it. He knew all about their recent marriages in Bangladesh so he knew they had the heart to travel to another country.

Twyla said, "Hell yeah, how much it pay?"

Elle said, "Word." They both looked at him.

"I figured y'all two would be interested." Bilal laughed and shook his head. "So if y'all with it, we gotta have a lil' meeting with Coco." He set it up for the following day.

The next day, Elle and Twyla accompanied Bilal for a face-to-face meeting with Coco. They sort of knew him already. Twyla knew him from back when she and Bilal were in a relationship and Elle had heard of him through her. Coco was a much loved Puerto Rican "businessman" in the neighborhood who owned a pool hall and a bodega that had been operating for years. It was speculated that he had the entire police precinct on his payroll.

Hearing so much about Coco made him seem larger than life but in person he wasn't that big at all. He was a good looking average sized dude in his early forties who stood around 5'9". He had a goatee and wore his hair cut low.

Coco's partner, Freddy, was there at the meeting as well. Freddy wasn't bad looking either. He was broad shouldered with a little potbelly and he wore his hair pulled back in a ponytail.

The sisters must've passed the initial test because the Hispanic gentlemen treated them like ladies and politely explained the conditions of the business they wanted to do together. They spoke first and then opened up the floor to Elle and Twyla for a little Q & A session. The girls had some questions too. They were too smart to just go somewhere blind.

They wanted to know what the odds were. And what would happen in the dreadful event that they got caught. And they wanted to know what happened to the last person who took that trip. Why was there somebody new needed?

Coco was upfront with them about everything. Without saying too much he patiently answered all of their questions. He carefully explained the scenario from A to Z and told them exactly what was expected of them. Then he told them about the benefits they stood to gain. He said smuggling was a risky profession but there were perks associated. Like the all-expense paid vacation they would be going on. He smiled and told them Venezuela was quite lovely.

Elle and Twyla had both been smuggling since they

were young teens, but that would be their first international drop. That was a whole new ballgame. To say they weren't nervous would be a lie. But the premise of earning fifteen large overpowered any doubts they had. They told him they were in.

In three days they would fly to Venezuela's capital city, Caracas, where they would spend five days at a five-star hotel resort. During their stay they would be wined, dined, and spoiled like divas – facials, massages, manni-peddis, and the whole nine. On the morning of their fifth day there, Freddy, who would meet them in Caracas, would come through with the shit. That way they would have a few hours to get comfortable with it and decide where it would be traveling.

They had two options for getting the stuff back. Carrying it inside their bags wasn't one of them. They could either swallow it, or stuff it inside what Coco referred to as their "chochas."

The sisters knew that whichever method they chose, they had to really be on point. International drug smuggling was not something to be taken lightly. The penalties of getting caught could destroy their lives forever.

The Venezuelan trip was dicey but Elle and Twyla were stepping out on faith. All they could do was be cautious and pray they made it there and back safely. Being HBIC involved taking huge risks. Both sisters believed that money was worth rolling the dice.

To be continued…

HBIC:
Head Bitch In Charge
A SERIES

Part 2

The Prodigal Daughters

Another Caroline McGill Exclusive

Chapter 1

Elle and Twyla prepared themselves for their upcoming international trip by praying every day. Finally, the time came for them to leave. Three days after their meeting with Coco, the sisters boarded a Delta flight to Caracas, Venezuela.

The trip wasn't bad at all. They got there in around five hours. South America was a lot closer than they thought.

Coco didn't exaggerate about the perks. In Caracas they were treated like royalty. Whatever they asked for, they got. Elle and Twyla received the star treatment and had a great time doing so. They spent the first two days just luxuriating at the resort.

Freddy turned out to be a pretty cool guy. On their third day there he called their room and told them to put on something nice that evening. About three hours later, he came over to take them out to this well-known ritzy restaurant called La Isla Fuego.

Elle wore a sexy, short, black cocktail dress that evening, and Twyla wore a red one. They both wore high-end designer high heels and matching purses. The sisters were showing lots of leg but they epitomized elegance. Twyla had styled their hair in appropriate up-dos for the dresses they wore, and she had also done their makeup. Freddy commented on how lovely they looked. He said they smelled even better.

The girls told Freddy he was sharp and smelling good as well. He was donned in a tailor-made beige linen suit with an Italian brimmed hat and lizard skin hard bottom shoes. You could tell that everything, including his aromatic

cologne, was expensive. Freddy was only about 5'6" and he was a little heavyset but he was definitely attractive.

That damn Freddy was a freak too. Over dinner and drinks, he told them about the way he had a thirteen year-old girl licking cocaine off his dick the night before. Elle and Twyla couldn't hide the shock on their faces.

Twyla was tipsy and told him how she felt. "Freddy, you're disgusting. She was young enough to be your granddaughter, wit' yo' old ass."

Elle made a stern face. "That's a damn shame, Freddy," she said, and popped him on the hand like a disobedient child.

Freddy just laughed. In his thick Puerto Rican accent, he said, "Man, we freaked the fuck off! I snorted and licked coke off that little chocha all night." He looked nostalgic like he was lost in the memory for a second. "And boy, she could take a dick too!"

Elle and Twyla were both thinking the same thing. He didn't look like he was packing that much with his short chubby self. They just shook their heads at Freddy.

Their disapproval only made him laugh. He bent over guffawing like he was watching Martin Lawrence doing standup in his living room. "Don't worry," he added. "I paid her well. Five whole American dollars for that pussy! And plus she got the golden opportunity to fuck with a cool ass nigga like me!"

The sisters had to laugh. Freddy was loud and presumptuous but likeable nonetheless. An underboss in his thirties, he had money, clout, and didn't give a fuck. He bought what he wanted and that was it.

But he wasn't that big of a creep. There was no way he would've done a thirteen year-old girl in America. Not even back home in Puerto Rico. But child prostitution was commonplace in Venezuela. He explained this to the sisters to redeem himself a little.

"Hey, I'm not the bad guy! It's like that out here, you know. Take a look around, and you'll see. And that five bucks I gave her is twenty times more than the last guy did.

This a poor fucking country – what you think? Mothafuckas here starvin' and shit! I got a friend who does business down in the fucking ghetto! Tomorrow I take you to there."

He looked over at Elle and raised his eyebrows. "But tonight - I take you to the moon, baby! Let me get between those sexy ass chocolate thighs. I know that pussy good and tight. C'mon Elle, I wanna test that shit out!"

Elle said, "I don't know whether to laugh or slap you. Something is wrong with you, Freddy. Stop talking to me like that. Because that will never happen."

"Christ, I love a fucking woman who holds out!" He grabbed her hand and stuck out his tongue in a lewd gesture.

She just shook her head and laughed. Freddy was a mess. He knew Twyla was off-limits because she was Bilal's baby mama but he didn't hesitate to make sexual innuendos towards Elle. Freddy was the type to say whatever came to his mind. He kept telling her what a great body she had and how much he'd love to sample her. She shut him down every time.

After dinner, they went dancing at this hotspot called Nocturna. The sisters had a few drinks and progressed to get their boogie on. They had lots of fun dancing with Freddy. He could dance his fat ass off. He taught them some Latin dances like the Rumba, Salsa, and Merengue. The girls had natural rhythm and knew how to move their hips so learning wasn't that hard. Freddy said he was really impressed. Especially by Elle. That fool had wandering hands so she had to keep stopping him from groping her. But it was all in fun.

Before the night was over Elle and Twyla even danced a bit with these cute Venezuelan dudes. They taught them a native dance called Joropo. When the girls got the hang of that dance they taught them another one that originated in Brazil. It was called Lambada - The Forbidden Dance. The guys didn't speak a lick of English but their body language spoke volumes. They came on so strong the sisters could see why their kind were called Latin Lovers.

They ended the evening with a nightcap. After that, Freddy dropped them off at the resort like a gentleman. They

all said goodnight and he headed back to wherever he was staying.

Twyla and Elle liked to smoke a little bit to mellow out sometimes. This was no secret. They were both curious to see how that Venezuela weed was looking. They imagined there was some good shit out there so they had asked Freddy about getting some. The following afternoon he came through.

Freddy arrived at half past twelve with the Venezuelan marijuana they had requested. It came in a small compressed block wrapped in foil. You could tell it was some potent shit. It was so good they wished they could take some back home. Maybe under different circumstances they could've, but that time it would be too risky.

Just as he'd promised, that day Freddy took them over to the underprivileged side of town. Along the way he directed the driver down this rundown strip that was clearly a hoe stroll. The strip ran through a marketplace so there was a lot going on out there. The thing that stood out most to them was the startling amount of under-aged girls standing on those shabby streets boldly prostituting themselves. In broad daylight. There were droves of them up and down the strip, scantily clad and wearing painted faces that cheapened and escalated their youthful appearance.

They were trying so hard to look grownup. Some of them were smoking cigarettes like they were sophisticated. To the sisters they only looked ridiculous. They were just babies but the red lipstick wearing nymphs were offering themselves to total strangers. Competing to sell what should've been their priceless virginity at that age. That was heartbreaking.

Elle and Twyla were bothered by seeing those child prostitutes, and it showed. Freddy noticed their reaction and pointed out that they were the children of dirt poor parents unable to feed and care for them. He said that was the only way some of them could eat. Some of them were out there to help feed their families but most of those girls were on their own.

Elle and Twyla wished they could take all the little baby faced hookers home with them and give them better lives. Over there those children clearly had no resources. The sisters didn't know what was sadder – the little girls having to do that for a living, or the fact that there was a market for it. If there were no paying customers they wouldn't be out there. Those girls were forced to grow up too fast.

Freddy pointed out some other things that proved the area to be poverty-stricken but the sisters could see with their own eyes how bad it was. It was a different world compared to the resort they were staying at. That was obviously a façade for tourists to proclaim the country beautiful. The naked truth lay in the streets they were traveling through.

They traveled through the city limits until they rode into these tall hills. That area was a more rural disaster. There they saw living conditions that made the projects in Brooklyn look like lavish condominiums. The Venezuelan slums were the slums of all slums. The housing was simply a mess of shoddy looking shacks all over the hillsides. There was trash strewn everywhere and diseased looking stray animals just roaming about.

The driver explained that those shoddy shacks were shelter for thousands of less fortunate families. The people were so poor they were forced to reside in those makeshift houses they built along the hillsides, and most of them had no running water or electricity. The saddest part was that during the rainy season mudslides often occurred, which sent the houses sliding downhill on top of each other. He said hundreds of people met their death that way each year, many of them children.

After hearing that, the sisters were quiet for awhile. Each was reflecting on their blessings and wishing they could change the world.

They finally arrived at their destination. Elle and Twyla were relieved that it was in a better location than some of the sections they rode through.

The driver stepped out and opened the car door for them. They got out and followed Freddy up a long walkway

towards a big white house. The courtyard out front was nothing fancy but it was broom clean.

There were two armed men guarding the entrance door. Freddy said something to them in Spanish. After curt responses they nodded and allowed them to pass. Both of them had the kind of eyes you could tell never smiled.

Inside they were greeted by an elderly woman dressed in black and white. Obviously a servant, she smiled warmly and welcomed them in Spanish. Elle and Twyla reciprocated the greeting using a couple of the few Spanish words they knew. The woman led them through a huge impressively furnished living room and dining area to the back of the house to an office.

Inside the office there was a young woman sitting at a mahogany desk talking on the telephone. She was speaking in Spanish. When she noticed them she cut her conversation short and then stood up smiling.

Grinning, Freddy walked over and greeted her with a kiss on the hand. You could tell they were familiar with one another. He introduced Elle and Twyla as his friends, and she greeted them cordially in English.

Freddy said, "This is Bella, girls. She's a good friend who's gonna show you some things. I'm gonna talk a little business so stick with her for a little while. She's gonna give you some pointers about that little job you gotta do."

Bella smiled and nodded. They were glad she understood English. And glad she spoke it too. Elle knew a little Spanish but she wasn't fluent in the language.

Bella led them to another section of the house, which was a huge sitting area. She offered them a seat and had another servant pour them a cold drink of lemonade. Then they got acquainted. She explained that her job was to teach them how to swallow – the product that is. If they chose to transport the stuff internally that skill would be necessary.

She gave them a demonstration using these huge black grapes she said were used for practice. Those were the biggest grapes they ever saw. She swallowed five of them effortlessly. Elle and Twyla laughed to themselves and

imagined what she could do to a dick.

They both knew they would gag on those damn grapes so they ruled the swallowing thing out pronto. And the thought of having to shit out that stuff was just unappealing. And what if the packages erupted inside of them? They graciously declined, opting to carry it the way they knew best.

Bella chuckled at their reluctance. She seemed pretty amused. Just then, Freddy and two gentlemen joined them. The men were slightly older but very good looking.

They were introduced as Freddy's very good friends, Charo and Nuevo. They greeted the sisters respectfully. Charo was from Bolivia, and absolutely charming. He praised their beauty with sincere sounding compliments. Nuevo was Colombian and equally charismatic. He kissed Elle and Twyla on their hands and murmured sweet Spanish sentiments.

The girls learned that Charo and Nuevo were real major players in the international drug trade. Both were actually considered tyrants in South America. But the drug lords seemed so kind and courteous it was really hard to tell.

Nuevo offered to fly them out to his homeland in Bogota, Colombia. According to him, it was just minutes away. He said he owned a house like a castle, and they would be his guests and want for nothing. He boasted of his political power too. He said people answered to him so nothing went on without his input or approval.

Charo was the more attractive of the two. He eluded a sense of power that was almost overwhelming. There was something about the way he stared at you. He was the type of mature man a young woman could get with. He too extended an invitation for them to be his houseguests. He promised them days of pleasure, fun and sun. He assured them that they would not want to leave Bolivia.

The men were really excited to meet the girls because they both wanted to proposition them about their services. The prospect of having a means of transporting their narcotics to America was promising. They were wealthy

already but anxious to corner new markets. There was no such thing as too much money.

Being around such ruthless men was nothing new to Elle and Twyla. They knew their types well. Seemingly gentle smiling creatures that would kill in the blink of an eye. It was just on a larger scale. The sisters knew how to play their positions.

They politely listened to the men's ideas and offers in their broken English, and then they told them they would think about it. The money they were offering was impressive but neither of the girls really wanted to go in that deep. That was a risky field and they were aspiring to be more than international drug smugglers. However, protocol was protocol. The sisters politely took the telephone numbers Charo and Nuevo gave them and agreed to keep in touch.

A few hours later, they were back at their hotel room. They needed to get some rest because it was countdown time. The next day was "D-Day." They were scheduled to take that trip. Elle and Twyla knew their fate was in God's hands. Both girls prayed about it before they went to sleep.

The next morning they both woke up full of nervous energy. They had butterflies about the situation but the money they stood to gain was the deal breaker. They were excited to be going back home. They just had to get from A to B with no interference.

They got up to shower so they could get dressed and get it together. When Elle sat down on the toilet to pee, she saw a crimson stain in the crotch of her panties. Wow, her period had started. That was bad timing at its finest.

"The devil is a fuckin' liar," she mumbled. What was she going to do now? Elle yelled, "Twyla, you ain't gon' believe this shit! I got my period!"

Outside the door, Twyla's eyes popped. "Oh shit! Damn… Well, don't worry, boo. We just gotta work it out."

Elle was relieved that she always carried tampons just in case. She seconded Twyla's last words with, "I know, sis. We ain't got no choice." It was time to go.

Freddy showed up with their package around ten o'clock. He told them he would be back for them in two hours. Their flight left at two o'clock.

They used the time he was gone to get situated. When they were comfortable and confident, they sat their luggage by the door and waited. Freddy called on time and said he was outside in a car. The girls called downstairs for assistance with their bags.

Before they left the room, they doused themselves with expensive perfume, each spraying between their legs in precaution as well. They weren't taking any chances. Afterwards, the girls joined hands and Twyla led them in prayer.

"Heavenly Father, we bow our heads in humble praises of Your mightiness. Thank you for life, God. We come to you honest, as we know you know all that we do anyhow, right or wrong. God, we beg that you forgive us for our wrongdoing. We are sinners, no doubt, who know better... But please forgive us for our transgressions. And please keep us safe, dear Lord. In Your Holy Name we pray. Amen."

Touched by the prayer and slightly teary-eyed, Elle added, "Amen." She squeezed her sister's hand and they headed out.

They arrived at the airport an hour early to check-in. Elle and Twyla were dressed in short, flowing, pastel colored sundresses and matching wedge heeled sandals. They purposely chose the dresses because they believed they created an optical illusion. They were so short it seemed unlikely that they were transporting neatly packaged pure heroin underneath. Each wore three too-small girdles to keep everything in place. While confining and uncomfortable, the undergarments served their purpose.

They boarded the plane with no problem. Other than the fact that Twyla's ears kept aching, they had a good flight. They arrived at LaGuardia in just over five hours.

When they got on the plane Freddy was acting like their buddy. But when the plane landed in New York he acted like he didn't know them from a can of paint. The

sisters knew just what that meant. If they got caught they were on their own. They didn't want Freddy making them hot anyway, so they were glad he distanced himself away from them.

To the naked eye, Elle and Twyla appeared to be young tourists coming off vacation. Their story for Customs was that they were art students who traveled abroad simply to explore different cultures.

After they claimed their luggage they headed towards the interrogation station called Customs. Along the way they saw a uniformed officer with a huge dog. They were heading their way. The girls didn't want to look suspicious so they held their breath and kept walking and talking, praying the canine didn't detect the abundance of heroin they were strapped with.

The dog must've smelled something because it lunged at Twyla and started barking. She placed her hand across her heart in fear and backed up a few steps.

The officer immediately grabbed his K-9 partner and commanded it to stop. Once it was subdued, he looked at Twyla apologetic. "Jeez, I'm sorry about that, ma'am. Are you okay?"

Twyla smiled and nodded demurely. "Yes, thank you so much." She noticed the approving onceover he gave her and made a mental note to thank her mama for giving her great lips and legs. She had to thank God too. Her looks had clearly distracted the officer's better judgment. He wished her a good day and he and the dog headed on.

That was a close one. She and Elle kept on. That dog had scared the hell out of them. Their feet were so heavy it felt like they were trudging through quicksand.

Just as the sisters feared, the U.S. Customs officers were hard on them. Much to their disgust, the most extra one of the bunch was a brother. He and this redhead bitch really gave them a hard time. Those two opened up their luggage and went though every single stitch of clothing, including their dirty panties. The black bastard kept peering at them with this annoying spiteful smirk on his face.

A few of the agents fired questions at them about the nature of their trip. They kept attempting to confuse them and make them tell something on themselves by asking the same questions over and over but in different order. The pigs grilled the girls about three things. They wanted to know who they knew in Venezuela, the reason they had gone there, and why their passports reflected that they had recently gone to Bangladesh. They kept insinuating that they were up to something illegal.

Elle tried to block the visions of prison that kept creeping into her head. She just maintained nonchalance and silently prayed. Twyla was doing the same thing. They were both shook but they kept their cool and stuck to their story. They were traveling art students, and that was that.

Customs humiliated them to their smug satisfaction and then they were cleared and released. The sisters gathered their belongings and dignity and made a beeline for the nearest exit.

They were curbside searching for a taxi when a yellow cab stopped right in front of them. The back window rolled down and Freddy sat there grinning.

"Hey there, sexy ladies! C'mon, get in!"

The girls smiled and shook their heads. With the cab driver's assistance, they loaded their bags into the trunk and got in the car. When they were situated inside they both leaned back and let out a huge sigh of relief. They were so grateful for making it through that frightful interrogation Unites States Customs had subjected them to, neither spoke for a minute. Elle and Twyla were busy thanking God. They wholeheartedly acknowledged that He was the reason they made it through. God was so good.

Freddy sat on the other side of them grateful too. He didn't stand to lose his freedom if they got caught but he had a hefty investment at risk. He was knee-deep in the game but he too was a God-fearing man. He had whispered prayers for their safety as well. They had taken so long to come out of the airport he started thinking they got caught. He was already in a taxi prepared to leave them for dead. He was ecstatic when they walked out.

Freddy had to admit he was fond of those girls. They were pleasant to be around and they had proved that they were about their business. As the car pulled off, he was still smiling at them. The driver began the short drive to Brooklyn.

Elle and Twyla didn't exhale until they were on the Brooklyn Queens Expressway floating in the sea of traffic. Customs had given them hell but they made it back safely with two kilos of heroin apiece.

Chapter 2

Needra sat in her bedroom alone in the dark listening to slow jams. "The Power of Love" by Stephanie Mills was playing and she was missing Bliss something terrible. She thought she was finally over the heartache, but that crippling pain in her chest was back with a vengeance.

When Barshawn, God bless the dead, came into her life she succeeded in forgetting about Bliss. But now the love she found was gone. Needra wasn't proud but she was so distraught over losing Barshawn she had allowed Bliss to comfort her one evening. They winded up having sex, which was beautiful and led her to believe that they were back on again, but he was still doing him.

So they were back to the same old shit. She wished she could just forget about him but it was hard. Hell, she was lonely. Sipping from a glass of Bailey's on ice, she thought about all the things she loved about him. Halfway through her bottle of comfort, Needra did some serious soul searching.

Later that night she gave in to the urge to pick up the phone and call him. When Bliss answered, she told him she had to talk to him about something.

He sounded alarmed and asked if she was okay. Needra said she was fine. With a hint of seduction in her voice, she told him she just wanted to see him. He caught it and told her he would be there soon.

Needra sat there waiting patiently for the first hour. Bliss didn't show up until the third. At around four o'clock in the morning she heard a car door slam so she peeked out through the blinds. She saw him outside so she looked in the mirror to check her appearance and hurried to the door.

She waited for him to knock but instead she heard keys jingling. She laughed to herself. Bliss didn't believe she changed the locks when she had put him out. Needra flung the door open. She startled him so he jumped. "Hey boo," she grinned.

"What up, Neej? What you still doin' up?" Bliss inquired. He figured she'd be in bed by then.

"I was waiting on you. I been thinkin' about you. Is there something wrong with that?"

He shook his head. "Nah."

Needra was in a freaky mood and prepared to go all out. That Bailey's had her feeling bold. She sank to her knees and undid his belt buckle, eager to give him a pleasure tour down her throat. Maybe that would make him straighten up and start loving her right.

Struck by intense pangs of guilt, Bliss stopped her and feigned fatigue. "Chill Ma, I'm mad tired. I had a long day… You ain't even gotta do that."

He'd just had a quickie with Nicole about two hours ago. That was the girl he'd been staying with since Needra put him out. He had hit it raw dog and hadn't even washed his dick good yet. He just wiped it off with a rag. He didn't want Needra tasting Nicole's juices on him. He wasn't that foul.

Needra was determined to satisfy him. It was her desperate attempt to salvage their relationship. She looked up at him and said, "No, I want to."

When he didn't protest, she unzipped his pants and freed his penis. It was limp, but not for long. She took to that blowjob like a fish to water. His hands dropped to his sides and his resistance faded. Leaning against the wall, Bliss completely lost his sense of reasoning and surrendered.

He guessed Needra didn't taste anything. Nicole was clean so she never smelled. Bliss convinced himself that it wasn't so bad. It was hard to feel horrible with Needra deep throating him that way. She'd been holding back so much lately he almost forgot what a pro she was. And he had taught her those skills. He had Needra since she was sixteen

years old. Reminiscing on those days, he smiled to himself.

Needra's head game was serious. Unable to stand it any longer, he grabbed the back of her head and wrapped his fist in her hair. "Aaghh, damn girl!"

He was about to bust so he pulled out of her mouth just before he erupted. Needra was the one girl he really loved so he respected her. That was wifey. They had been together for like eight years.

She wasn't with all the cum guzzling either so it winded up in her hand. She smiled up at him happily and rose to her feet. Pleased that she'd pleasured him, she told him to get comfortable while she went to get cleaned up.

Bliss leaned against the wall for a second and caught his breath. He stared straight ahead at a framed 8 x 10 of him and Needra. That picture was taken four years ago. Guilt and shame flooded him again. That was some good head but he felt like shit for doing that to her.

For the ten thousandth time, he wondered if he should just go away and leave her alone. He had singlehandedly destroyed her trust over the years. It wasn't her fault. She deserved better than that. She needed a man she could depend on to be faithful. Bliss was a good provider but he was the first to admit he fell short when it came to loyalty. Needra shouldn't even have to worry about sucking some bitch's cunt juice off of the man she gave her heart to. He wasn't even worthy of her.

Heavyhearted, Bliss dragged his weary oversexed self to the bathroom. He felt dirty now and really needed to shower. He was just grateful that Needra didn't find out anything.

Needra didn't find out anything before she hooked him up but she found out afterwards. While he was in the shower she heard a buzzing noise coming from his pants pocket. She checked and saw that his pager was going off. It was on vibrate only. The number showing on it had a 718 area code so it was somebody local. Needra's curiosity got the best of her and she dialed the number on her house phone.

To her chagrin, a female answered. And the bitch had an attitude.

Nicole was brave. She said Bliss was her man and then she said he lived with her. She told Needra he had just left her house an hour ago after they had sex.

Needra literally felt faint and almost dropped the phone. She was at her breaking point but she needed to know one thing. "Did y'all use protection?"

"Didn't I just tell you that's my *man*? We *been* stopped using rubbers!"

Needra was sickened by her last statement. She just hung up because she was at a loss for words. She couldn't have spoken at the time if she wanted to. Nauseated, she started vomiting up that Bailey's she'd been drinking and everything she had eaten that day.

She got herself together and wiped her mouth and her tears. Blinded by vengeance, she hurried to the kitchen to retrieve her sharpest butcher knife. In a flash, she was inside the bathroom. She hid the knife behind her back and snatched back the shower curtain.

Bliss assumed she had come to join him in the shower but the closer he looked at Needra the more he could tell she was upset. He reached for his towel, trying to figure out what the deal was.

Before he grabbed the towel she reached over and grabbed his dick. Then she revealed the butcher knife she was hiding. He gasped when she pressed the blade into his shaft. The look in her eyes said she wasn't playing. That's when Bliss figured it out. She knew.

There were sparks shooting from her ears and death rays from her eyes. When Needra spoke her voice trembled with emotion. "You dirty mothafucka! How could you come over here after you been laying up with a bitch? You fucked that hoe raw, and then had the nerve to come put your dick in my mouth?! Like I ain't shit to you, nigga! You disrespectful piece of gutter shit, I should cut your fuckin' dick off! Nigga, I will fuckin' kill you!"

He was afraid to move with that knife on his shit so

he played it cool and tried to reason with her. That would probably be an impossible task at the time but it was all he could do.

"Listen, you buggin' right now. As much as I love you, why would I disrespect you that way? Are you fuckin' serious?"

Wanting to believe him, she hesitated for a second. That bitch Nicole could've just been lying to get a reaction out of her. They had to call that bitch back so they could clear that shit up.

"So let's go call her back." She tugged at his penis roughly.

"First of all, let go of my dick. And put that fuckin' knife up! You know better than this! And what the fuck you doin' answering my pages anyway? Going through my pockets and shit... You violated me right there!"

That's when she knew it was true. The nigga was trying to use reverse psychology and that was a sure sign of guilt. The no good bastard.

Needra knew just as well as Bliss did that she would never cut off his dick. But she would do herself one better and cut their ties. If he could disrespect her that way then he wasn't worth being around. "You dirty dick mothafucka! Get the fuck outta my house! Now, nigga!"

For some reason those words really upset him. She wasn't putting him out again. Not after she had called him. He wasn't going anywhere. He wiggled out of the vise she had on his penis and hopped out of the shower. He had the audacity to grab Needra by her neck to chastise her.

That was when all hell broke loose. She started hollering and swinging that butcher knife like a crazy woman. He had to pull some serious acrobat moves to avoid being cut. He managed to wrestle the knife from her hands and then they got into a big fight.

She struck him in the face and dazed him so he backhanded her across her jaw. She started bawling like someone was killing her but the girl wouldn't back down. She kneed him in the nuts and clawed his eyes with her acrylic French tipped nails. Needra was vexed and

humiliated so she was out for blood. She got up in his face again and he slapped her down.

Needra hit the floor hard but she jumped up and ran for the phone to call the police. Bliss saw her dialing 911 and agreed to leave the house. She put him in the hallway butt naked and tossed his clothes out after him. But not before she dug in his pants pockets and took the roll of money he had. She would later find out that it was sixteen hundred dollars.

After their battle, she sat there crying for a few minutes. Bliss kept knocking on the door for a while harassing her. After about thirty minutes he gave up and left. Needra didn't want to be alone so she got dressed and called a cab. She made her way to her cousins' house. She was glad Elle and Twyla were back in town because she needed a shoulder to cry on.

$$$

A few days after Elle and Twyla got back from Caracas, they learned that Big Joe and Cliff's record label was officially shut down. The police had already seized the DATs that Barshawn recorded but now they had also picked them niggas up one by one for questioning. God didn't like ugly so their greed had ultimately put them out of the game. Sony reneged on the deal and voided that multimillion dollar check they had released.

Elle and Twyla were up real late at night smoking a blunt and thinking of a master plan. The thought of Barshawn's legacy being stuck in the evidence room at the police station really bothered them. They wanted to change that so they needed another come-up. They were running through their Venezuela money fast as hell so they knew they had no where enough to fund their musical endeavors. They had spent over five grand apiece in barely two weeks. At that rate they would be broke in a month. They didn't want to spend out so it was time to do something else. But another international run was not an option.

They were grateful to God that they made it back safe but their experience with Customs really left a bad taste in their mouths. That was scary. They'd been just seconds away from going to jail until they were old, gray and forgotten, so they didn't want to press their luck.

Those international trips they took had really affected them. Even though they had gone to Bangladesh and Venezuela for illegal purposes, those experiences had triggered sort of a spiritual awakening inside of them. Elle and Twyla were compelled to get rich so they could do something great for the have-nots of the world.

Coughing, Twyla passed Elle the el. "We gotta make a power move, sis."

Their finances were depleting so Elle nodded in agreement with her sister. "I know. Before our money get real funny."

Twyla said, "Fuck this shit, let's get some work and get up outta here. Our *own* shit. I'm sick of us having to depend on niggas to eat. We takin' the risks transporting the shit anyway."

She was right. "Word, Twyla. Time to make a move."

After they went to Venezuela, the girls were connected. All they had to do was make the decision to utilize their resources. Anything they needed, they could get.

"It's time to get some money, Elle. We could flip a coupla' times before the summer ends and be back before school starts." Twyla's daughter was going to kindergarten that year. By then they could be right.

"Elle, Bilal's cousin Ken is out in Norfolk gettin' it. He fuck with that dope shit. We need to get some and go down south too."

Twyla was referring to North Carolina, which was like their second home. They knew there was money down there from their past little hustling endeavors.

Just then, the telephone rang. It was Needra, calling from a pay phone down the block. She sounded like she was glad they were still up.

When she arrived at their crib she informed them about the fight she just had with Bliss. She told them about the way he came over her crib right after he fucked some hoe. Too embarrassed to admit she had sucked him off, she skipped that part and told them she called back a number on his pager when he was in the shower.

To her surprise, nobody said "I told you so." Her cousins didn't judge her for her moment of weakness and insanity, and for that she was grateful. When Needra found out they were planning to go out of town she wanted in. She was in dire need of an excuse to get away.

Needra said, "I'm coming too, y'all. I got a thousand dollars."

She looked serious, so Twyla gave her a pound. "A'ight, bitch. It's time for the takeover."

Elle grinned. She liked the way that sounded. "That's right, we gon' be them bitches in charge! From this point on. HBICs up in this mothafucka!"

Chapter 3

Across town, their homegirl Pringles was pacing back and forth waiting on her doorbell to ring. She was bothered by the absence of her new lover so she wasn't exactly a happy camper.

Her friends didn't know but she had a secret. Pringles loved pussy. She loved it ever since she was nine years-old and had her first taste. At the moment she was waiting on her new girlfriend to come home. Chelsea was two hours pass the midnight curfew Pringles had given her.

When she was young, Pringles wasn't your average kid. At seven, she'd already discovered her joy button, and would masturbate for hours after her mother tucked her in at night. Even while she'd be having a bedtime story read to her, her little mind would be thinking of sexual fantasies a child would be expected to know nothing about. She had once watched a porno movie that belonged to her older cousin Beverly.

Pringles glanced at the clock impatiently and recalled that incident, which had pretty much changed her life.

One weekend Beverly was babysitting Pringles and her sister, Sandra, when their mother was out of town. Beverly's boyfriend came over that night after she thought the girls were sleeping. Sandra was asleep but Pringles crept down the stairs and spied on them. There was a porno tape playing in the VCR and they were on the couch entangled in each other's arms. Beverly's legs were up in the air and Pringles could hear her making these sounds like he was hurting her. Pringles had heard those same sounds coming

from her mother's bedroom when her ex-boyfriend Curtis used to live there.

Pringles was more interested in what was on the TV. She walked in on a girl-on-girl scene with two busty blonde women. One was laying down stroking the back of the other's head as she licked between her legs. As Pringles saw her face buried in the furry blonde and pink patch, she began to experience these feelings. She longed to bury her face down there in that woman's patch. She stood and watched for a while. The longer the woman got her pussy licked, the more she squirmed and begged. She cried, "Yeah baby, eat me. That's it, lick my pussy! Eat me," and wrapped her legs around her partner's neck.

That day Pringles was educated on oral sex. She was only seven at the time but she couldn't wait to eat her first pussy. She hurried back up to her room to touch herself.

Pringles looked outside again. There was no sign of that bitch yet. She was ashamed that a girl had her that open. She cursed the day she fell in love with twat. Getting angrier by the second, her mind went back to her unusual childhood. She could remember like it was yesterday.

Her older sister, Sandra, was having a slumber party for her sixteenth birthday. She'd invited her four closest friends, including her best friend and study partner, Julissa, whose birthday was a day later. Pringles' bedroom was directly across the hall from Sandra's and she could see right inside. She saw the girls changing into their pajamas.

Her eyes were drawn to Julissa. "Julie" was a Butter Pecan-Rican. She was tall and slim with reddish brown hair that hung down to her round behind. Pringles saw that Julie had on white panties and also caught a glimpse of her breasts. She put on a pink pajama short set with white lace trim. Pringles longed to remove that clothing and kiss her body. She yearned to see the furry patch she knew was inside of those white panties.

All evening she watched Julie parade around in those

pink pajamas at the slumber party. She and the other girls appeared to be enjoying themselves. They let Pringles stick around for a while because she was the adorable little sister. They played Truth or Dare, had fun dancing, ate cake and ice cream, and even had a pillow fight. Finally, at three AM they laid in their sleeping bags which were spread out in Sandra's room.

Pringles had been forced to go to bed earlier but she laid awake thinking about Julie. She knew she couldn't sneak into her sister's room so she waited for the opportunity to corner Julie alone.

She got her wish about an hour later. Sandra's bedroom door opened and Julie stumbled sleepily down the hallway to the bathroom. Pulse racing, Pringles got up and followed her. Julie went in the bathroom and half closed the door. She didn't see her.

Pringles could hear her urinating. Eager to satisfy her curiosity, she slowly pushed open the door. Julie was standing up wiping herself. Almost drooling, Pringles stared at her pussy. It looked fuzzy and soft, just like the woman's in that movie Beverly had that night.

Julie looked at her and began to pull up her panties. "Sorry, mami, I forgot to close the door. Do you have to pee?"

Pringles shook her head. "No, I wanna show you something. It's in my room."

"Honey, I'm so sleepy. Tomorrow, okay?"

Pringles smiled and said, "I wanna give you a birthday present."

Julie sighed and started to wash her hands. "Aww, sweetie that's nice."

She dried her hands on the front of her shorts and pinched Pringles' cheek affectionately. "C'mon, let's go."

Pringles grinned and led Julie to her bedroom. Inside, she closed the door behind them and offered her a seat.

Julie sat on the bed. "So what kind of birthday present do you have for me?" She expected it to be some type of childlike handmade craft.

Innocently, Pringles stated, "I wanna lick your pussy. I can make you feel good enough to scream."

Julie just sat there with her mouth hanging open for a minute. Pringles got bold and knelt between her legs. She began to feel very excited. Julie's femininity was so close to her face.

Julie was in total shock that a nine-year-old girl was coming on to her that way. She snapped out of it and pushed Pringles away. "No, Pringles!" Her tone was stern but hushed because she didn't want to wake up anyone.

"Where did you learn that? That's wrong, Pringles! You hear me? I'm a girl like you, and you're too young to know about stuff like that anyway. Where did you learn that?"

"I learned it on TV. Please, can I lick your pussy? I won't tell nobody, I promise."

Julie stood up. "Come on, you're going to bed." She made Pringles get in the bed, and then she went back across the hall and tiptoed inside Sandra's room.

Pringles lay there disappointed that she blew her first opportunity to taste a girl. She was so close she just knew her plan would work. She decided to touch herself until she fell asleep.

About twenty minutes later, Pringles' door opened. She figured it was Sandra and assumed Julie had told on her. She anticipated being in big trouble. When she saw who it was, Pringles smiled.

It was Julie. She came in and locked the door, and then walked slowly towards Pringles' bed. She stopped a few feet away and undressed under the moonlight shining through the bedroom window.

Pringles was awestruck. She just stared at her open-mouthed. In seconds Julie stood there naked in her bedroom. Her little hormones were all over the place. She got up on shaky legs and went over and ran her hands along Julie's lovely body, and then rubbed her pussy with both hands. The hair was soft and fuzzy. Pringles was fascinated.

She knelt in front of Julie and parted her lips with her

tongue. Julie erupted again so she got to savor her juices once more.

Pringles was a pro at pleasing the ladies already but she didn't know it yet. All she knew was the fact that she loved the way pussy tasted. She couldn't get enough. She ate Julie out for two hours. She only stopped because the sun was coming up and she knew her mother got up early.

At six AM, Julie stood up on wobbly, unsteady legs. She was completely exhausted. She bent down and lightly kissed her nine-year-old lover's lips. She whispered, "That was wonderful, sweetie. Don't ever tell anybody about this, okay mami?"

"I won't. Just promise to let me do it again."

Julie nodded. "Okay, now go to sleep, mami." She unlocked the door and peeked out to make sure the coast was clear, and crept out of Pringles' bedroom. After going to the bathroom to clean up, she slowly opened Sandra's door and tiptoed back to her sleeping bag.

Pringles decided not to wash her face. She fell asleep with Julie juice all over her and dreamed of their next encounter.

That was how Pringles came to love pussy. She loved its taste, its feel, and its smell. She wasn't an out-of-the-closet lesbian yet but sometimes sex with men repulsed her. You'd never be able to tell that from the way she carried on in the bedroom with a dude, though. She could make a bedspring sing a song of mercy.

Chelsea still wasn't back. Pringles was pacing and thinking of evil shit to do to her now. That bitch must've thought it was a game. Pringles knew she was out sucking and fucking her baby father, Ralphie, but she had a trick for her. She was going to fix that bitch.

Pringles felt straight disrespected. She didn't play that shit. She had warned Chelsea but that bitch got out of pocket, so now she needed to be put in line. Since she needed to get fucked so badly, she was going to get it like she never got it before. That pussy was going to be black and

blue when Pringles was done with it.

Earlier, she had filled a liter-sized Coke bottle with water and placed it in the freezer. That was a makeshift frozen dick she planned to ram up Chelsea's twat after she tortured it with all the inanimate objects she had in mind. That bitch had her twisted.

They first met downtown Brooklyn when Pringles was shopping one day. At the time, Chelsea and her kid were living in a shelter because she was on the waiting list for Section-8 to subsidize her an apartment. Possessing a weakness for longhaired Latinas since her childhood, Pringles pushed up on her. While they were downtown she took Chelsea in a store and bought her a pair of Reeboks. Her antics worked because homegirl was a sneaker whore.

Now Chelsea and her one year-old daughter Destiny had been staying with Pringles for three months. Her nosy neighbors were starting to suspect that they were a couple, even though Pringles never let anyone know about her sexual preference. But truth be told, she was getting tired of living a lie.

She was in love with Chelsea. That was her wife and the baby was hers too. She took care of that kid better than she took care of her own children. Pringles had three that were all in her grandmother's custody. She'd started having babies at thirteen but she was never maternally inclined. And she'd only been fast with men as a child to cover up her attraction to girls.

Finally, Pringles heard Chelsea's key turn in the door. She hurried to the bedroom and plugged in the iron and then she plugged in a big barreled curling iron she used on her bangs. She put both on their highest settings. While inside the bedroom, she heard Chelsea's footsteps go straight to the bathroom and then she shut the door. She was probably going in there to gargle that nigga's cum out of her throat.

Minutes later, Chelsea walked out of the bathroom smiling brightly. "Here you are! Hey baby, I missed you."

Fake ass bitch. Pringles was standing in the bedroom pretending she was ironing a pair of jeans on the ironing

board. Chelsea strolled over and tried to give her a kiss but Pringles turned away from her.

Detecting the attitude, Chelsea started to explain. "I took Dessie to my mom's house. That's where we were all night. She fell asleep so I just left her over there."

"Word" Pringles asked. "So what time you left your mother's house?" She was praying to catch her in a lie. She knew exactly what time she left because earlier she had called her mother, Mrs. Santos, and found out. That was hours ago.

"I just left there like twenty minutes ago," Chelsea lied. "You can ask my mother."

She didn't think Pringles would go that far because their relationship had been pretty cool so far. But Chelsea was about to see a side of her she had never seen.

Pringles reacted to that lie so fast she even surprised herself. In a split second, she grabbed Chelsea's throat with one hand and grabbed the hot iron in the other hand. She shoved it a centimeter from her face and hit the steam button three times.

Terrified, Chelsea screamed at the top of her lungs.

Pringles wrapped her fist in her hair and yanked her head back. "You fuckin' spic *bitch*, if you lie to me again I'll fuckin' kill you! I know you was wit' that nigga Ralphie! Bitch, I'll stick this iron on your fuckin' face. Take off your clothes! Now, bitch! Take them mothafuckas off!"

Chelsea was crying hysterically. "What's w-w-wrong with you?" she stammered. "Why are you d-d-d-doing this to me? You know I l-l-love you!"

Pringles laughed coldly and shot some more steam in her face. Chelsea tried to get away but her hair was wrapped around her fist. Pringles threateningly waved the iron in her face. "Take off your clothes now, you stupid bitch! Before I take the skin off your face!"

"Okay, okay! Please don't burn me! I'll take 'em off!"

Pringles released her hair and Chelsea undressed in a hurry. She acted like she had a loaded gun pointed at her.

Seconds later, she stood in front of Pringles naked. Teary eyed, she crossed her arms over her breasts and pled with her. "Put the iron down *please*, and I'll do whatever you want."

Pringles sat the iron down on the ironing board. "That's my good little slut. Lay down on the bed for me, mami. Let me take care of that pussy for you. My pretty ass, sexy little bitch. Lie down and open them legs."

Chelsea thought Pringles was acting weird but she also knew she loved eating her. She obeyed and lay spread-eagled on the bed. She had to play along with whatever Pringles wanted to do. She took care of her. Chelsea couldn't go to her mother for anything. The poor woman didn't have it to give. And her sorry ass baby father couldn't give her a pot to piss in. He probably wouldn't if he could.

She looked down at Pringles crawling between her legs and started to get a little turned on. Being submissive was fun sometimes. Chelsea was pretty much unsatisfied after that quickie she had with Ralphie a little while ago so she wouldn't mind having her pussy licked.

Pringles paused and admired the folds of Chelsea's feminine flower. She actually felt a little bad about what she was about to do to it. She smiled at her. "Scoot down to the end of the bed and hold that pussy open for me."

Pringles glanced at the curling iron on the dresser. It was just two feet away, piping hot and ready. She leaned in and started eating Chelsea out, hungrily sucking on her clit to make her pussy real wet. She purposely left a lot of spit down there too.

Soon Chelsea couldn't take it anymore. She was moaning and her eyes were rolled back in ecstasy. The tongue massage her pussy was receiving had her on the verge of climax. She squeezed her eyes shut and rode the orgasmic wave that swept over her.

Pringles kept pleasuring her and reached for the curling iron. She swiftly replaced her warm lips with the hot curler. Delighted by the way it sizzled on her juices, she laughed.

Chelsea let out a blood curdling scream and started hollering like someone was butchering her. Writhing in pain, she cried, "Oh my God, you're fuckin' crazy!"

Pringles' goal was to put her pussy out of commission for a while. Satisfied, she put the curling iron down. See how much dick that bitch could get now.

Chelsea kept hollering so she gave her a warning look. "Shut up, bitch! Shut the fuck up! Give my pussy away again and I'ma *kill* you!"

Chelsea laid there sobbing, afraid for her life at that point.

Pringles just stared at her and smiled. She was beautiful when she cried. She got up and went to retrieve her liter-sized ice dick from the freezer. When she got back she rubbed it on Chelsea's blistering cunt.

Pringles comforted her girlfriend with soothing words. She softly said, "You made me hurt you. Baby, you know I love you so don't make me hurt you again."

Chapter 4

Twyla and Elle made some calls and then made the necessary moves to put their plan in motion. They had a meeting with Coco two days later. They sat on either side of him at the bar in his place laughing at his jokes politely. The jokes were actually funny. And it was pleasant to be beside a man of such power. Coco was charismatic, which outweighed the intimidation factor by far.

He knew why they came but he insisted on them all having dinner before they talked a word of business. They relocated to his private dining area in the back, where a table was set for royalty.

Coco was a self-made man who once had nothing. He had eaten rice and beans from an old battered wooden bowl for almost every meal during his childhood. He had earned the right to enjoy himself so he enjoyed himself as much as he could. He did dinner big now so the candlelit ambience wasn't there to impress them. If he'd been dining alone there would have been the same fancy setup.

The girls learned Coco was also into fine wine. He referred to himself as a connoisseur. He had a servant who brought out a bottle of vintage merlot that he was excited about opening. He said he had it for seventeen years and believed it had aged perfectly. He insisted that the sisters join him for a tasting.

The server poured a swig in his glass, which Coco waved under his nostrils and smelled before he tasted. He nodded at the server, who then poured a swig in the ladies' glasses. He and Coco both waited patiently for their opinion. The sisters smiled and mimicked Coco's method of smelling and tasting the wine, and then they each gave them a nod of

approval. After the initial tasting, the server filled each of their glasses and Coco made a toast.

After they were done with their meal he leaned back and lit a cigar. After the help took their plates away, Coco asked them what their plans were. It was time to talk turkey.

The girls were honest and told him they wanted to flip some dope out of town. He smiled and asked what direction they were heading in. They just told him south. He nodded and asked them how much they wanted. The sisters said they just wanted something small to start out with because it was new territory to them.

Coco told them what he could do for them. He was willing to front them all it took to build their operation. The girls both knew a little something about cutting dope but they opted to get it prepackaged. They didn't want to take any chances of messing the work up because, as Coco reminded them, too much of this or too little of that could destroy the whole batch.

At first he suggested that they partner up so he could keep them supplied. He said all they had to do was move the shit he would front to them. His price for that was seventy dollars a bundle. That was marked up a little because it included a "small convenience fee."

The sisters were too smart to give away a percentage of their profit. They asked him what the price would be if they paid for the work upfront. He laughed and said he liked them so he'd give it to them dirt cheap. Just forty dollars a bundle. A bundle consisted of ten bags.

To the girls that seemed like a win-win situation. In their part of New York a bag of dope sold for ten dollars, but it was worth more outta town. The sisters made a deal with Coco and they shook hands.

After they copped, they made preparations to blow town. Elle was the only one of them with no real obligations so she could come and go as she pleased. Twyla had two children but she made arrangements for Etta to watch them, and agreed to pay her for her services. Needra had a job but she took a short leave from work. Two days later they were

scheduled to break out.

Thursday was the big day. They chose then because they wanted to get down there for the weekend. The three girls packed up and traveled by Greyhound down to Raleigh, North Carolina. They chose Raleigh because it was a big city where they knew there was a lot going on.

They arrived early Friday morning and checked into a hotel room so they could shower and get ready. The first thing they did was carefully stash the work inside the room.

After the girls were dressed, they hit the streets with a few testers to show people what they were working with. Twyla, Elle, and Needra weren't new jacks to the hustling game but none of them had ever dealt in heroin. They had transported a grip and they'd all had boyfriends who they learned a few things from, but that was it. So they were winging it and playing it by ear. They figured if they could hustle one thing, they could hustle another.

To their disappointment they found out there was no market there for the product they had invested in. They spent two days combing the ghettos of Raleigh for an outlet but they were unsuccessful. At the mention of heroin people were looking at them like they were crazy. Everybody they hollered at told them they'd have better luck in that city if they were hustling cocaine.

On the third day there, they met these dudes who pointed them to some old timers they said probably knew what was up. The girls hollered at this old head named Jimbo who was a real cool cat. He advised them to pack up and head for Durham, which was another city about thirty miles away. According to Jimbo, they would find all of the customers they needed out there in a housing project development called MacDuffie Terrace. He insisted that the heroin market was booming out there.

The girls were frustrated and on the verge of regretting their decision so they were grateful for that tidbit of knowledge. With nothing to lose, they called a cab and headed to Durham. The cab ride was thirty two miles and cost them $44.

As soon as they touched ground they attempted to set up shop. It wasn't that they were so bold. Their asses had no choice. They had to get that dope off before it fell and lost its potency. They all walked down a hill to this park they saw ahead. It was buzzing with adult activity.

Elle said, "It looks like that's where all the action is."

"Word," Twyla said. Needra nodded in agreement.

Unbeknownst to any of the girls at the time, they had stumbled upon a goldmine.

Before they walked inside the park, Twyla motioned for this dude in there to come over so they could ask him a few questions. The guy introduced himself as J.R. He was clearly handsome at one point but you could tell he was on heroin because it had started to take its toll on his body. You could see it in his posture and yellow eyes.

The girls let J.R. know what they were working with and asked if he could point them in the right direction. He assured them that they had come to the right person. He requested a tester so he could try it out before he assisted them. Elle pulled a bundle from her sleeve and passed him a bag. He thanked them and said he'd be back with a grade in no time. Then he disappeared into the woods to their left. Elle, Twyla, and Needra just sat on a park bench and waited with high hopes.

J.R. was a snorter. He simply tore the bag open and sniffed it through his nostrils.

He returned a few minutes later and gave them a thumbs up. "Hot damn! Y'all got some powerful shit! Let me help y'all get rid of that dope. I'll run for you, and all y'all gotta do is sit back and collect money."

He insisted that he knew all the users and key players so the girls decided to gamble. They really didn't have much of a choice. They were new faces and didn't know who to trust yet. They hired J.R. and he quickly circled the park and put the word out to the other heads about the new dope from New York.

In just seconds there was a small crowd formed around the girls. The people were asking for testers. Elle

gave out the other nine bags left in that bundle and they waited again. They laughed amongst themselves as they watched J.R. go into a little nod, but they were all on point. They were in unfamiliar territory so there was no sleeping.

Within minutes, the verdict was in. The first person to report was a shooter who pulled out his works and shot up back there in those woods J.R. had gone in. The second was a snorter. After he sniffed a bag he exclaimed, "Damn, y'all girls got a smoker!"

It was on after that. The crowd reacted in a flash. People lined up like they were giving away free cheese. The words "Chinese Dragon" and a dragon logo were stamped on each bag they had. That was Coco's brand of heroin, and they were screaming for it. The girls sold the other four bundles they had in just minutes. That was forty bags at $25 apiece. That was the quickest thousand dollars they ever made in their lives.

The local hustlers looked on somewhat amazed that three pretty bitches had just set up shop on their turf. They figured they had to be Five-O to have all that heart. Nobody fucked with the girls that day because they believed they were undercover cops.

Within an hour there was a buzz around the projects about that Chinese Dragon. Heads were showing up one after another trying to cop. But they were disappointed to learn there was no more. Overwhelmed by the response, Elle, Twyla, and Needra got ready to make a move.

The laws of supply and demand said go, so the girls hired this lady they met to drive them to Raleigh to get their things. The rest of the work and all their luggage was back there at the hotel room. They made a unanimous decision to relocate to a hotel in Durham so they wouldn't have to commute so far. They had a feeling they would be there for a while so being closer made more sense. They had to be able to watch their money.

The woman who drove them was very decent looking and surprisingly an educated sister as well. Her name was Nancy and she admittedly had a heroin addiction. She was so well kept it was hard to believe that she was on that stuff.

She missed the testers they had passed out but she was anxious to try out their product, so she offered them a ride. For her services, she would receive two free bags.

J.R. did all the running for them and they got rid of what they thought would last at least a week. A day and a half later they were completely sold out. J.R. had earned their trust but then temptation overruled. He ran off with the last two bundles they gave him to sell. He beat them for a few hundred bucks but they had still profited substantially. They were amazed at the opportunity they had stumbled upon. Financial-wise, that city was ghetto heaven.

$$$

Elle and Needra stayed in a hotel while Twyla went back to New York to re-up. All she had to do was take the bread to Coco and cop more product, so she could handle that alone. They decided to quadruple the quantity they had initially purchased because running back and forth to New York every two days would be asinine. And they were paying for their shit upfront again.

Twyla left her gun with Elle and Needra for protection and got on the bus. She had opted to take the trip because she missed her kids. She was going to spend a day with them and take them out to do something fun. And then she was coming right back.

When she got up top, she handled the business first. After she got that out of the way, she took her babies to Discovery Zone.

The kids were so happy to see her she felt guilty. They had almost knocked her down running to hug her. She knew she didn't spend enough time with them but she made sure they were with family who cared about them and loved them just as much as she did. Her mother and her sister took great care of her kids. She wouldn't have left them in their care if they didn't. But Twyla knew for herself that there was no other like mother. She wasn't proud that she was hardly there but at least she was out trying to give them a better life.

Twyla was into labels so she liked to dress them in name brand clothes everyday. She also liked to buy them the latest toys, video games, bikes and cars. Stuff like that cost money. So she offered no apologies for the things she did to pay for it.

After spending the day with her babies, Twyla couldn't resist the temptation to get up with Rome that night. She was leaving town the following day so she figured she might as well get her shit off while she was up there. Elle and Needra weren't around to talk her out of being stupid and weak for him, so she decided to revel in the forbidden guilty pleasures of sex with him that evening.

A few hours later, she was sweating in the sheets with Rome. Against her better judgment, Twyla told him about the town they found. Rome was impressed and interested. The opportunist in him made him start talking right after that. He told her he wanted to try and make their family work. She knew deep inside that he was full of shit but they had a little boy together, so she wanted that too.

Chapter 5

Meanwhile, Elle and Needra were down south strategizing how they would run their operations. They wanted to be on point and ready to roll when Twyla got back. So they did some research and observation so they could figure out the best way to shake and move. Whatever it took, they had to make it work.

After that dude J.R. beat them for that bread they were leery about trusting anyone else. They knew they needed runners but they were careful in the selection process. As they were canvassing the park for candidates this dingy looking dude who smelled like he needed a bath walked up to them.

Funky Underarms McDirt boldly asked, "Ay, I know y'all girls from New York. But who is y'all?"

Elle was in a silly mood so she decided to fuck with him. She looked around like the information she was about to disclose was top-secret. Just kidding around, she put on an important voice, and said, "We're HBIC. The head bitches in charge. And we mean business."

The fiend ate it up. He nodded his head like he was astonished. He went on about his business but he talked about them for the next three hours at every pit stop he made. The people he told each told a friend and the word spread like it was gospel. HBIC was in town to take over. And they meant business.

The following day, they caught the attention of a well respected dude named Turbo. Turbo had heard about them and knew it was only a matter of time before they crossed paths. There was so much talk about these new brave and

crazy chicks he wanted to see for himself.

When he finally saw them, he was amused by how harmless they looked. For some reason Turbo was moved to do something he normally didn't do. He approached them and introduced himself.

Elle and Needra got a good vibe from Turbo so they were pleased to gain his acquaintance. And they were lucky too. Turbo knew everyone and everything that went on in that city. They later found out that he was a pretty big-time local dealer who had the powder and rock cocaine market on smash. Turbo was the go-to dude for weight.

When Twyla returned and learned Elle and Needra had made friends with him she was leery at first. Twyla always had trust issues. But when she met him all of that changed. Turbo was charming and good looking, and he had a way of making you feel safe when you were with him. He was lovable and seemed to have their best interest at heart.

Since they were dealing in heroin, Turbo didn't view them as competition. So he made it a point to help them in every way he could. He took them on as honorary little sisters and then he put the word out that they were his family, and not to be touched.

Turbo schooled the girls on a few things, including but not limited to who they should and shouldn't fuck with, and the normal hours of operation for their market. Then he found them some dependable runners he said were loyal workers, and even set them up in a safe house for business.

The crib belonged to this lady named Annette. It was in the projects they were hustling in, but it was way in the back on the quiet side. They were allowed to chill in there so they could stay out of harm's way and keep their dope runners supplied. Annette got high off cocaine but she seemed decent and her house was clean. All they had to do was hit her off with a few dollars so she could smoke her "ready rock," which was their terminology out there for crack cocaine.

Turbo was a real dude who turned out to be nothing short of a Godsend. He was sort of flirtatious with Twyla but he treated them all with the utmost respect. Twyla could tell

he had a little crush on her. She sort of liked him too but they never took it there. Turbo was like their guardian angel.

Another nice thing he did for them was introduce them to a guy they hired to fix J.R. for running off with their money. When you got beat in the street you had to answer. That was how the game went.

Folks down there called their fighting friend Turk. Turk was a married family man who was cool but he had a dope habit. The girls agreed to pay him two bags, one upfront and one after he delivered the ass whipping he promised to give J.R.

Eager to impress them, Turk went on a mission to locate J.R. One morning he spotted him walking to the store down the hill and stealthily crept up behind him.

When J.R. saw Turk, he actually spoke to him first. They never had any problems so he believed he was more of a friend than a foe. He knew he ran off with that money but he figured that shit had died down by then. It had been a few days. He was hoping that those damn girls were long gone. He didn't expect them to survive out there. Not in those projects. It was like a jungle out there so he was sure somebody had run them out of there by now.

J.R. said what's up to Turk and Turk responded with three words. "You dirty mothafucka!" He followed those three words with three punches.

Surprised by the three-piece he received; J.R. stumbled and grabbed his hurt jaw. It didn't take him long to figure out where it was coming from. He knew who he had ripped off. He made the decision to fight like a man and threw up his hands.

Turk was a former Navy boxer who loved a good fight. He was thrilled that J.R. had a little heart. Amped, he stepped in and bombarded him with a series of haymakers. That was too much for J.R. He hit the ground with a thud. He made the mistake of getting back up and trying to swing again. Turk moved in on him and lumped him up something terrible. And then he delivered the winning punch. J.R. hit the ground again but this time he was out cold. Turk had

finished that nigga.

And after he knocked him out, Turk put his foot on his chest like a victorious bullfighter. He looked around at the bystanders and proclaimed loudly enough for all within earshot to hear, "Listen here, them three girls with the Chinese Dragon is the wrong girls to fuck with! I'll *kill* a mothafucka over them girls! So *nobody* better not mess with 'em!"

Only a few people actually witnessed it but word spread through the projects like a wildfire. That bloody beat down Turk gave J.R. sent a message to all of the other runners. Now they understood that those New York girls were not the ones to be fooling with.

Turk was a former boxer who still had a pretty nice form. He had always been nice with his hands but his boxing dreams were deferred and destroyed by the horse he had started riding at nineteen. He tried heroin once, and hadn't been able to get that monkey off his back since. Turk was a shooter. He preferred his heroin intravenously, and it had taken its toll on his teeth and bones.

To earn a bag every morning and evening, he became the girls' self proclaimed bodyguard from seven AM to six in the evening when they shut down. It worked out at first because Turk was an O.G. who was respected by heads around the city. An addict would hurt you for a fix, so his being around made the niggas known for robbing and stealing think twice.

$$\$\$\$$$

Turbo had a homie named Jimmy, who was his right-hand man. Tall, lean, and very light-skinned, Jimmy was a cool cat who was equally warm to Elle, Twyla, and Needra, so they all clicked too. Jimmy just happened to have a nice crib with two extra bedrooms. He and Turbo suggested that the girls move in there with him for a while. They said living out of those hot ass hotels was a sure fire way to get trapped off, so they would be better off. A lot went on at the hotel they were staying at, and the police were on to it.

The girls discussed it amongst themselves and they decided to accept the seemingly heartfelt offer. They assured Jimmy that they would pay him every month for staying there.

Jimmy's crib was in a nice and quiet complex located on the outskirts of the city. It was in a completely different environment from the projects. Staying over there would allow them to rest their heads in peace. Things were working out well. It almost seemed too good to be true.

Chapter 6

Over the next few weeks it was all good. The girls were stacking bread and keeping a low profile. Jimmy was cool too. He seemed to love having them stay with him, and kept refusing their offers to pay him.

Jimmy was a lighthearted dude who liked the fact that there were three hot girls living with him. It made him feel like he was the man. When he came in he would jokingly greet them with "Honeys, I'm home!" The girls would all just snicker. Jimmy flirted with each of them shamelessly but they would all just laugh it off and punch him in the arm or something. Especially Twyla and Needra, because it was no secret which of them he really wanted. It was Elle. He wanted her in the worse way but he was a gentleman about it.

But it wasn't long before Jimmy got bold. One night he asked Elle to sleep in the room with him. She was hesitant but Twyla and Needra gave her a little pep talk. Through a fit of giggles, they basically asked her to take one for the team.

Upset about the notion, Elle crossed her arms and pouted at them. "But I don't like him like that. I don't wanna fuck Jimmy, with his Pink Panther looking ass."

"So don't," Twyla stated. "You don't gotta do nothin' you don't wanna do. It ain't like that nigga gon' rape you, or somethin'. Jimmy ain't stupid. We'll fuck him up in here." She and Needra hit five on that.

Needra laughed, "You know the boy likes you, Elle. He probably just wanna cuddle with you. Just let him squeeze on them big old cannonballs 'til he fall asleep."

Twyla fell out laughing but Elle wasn't amused. They got on her nerves. Reluctantly, she agreed to go. Those bitches literally pushed her out into the hallway. Elle's mouth was poked out the whole time.

Before they closed the door, Twyla whispered, "Let us know if his dick is pink too."

Elle just scowled at that fool. She looked down the hall at Jimmy's room door like it was the principal's office to a kid in trouble. She took a deep breath and grudgingly made treks towards it.

Inside the bedroom with him, she played it off and smiled. Just as she figured, Jimmy tried to smash. Elle held him off by saying it was too soon. She promised him that they would get to that in time, just because she didn't want to hurt his feelings. He didn't even protest. He was a good sport about it and just asked if he could hold her. She smiled and agreed, and then fell asleep in his arms. It actually wasn't that bad.

But after that, he wanted her to sleep with him every night. Elle didn't get offended because she knew he liked her. The problem was she didn't like him back. Not like that. Twyla and Needra knew this but they made the situation awkward every opportunity they got. They played entirely too much. Those bitches would joke around and say stuff like, "Elle, there go your boo, Jimmy. Y'all make such a nice couple!" And at nighttime they would be like "Elle, go to bed. You know your hubby in there waitin' on you."

Jimmy would beam every time they said something. He loved it. Elle would just do the fake smile thing, but she would narrow her eyes at them to let them know she was going to kill them for their damn sarcasm.

One thing Elle couldn't front on was the fact that Jimmy had these full, soft ass lips. She would let him hold her from behind, and as nights went by, he started getting bolder. He would kiss her on the back of her ear or neck. She would usually shift positions so he would stop, but one night she just laid there. He went from kissing her neck on down her back and continued around her belly. Then his trail of

soft kisses made its way up to her breasts. He licked and sucked her nipples until they were standing up like Jujubes. Elle laid there quietly and breathing heavily. She tried to hold back the moans that kept threatening to escape from her throat.

Jimmy started working his way south. He pulled off her pajama pants and panties so he could get to her hidden treasure. Neither of them said a word. Elle laid there still as death while he took it upon himself to get to know her a little better. He explored her with his hungry mouth and tongue and made her squirm in pleasure. Each delightful stroke of his tongue took her closer and closer to climax. Finally, Elle could no longer endure the pleasurable torture. She grabbed the back of his head and began wildly bucking and grinding on his face.

Jimmy just kept licking, and then he dipped his tongue in and out of the honey. That pushed Elle off the cliff. The next thing she knew she was falling and then floating in space. She shook and quivered and cried out in bliss, cumming all over his face.

Jimmy smiled to himself in the dark, proud that he had her body reacting that way. He reached under his pillow for the condom he slept on top of with high hopes every night. He was finally about to beat. Jimmy knew he'd better move quickly and take advantage of Elle creaming in front of him. The way she had been holding back on those cookies, there was no telling if he would have another opportunity. With plans to sex her resistance away, he ripped the rubber open and rolled it on.

Elle laid there waiting on what came next. She could see Jimmy through the window light. He was putting on a condom. She hadn't had sex in so long she was curious to see what he had to offer. He had made her feel good so he deserved a little pity pussy. They were already out there now.

He commenced to enter her, and Elle gave him a mercy fuck that she actually enjoyed very much.

$$$

When it seemed too good to be true, it usually was. Jimmy loved the idea of the girls staying with him, but he had a fraternal twin brother named Rick who hated it. Rick was the evil twin. The complete opposite of Jimmy's paleness, he was dark brown in complexion. Set aside their skin color, they looked a lot alike. But for every ounce of good heartedness Jimmy possessed, Rick matched it with malice.

Rick was salty about Jimmy housing those money getting bitches, so he attempted to persuade his brother to view the situation like he did. The way he saw it, those girls were taking food out of his mouth.

Truthfully, Rick didn't even hustle like that. He just didn't want to see those bitches getting fat off their town. Rick was a smalltime dealer, but he actually snorted a little heroin himself. He didn't consider himself an addict because he dressed nice, held it together, and tried to take care of himself.

Rick had started snorting dope ten years ago at fifteen years old. He was just like a lot of folks in that area. Heroin use was as popular to the youth as smoking marijuana was. It was a whole new world.

Rick managed to corner his brother, and took a shot at getting through to him. Jimmy said he didn't want to hear it so Rick started clowning him about being a sucker.

"Jimmy, you a fool, boy! Them bitches livin' off you, eatin' all that cake, and you 'round here like a lil' lost puppy wit' ya' tail between your legs. You ain't taxin' them mo'fuckin' bitches, and niggas out here starving and shit. Them New York hoes eatin' all the food, and we hungry as fuck! Man, we 'posed to take they shit, and run them hoes the fuck up outta here!"

Always the good son, Jimmy told his brother he wanted no parts of that. He told him he was looking out for those girls because they were good people. He left out the fact that he was really into one of them.

Rick was extremely displeased by his brother's

decision, but he left it alone... for the time being at least.

$$$

Seeing that he couldn't get through to his brother, Rick decided to play dirty. He showed up one day at Jimmy's claiming he just came to smoke a blunt with his twin. He said he wanted to call a truce, and the blunt was the peace pipe. What he didn't tell his brother was that it was laced with ready rock.

Rick laughed to himself as he watched Jimmy pulling on the hard cocaine laced marijuana.

After Jimmy hit the blunt the second time, he said, "Rick, man, I don't feel right. Somethin' ain't right. This shit here don't taste like no regular weed, man. What the fuck is this?"

"Man, that's weed! It's just loud like that. Just smoke the shit, boy. That's some of that good *good* you puffin' on."

Just then, Jimmy felt a rush. He began to experience a high he had never experienced. It started at the tips of his toes and then spread all the way up to the very top of his head. His body seemed to just come alive. Every single hair on him. It was awesome. He grinned and told Rick that was the best weed he ever smoked.

Doubled over in laughter, Rick told him he had tricked him. When he informed him that the blunt was laced, Jimmy turned bright red. He looked afraid at first, and then real disappointed. He wondered how his brother could do him dirty like that. He couldn't believe Rick.

That was a cruel trick but it made Jimmy realize he loved the effect cocaine had on him. On the low, he started lacing his blunts with it. It wasn't long before he left Mary Jane alone for that white girl. Before he knew it he was smoking ready rock from a pipe.

Sadly, Rick was glad Jimmy got turned out. That was his plan. He had always been a little envious of the fact that his brother had remained strong when he got weak and fell victim to the demons that dwelled in their community.

Jimmy being on the stuff clouded his brain enough to start listening to Rick. That shit made him real paranoid. And that was just what Rick wanted. He finally managed to get into his brother's head.

Twyla, Needra, and Elle were oblivious to the fact that Jimmy was smoking. But they did notice something was strange. Now that he was getting high, he was acting sort of different. He was changing up on them.

One Friday night, Twyla and Needra were hanging out with some dudes they met, so Elle was at the house alone with Jimmy. He left out for a while, and when he came back she noticed he was acting weird. He was moving all fast and just kept on pacing. When he finally sat down, he kept hopping up every few seconds to look out the window. Elle asked him if he was expecting somebody, but he said no.

Jimmy had been avoiding eye contact with her all evening. When Elle finally got a chance to look in his eyes, she saw that they were glassy as hell. She had been around, so she knew the look of a person on that shit. And she knew the signs. That nigga was high. She couldn't believe him.

Elle was disturbed but more disappointed than anything. She didn't want to be around him while he was like that. How did she know she could trust him? Determined to put as much distance between them that night as possible, she got up out of there. She couldn't wait to see Twyla and Needra to let them know the deal.

$$$

The girls were getting mad money but their social lives sucked. Accustomed to the upbeat pace of New York City, they were almost bored to tears. So against their better judgment, they started mixing and mingling with a few dudes. Lots of them tried to holler but just a few of them were actually attractive.

Twyla and Needra were M.I.A. because they had spent the night fraternizing with some cuties they met. The dudes, D-Rock and Tony, were known for getting cocaine

money on the north side. Ironically, both Needra and Twyla found out their dates got high. D-Rock and Tony were both on that "boy."

Twyla found out about D-Rock's weakness the morning after they had sex. She was into well dressed, clean cut guys with waves, so they went out for dinner and drinks, and then she fucked him. They had a great time but he woke up dope sick, and asked her if she had a bag on her he could buy. He had apparently been trying to hold out, but couldn't. Twyla threw him a bag on GP, and he turned his back and tore it open and snorted it right there. It was weird watching him do heroin, but after that he seemed good. She guessed he needed it to feel normal. Before they parted, he copped two more bags from her full priced.

Needra and Tony spent their evening a little differently. They got to know each other and just talked until the sun came up. During their heart-to-heart, Tony admitted to her that he was battling a heroin addiction. You could've knocked Needra over with a feather when she found out. The tall, dark, handsome gentleman with a touch of bad boy in him who she dug so much was a dope fiend. The first thing she said was "so get some help."

Tony told her she was right, but he admitted it wasn't easy. He was actually feeling sick at the time. He explained to her that when a person was addicted, there was a chemical reaction to the lack of the presence of heroin in their body. Needra understood and sympathized with him. He tried to hold out but the dude was so pitiful she felt sorry for him. She gave him a bag on the strength. He took it but he was too shy to snort it in front of her. He went in the bathroom.

Heroin really had those mothafuckas out there by the balls. Young people in Durham used it like it was no big deal. It was commonplace and socially acceptable. They handled it like young people in Brooklyn smoked weed. It seemed like all of the hot boys were hooked on that shit.

When Elle got back up with Twyla and Needra, they told her all about their crazy evening. When she was done listening, she told them about Jimmy. They were all shocked at each other's stories, but that Jimmy issue superseded all

else. If Jimmy was weak, he could really turn out to be a problem because they were staying in his house. That made them susceptible to his actions.

The trio decided it was time to move on. They had to find a place of their own. They were wise enough to know that everybody didn't have their best interest at heart. They knew it could happen so they were going to play it safe.

Chapter 7

Twyla, Elle, and Needra were in the south dealing with that drama, but in New York their homegirls were on some other planet shit. One day an incident occurred that was so bizarre you would swear it was made up.

Pringles was out of the closet now, and she was trying hard to look the part of a "boi." She had cut off all her hair and commenced to taping down her breasts and wearing sagging pants like a dude.

One day she was bored and lonely. Chelsea had left about two weeks before. There had been two more incidents after the curling iron episode, so she finally got fed up and bailed. Pringles was feeling a lot of emotions about her departure, and she didn't like that one bit.

Determined to beat the fog she was in, she called Mena on the phone and asked if she wanted to come to her crib and puff an el. Mena was the type of girl you could lure with a blunt and a forty so she leapt at the opportunity to get high for free. She told Pringles she would be there in fifteen minutes.

Pringles never made a formal announcement to Mena about her sexual preference but she made no secret about it. She walked around dressed like a dude and wearing a strap-on, for God's sake. So it wasn't beneath her to assume that Mena showing up at her crib wearing a miniskirt and a g-string was an indirect invitation to sex.

When Pringles laid eyes on her, all types of mischievous thoughts invaded her mind. In the tiny little denim skirt she was wearing, you could see her buttocks while she was standing up. Pringles was no fool. She knew

immediately what Mena wanted. She decided to play it cool until they were a little more intoxicated.

She had directed a few lewd jokes towards Mena in the past about her ass and tities, just as she had done to most of their homegirls. Mena always pretended to be offended, but now she had the nerve to show up at her crib half dressed.

They didn't have much in common so they mostly talked shit about Elle and Twyla thinking they were all that now. After they smoked a blunt and had two drinks, Pringles changed up her whole demeanor.

She smirked at Mena, and said, "Bitch, you parading around in front of me in that little ass skirt, and shit. I know what you want. You want me to fuck that pussy, right? I know, bitch. Don't worry, I'ma ram this big ass dick inside of you!" She was referring to the big black strap-on she was wearing. Strangely enough, it empowered her.

It was hard for her to admit, but in the back of Mena's mind she was bi-curious. She had worn the skirt on purpose. She was guilty. But what she had in mind was more along the lines of cunnilingus, not the beast fuck Pringles was indicating. She figured she might get eaten by a girl for the first time, or maybe get her tities sucked, but that bitch was talking crazy. Warning bells went off in her head.

Mena planned a quick exit. She didn't like the way Pringles was leering at her. She had this crazed look in her eyes. "Yo, good lookin' on the smoke, bitch. I got you on the comeback. Next one on me. I'ma get ready to go, girl." Mena stood up.

Pringles stood up too. Laughing evilly, she grabbed Mena by her shoulder. "Nah, where you going? Don't leave yet. Lemme taste that pussy."

That sounded more along the lines of what she wanted to hear. Against her better judgment, Mena grinned and followed Pringles into her bedroom.

Wearing that false dick, she felt like she could conquer the world. Pringles laughed to herself as she thought of how much she would make Mena regret her decision to

stay.

She played with Mena's nipples for a while and then she made her lie down on the bed spread-eagled. She told her to relax, so Mena leaned back and closed her eyes in anticipation of the licking she assumed she was about to receive.

Suddenly, Pringles pinned her down and managed to slap a handcuff on her right wrist. The handcuff was attached to the bedpost so it prohibited her from using that arm anymore. Mena struggled to get free but it was in vain. Pringles subdued her until she got her cuffed on the other side as well. She tried to fight back but those handcuffs were a huge disadvantage. Both her arms were secured so there was really nothing she could do.

The helpless look on her face just intensified Pringles' lust. She loved to overpower bitches. She chortled demonically. She wanted to hurt Mena so bad.

Even though Mena was protesting, a small part of her was curious to see what Pringles had in mind. She was a no-holds-barred type of bitch, and had entertained some freaky shit in her lifetime.

Pringles snatched the flimsy g-string she wore off and shoved it in her mouth. After she gagged her with her panties to muffle her cries, she superseded Mena's expectations of freaky. She plunged inside of her with her strap-on until she hit the bottom of her pussy. Trying to make that plastic dick come out her throat, she mercilessly slammed into her cervix.

After repeating this several times, Pringles didn't get the reaction she felt she deserved. She took that as an insult and wrote it off to Mena's twat being overused and stretched out of proportion.

Pringles spat, "Your pussy raggedy, bitch! You ain't even got no fuckin' walls no more!" Disgruntled that her strap-on had not allowed her to make Mena scream for mercy, she quickly thought of a plan B.

That crazy bitch rolled a condom on a Totes umbrella and lubed it up, and she shoved it inside of her. Pringles grinned wickedly and hit the button, shooting the umbrella

deep inside her tunnel. Mena screamed when it crashed into her cervix but her cries could barely be heard through that panty gag. Pringles repeated her newfound torture method until she was tired. She put a pounding on that pussy that would leave her insides sore for weeks.

Tears ran from the corners of Mena's eyes. The experience was horrible. Pringles didn't stop until the ongoing pressure on her cervix triggered a bowel movement. To Mena's dismay, she shitted all over the sheets. Pringles had literally fucked the shit out of her.

$$$

Back in North Carolina, Elle, Twyla, and Needra got wind of some disturbing news. Turk, their self-proclaimed bodyguard, had died from an overdose. He had been shooting heroin mixed with cocaine, which was referred to as a speedball. The girls were really sad to learn that. They were almost a hundred percent sure that it was their dope he'd been shooting.

The girls also learned that Turbo took a nosedive after he got pulled over for a DWB - Driving While Black. The pigs that stopped him ran his name and learned he was also driving with a suspended license. Then they discovered that there was a warrant for his arrest, so they took him in. That warrant made him ineligible for a bail so he just had to lay up.

Turbo's absence was a wakeup call for them. They were out there on their own so there was no margin for error. The girls had put their relocation plans in motion. They were looking for a house to rent, but they played it cool with Jimmy and didn't mention a word to him. He acted pretty cool when he wasn't smoking that shit, but they knew they couldn't trust him. When the time came, they would just gather their belongings and leave.

The night before they were scheduled to meet with this realtor to sign a lease, Jimmy informed them that he had to take a ride a few towns over to handle some business. He

was fucking around but he still had responsibilities that Turbo left him in charge of when he got locked up. Jimmy was acting normal for a change so the girls had no reason to doubt what he said. He assured them that he would be back as soon as possible, and then he left.

Later on, the girls were all sound asleep. Jimmy still hadn't come back. Elle was tossing and turning in the middle of the night so she got up to go use the bathroom. The clock read 3:12 AM.

When Elle sat on the toilet she peed for almost a whole minute. "Damn," she mumbled sleepily. That was that huge sweet tea she drank before she laid down.

Elle wiped herself and washed her hands, and then she headed back to bed. Before she laid down she peeked at her sleeping partners in crime. Twyla and Needra were okay so she got in bed.

Just seconds after her head hit the pillow, Elle thought she heard something. She sat up in bed and listened closer. It sounded like somebody was messing with the doorknob like they were trying to get in. Everybody who stayed there knew that you had to jiggle the key a little bit to turn the lock. Especially Jimmy, so it couldn't have been him. And he would've rung the bell if he had trouble getting in.

It suddenly dawned on Elle. Somebody was trying to break in the house! She quickly woke up her other two thirds and frantically informed them. "Get up, y'all, somebody try'na break in!"

Needra and Twyla woke up startled but they got on point fast and got in attack mode. Twyla jumped up and grabbed the .45 she always kept close. That was usually her second instinct. She always prayed first. Elle grabbed a baseball bat from the corner and Needra went in her purse and got the big ass Ginsu knife she always carried. The pajama-clad, weapon toting trio made their way to the kitchen where the back door was. That was where the noise was coming from.

Each of their hearts was racing with fear combined with adrenaline. Nobody was going to just run up on them

and hurt them. Fuck that. Their defense mechanisms had kicked in.

They got to the door just in time to see a figure dressed in all black entering the house. Twyla didn't hesitate to cock and squeeze. *BOOM!* The first was just a warning shot she hoped would make him take heed and run.

The assailant was surprised by the gunfire but he didn't run because he was armed too. He raised his gun at them but Twyla didn't give him a chance. *BOOM BOOM*!!! She put two holes in that nigga. The gun he was holding must've jammed because he tried to shoot but nothing happened. He just turned around and ran. Twyla thought about finishing him but she didn't want a murder charge.

They could tell the bastard was hit in the leg because he was running funny. He hopped in an awaiting dark colored sedan and the vehicle screeched off. The girls were relieved to see that creep go. They were a little shook up but they were glad it didn't end with one of them getting shot instead.

They checked the door to assess the damage, and what they discovered was unnerving. There was a key inside the lock. The mothafucka had a key. It was a setup. That nigga Jimmy was living mad foul. The girls secured the door and quickly got dressed. Then they started gathering all their shit. It was time to get the hell out of there. They had been too trusting but that was a big lesson for each of them. No one would ever get close enough to set them up again.

After they were packed, The girls gathered their belongings and all the work they had, and took a cab to a hotel in Cary, the next town over. After they were settled in, Twyla called Bilal, who was in Virginia just an hour away. Using code words, she let him know she had popped a nigga that was trying to break in. Bilal was alarmed but calm as usual. He told them to lay low and assured them he would be there in the morning.

The trio laid across the hotel's double beds discussing their plans and passing around a lit blunt. They had to tighten it up and get their shit together. The attempted

setup at Jimmy's was alarming but they all agreed they were staying out there. They had struck oil in that town, so walking away wasn't easy.

$$$

Bilal showed up at their hotel room bright and early the following morning. Twyla opened the door for him and gave him a big hug. He laughed and smacked her on her ass, and then he picked her up and spun her around. Bilal had lived a life of crime you could write a book on, but he was an easygoing dude.

Poking fun at Twyla, he said, "Look at you, wit' your little scared self. Done had to shoot somebody, now you shakin' in my arms. Daddy here now, baby. Don't worry. Daddy here."

Twyla laughed, "I *am* glad to see yo' ass. What up, nigga?"

He grinned. "These damn prices." He was referring to the current rate of weight.

Twyla and Bilal had a unique baby momma/baby daddy relationship. The two of them had been through a lot but they got along great. She was just fourteen when she got with him, and it was him who had taught her how to operate a gun in the first place. An affluent hustler five years her senior, Bilal had rescued Twyla from an abusive "relationship" with this crazy ass loon named Kincaid, who used to slap her around when she was mad young.

Twyla was fast back then, so Bilal took her on as a work-in-progress and tamed her. She won his heart, which led to the role of his leading lady. Against her parents' wishes, she left home and moved in with him at fifteen. Her father disowned her and blamed her mother for letting her go, which contributed largely to her parents' failed marriage.

Twyla got pregnant soon after and gave birth to her daughter at sixteen. The baby was adorable, and pulled the family back together somewhat. Pop let go of the resentment he had about the situation and embraced his first grandchild.

He and their mother took turns keeping her while Twyla finished school.

When the baby turned two, Bilal had to go do some time. Twyla stood up for the first year, but one day she bumped heads with his mistress on a visit. She was so hurt she wanted some get-back at Bilal. Twyla had a couple of flings, and then she gave in to the advances of Rome, a younger guy who was aspiring to be the dude Bilal was. He also happened to be one of Bilal's former workers.

When Bilal got out three years later, Twyla was six moths pregnant by Rome. The streets whispered assumptions of a blood bath in the making. Dudes swore Bilal was going to kill someone. Twyla was terrified because she knew she had basically disgraced him by fucking with the help. But Bilal surprised her and everyone else. He was really a good dude. When he came home, his main concern was taking care of his daughter. He was annoyed by the situation but he knew he had locked Twyla down at a young age, so she had to live and experience something other than what he had to offer.

Bilal let it ride but a few folks in the neighborhood joked about the downgrade Twyla took. One guy had the nerve to tell her she went from sugar to shit. And she couldn't even deny it. Rome was nothing like Bilal. He may have been more of a ladies' man, but looks certainly couldn't pay the bills. He did what he could, but he was nothing like the provider Bilal was. God only knew why she loved him so much.

When it was almost time to have their son, Rome was fucked up financially so Twyla got money from her parents to buy things the baby needed. Against her better judgment, Rome took the money and attempted to flip it. He tried to double the money but the work he bought turned out to be no good. So they took a loss. Bilal had so much love for Twyla he bought her new baby a crib and everything else he needed. She and her new beau were struggling at the time, so she really appreciated that. Bilal had a heart of gold. Now they were like sister and brother.

Elle and Needra smiled at the display of affection between Twyla and her first baby daddy. They loved Bilal as well, so they got them a hug too. He looked around sincerely at all three of them and asked if they were okay. Knowing his concern was genuine, they assured him that they were fine. They were really happy to see him. Being around Bilal made them feel safe.

He had a seat across from the girls and proceeded to preach. And he schooled them on some real shit. It was Hustling 101 up in there. Bilal was an O.G. who had been in the money taking and money making business since he was a young man, so they hung on to his every word. Having a mentor with such a résumé was definitely a bonus. He had seen and done it all.

After Bilal gave them some pointers, he pointed out some changes they needed to make. He thought it was unwise for three women to be all alone out there. He suggested that they get some loyal shooters around them so mothafuckas would think twice. He said he wasn't belittling their authenticity or hustling acumen, but niggas looked at females like birthday cake – sweet.

Then Bilal addressed the shooting the night before. He was so real he took the dirty hammer Twyla had busted the would-be thief with, and said he would get rid of it. In exchange, he awarded her with a spanking brand new one. He told Elle and Needra he would get them one too, but he wanted them to come down to this private shooting range to practice a little bit. He said a friend of his owned it, and it was located just across the Virginia state line.

Bilal believed that they should put a hold on their plans to rent a house for the time being. He said the shooting was still fresh, and reminded them that they didn't have any fake ID, so putting a crib in their real names wasn't wise.

Bilal also told them they needed to get a little hooptie to get around in. That way they wouldn't have to depend on anyone to take them places. And they would save a lot of cab money too.

The last thing Bilal addressed was their method of acquiring their product. He let them know they had options,

so they didn't have to keep running back and forth up top to cop. He said he would be happy to supply them with all the dope they needed, and would give them better prices.

The girls were honest with him and told him they fucked with Coco because the fiends said that Chinese Dragon was the best dope in town. They worried that if they changed up, they would lose clientele. Bilal understood their fears but he just laughed. He got most of his dope from Coco, so he sold the same shit. He knew the tricks Coco's peeps used to hype up the work, so he informed the girls that there was nothing spectacular about that Chinese Dragon, other than the stuff they cut it with.

The trio knew Bilal knew what he was talking about. They assured him that they were willing to buy from him, but they had to end it with Coco on good terms. That wasn't a bridge they wanted to burn. Being affiliated with a man of his stature had too many advantages. It was always who you knew.

Bilal understood and he respected the way they decided to handle it. There were rules to the game, and the winners usually abided by them. He secretly gave the ladies props for having principles and respecting the game that way. They had scruples, which was a necessary component for longevity. Real recognized real.

Chapter 8

After Bilal left, the trio discussed the move they were contemplating. Twyla, Elle, and Needra all agreed that dealing with him would be a win-win situation. Bilal was always on the up and up so they were comfortable with their decision.

It was time to re-up so they were going to deal with Coco one more time. The girls voted that Elle would take the next trip. They would be seeing Bilal again in just a few days so she would be bringing back less than usual.

Elle took the train to New York and arrived the following morning. When she got home, she was delighted to see the prettiest woman on earth sitting in the kitchen.

She grinned and greeted her mother with a big hug. "Hey Lady!"

Genuinely surprised to see her baby daughter walking in, Ellen hugged her and exclaimed, "Oh my goodness, hey there, country girl! What are you doing in New York?"

They both laughed and then walked to Elle's bedroom to put away her luggage. Ellen asked where Twyla was, and started bombarding Elle with questions. Her main concern was their recent illegal activities. She said she knew what they were up to, and gave Elle a talk about doing the right thing in life.

Elle stood there and listened to the advice. A part of her felt guilty because she knew better. Her mama would probably have a heart attack if she knew they were dealing heroin. Elle lied and said she and Twyla were just selling a little weed, just to keep her from worrying so much.

After she was done talking, Ellen remembered that she had some mail for Elle. She went in her bedroom for it

and then returned and handed the envelopes to her daughter. Amongst around eight were two letters with hand written addresses on the front. You could tell they were from someone incarcerated.

Ellen pointed them out and said, "I don't know who those are from. Somebody in jail, it look like."

Elle looked at the mail closer and realized it was from Blaze. What a nice surprise. Her mother didn't recognize his government name because she only knew him by his moniker, Blaze.

Elle grinned. "Lady, they're from my friend Blaze. He got locked up, remember?" She decided to read the letters later on when she was alone.

A few minutes later, Etta came walking in the house with their little brother, her daughter, and Twyla's kids. Elle hid when she heard them coming and jumped out and surprised them. They were all thrilled to see her. She kissed and bear-hugged the whole team one by one.

Twyla's kids looked at Elle expectantly. Nay-Nay asked where their mommy was. When they learned she wasn't there they looked sad. Elle hated to see their long faces. She hugged them again, and promised that Twyla would be calling soon. She apologized on her sister's behalf and felt a pang of guilt. Twyla had to spend more time with her kids. She was hustling to provide for them but children didn't even care about that.

Junior pressed Elle and demanded the money Twyla had promised him for babysitting. Etta had her hand out too. Elle just laughed and started playing Santa. She came up off a few hundred dollars before it was over.

The kids cheered up when Elle promised to take them out to a movie. She and Etta made plans to roll out around seven o'clock. Ellen decided to sit that one out. It was her day off and she just wanted to take it easy.

After she played catch-up with her family, Elle went to handle that business with Coco. Their meeting went well. He understood their decision to stop traveling so much. They ended it with him telling her that he would always be there if

they needed his assistance. Elle kissed him on the cheek and thanked him. Then she took a cab home to stash that work for safekeeping until she left town.

That night she hung out with Etta, Junior, and the babies until about eleven. After the movies, they went out to eat at BBQ's. Elle picked up the almost $200 tab. When they finally called it a night, the kids were all good and sleepy.

$$$

Elle knew she needed to get back to NC with the product but she decided to make a little pit stop before she left. She wanted to go upstate to visit Blaze. The letters he had sent her had stirred something inside of her. Now she couldn't leave New York without seeing him.

She made arrangements to travel the two-hour trip upstate with this van service he had mentioned in his letter. She called them the night before and scheduled a pickup for the following morning at five AM.

Blaze wasn't expecting a visit that day so he didn't know who had come to see him. He was surprised to find out it was her. She could tell by the look on his face when he walked out. Elle tried to be cool, but when she saw him she was moved to run over and jump in his arms. It probably had a lot to do with his fresh haircut and bulging biceps. Damn, he looked good.

Happy to see her as well, Blaze picked her up and swung her around. He smelled so good. And he was holding her so tight. He had really filled out since the last time she had seen him. That lanky, baby faced kid was gone. He was a man now. But he still possessed that boyish charm. When he smiled, something inside of Elle melted.

When he put her down she planted a little kiss on his lips. Blaze just stood there blushing for a moment until he caught himself. He took a step back and sized her up. "Damn, you look good, girl. Turn around real quick."

Laughing, Elle did a little sexy spin for him. "You like?"

He shook his head and bit his lip. "Damn, that thang lookin' ripe. You lookin' like a juicy ass peach right about now, ma. You gon' make me bite yo' ass."

She smiled at that. "That's wishful thinking. You lookin' good too, boo. I see you been workin' out." Undressing him with her eyes, she removed his Polo shirt and visualized his six-pack.

"I ain't been doin' too much weightlifting. Mostly calisthenics, like dips, pushups and pull-ups. I don't wanna get too bulky. That swole shit slow you down. At this size, I'm nimble. And I'll put a big nigga on his ass quick."

Turned on by his confidence, Elle just laughed. The two of them had a seat and they just stared at each other for a minute, both feeling the connection.

Then Blaze looked real serious for a second. He took her hand, and asked, "So what took you so long to get up here?"

Elle looked apologetic. She explained that she'd been out of town a lot lately. They began to play catch up, and amongst other things, she told him about her latest hustling endeavors. She was modest about the money they were getting, but she basically told it all. When she got to the part about Twyla shooting that dude who tried to break in and rob them, Blaze really looked concerned. He listened intently, and then told her to be safe out in those streets. She knew he was genuine so she assured him that she would.

Elle said, "Oh yeah, I tried to leave you some bread, but they told me I could only leave fifty dollars. They said I could mail the rest in a money order, so I'ma get one and send it up here."

He made a face and shook his head. "Thanks, but I'm good. Keep your money. You could've kept that half a man you put in my commissary too. I *get* money, ma. Trust me, I run this shit."

His last words were a statement, but he didn't come across as bragging. That was sexy too. Elle loved his confidence because it wasn't boastful. She leaned in and looked in his eyes.

"So, you got a lotta girls coming up here to see you?"

He shook his head. "Nah. What kind of dude you think I am?"

Elle laughed but she kept on. "Well, I know you got a girlfriend. What, you gon' get married so you can get them conjugal visits?"

Blaze laughed, and leaned back and crossed his arms. "Nah, I'ma wait on this pretty chocolate chick. I'ma marry her when I touch ground." He winked at her.

Elle blushed. Damn, she liked him. He kept saying all the right things. "Who knows what the future holds…"

"Word. You gon' make me wife you." He grinned and grabbed her hand.

They had a great visit that ended with a long kiss on the lips. Elle left there feeling giddy and full of mixed emotions. The connection they had was undeniable. She wondered if she could wait the 5 to 15 years he said he was sentenced to. But her lifestyle wouldn't allow her to be there for him the way he deserved. She couldn't give him her whole heart. Most of it belonged to the game.

$$$

Later that day, Elle bought a money order from the check cashing place. Even though Blaze told her not to, she mailed him the rest of the two hundred she'd planned to give him. After she put the letter in the mailbox, she decided to go visit her father before she left town that night.

Along the way, Elle ran into Pringles. Unsurprisingly, she was on her "boi" shit again. She had cut off all her hair, and wore her pants sagging below her waist. She had a pair of Ralph Lauren boxers on display like she was a real dude.

Pringles said, "Oh shit, I been lookin' for y'all bitches! Where the fuck y'all been?"

Elle grinned and shrugged. "We been O.T."

"Oh, word? Where my bitch Twyla at? "

"My *sister* is outta town right now, hoe."

Pringles laughed and grabbed her crotch. "I got your fuckin' hoe right here. This big black dick!"

Elle looked at her like she was crazy.

She adjusted the strap-on she was wearing and continued. "Yo, Elle, lemme tell you, I took some pussy from your homegirl the other day."

Elle raised an eyebrow. That bitch had gone stark raving mad. "*What*?"

"I raped the shit out that bitch Mena," she laughed. "I tore that raggedy ass pussy apart!"

Elle just shook her head. "Spare me the gory details, boo." She didn't even want to know.

Pringles laughed and just ignored her. She proceeded to give her a graphic, detailed account of the lewd and taboo sex act she'd initiated on Mena. From the sounds of it, Mena had been straight violated. Elle didn't understand how she could've allowed another woman to do her like that, but she was staying out of that one. Both of those bitches were crazy anyway.

When Pringles got to the part about fucking Mena with an umbrella, Elle wondered if she was fabricating the story. For Mena's sake, she hoped at least that part was a lie.

"Pringles, you is one sick bitch," Elle said. "Girl, I gotta go."

Pringles said, "I be fuckin' the shit out these bitches." That fool grabbed her crotch and showed Elle her "dick" print.

"Yo' ass is crazy. Bye, bitch."

"Hold up! Yo, ain't nobody tell you? I got that weed now. Some *fat ass* nicks and dimes. A bitch blowin' up, Elle. I'ma cop me a whip soon. One of them Jeep Cherokees. And get me a bad ass White bitch to ride around in it."

Pringles was jealous and competitive so Elle knew that bitch was trying to give her fever. She ignored all the other bullshit that came from her mouth and addressed the weed. "Fuck it, I'll support yo' ass. You got somethin' on you now? Lemme get a dime."

Pringles nodded and looked around, and then she

progressed to serve her like she was pushing mega weight. She was fronting so hard, the devil in Elle decided to floss on her. Just to cut her down a little bit. She had two ten dollar bills and three fives in her wallet but that was the perfect opportunity to shine on Pringles. She pulled out a bankroll on that bitch, and innocently asked, "You got change for a hundred?"

Pringles' eyes got big as golf balls when she saw that money. The bitch started stuttering and shit. "Wh-where you get all that bread from?"

Elle looked in her eyes and saw how mad her frenemy was. Her deep seeded dislike for Pringles made her pick at the festering sore of her resentment. "I told you I been outta town. Bitch, we *gettin'* it. Shit, this just my pocket change."

From the look on Pringles' face, she didn't like that one bit. She was green with envy. Elle just laughed to herself. She didn't give a fuck. She had a wad of cash and was feeling herself.

Pringles said, "Oh shit, what the fuck y'all bitches into? Put me on, Elle! 'Least lemme come out there and sell some weed, and shit."

Was that bitch crazy? Nobody trusted her ass like that. To get Pringles out of her face, Elle lied. "Lemme check on a few things, and I'll get back to you."

Pringles nodded enthusiastically, already counting money in her head.

$$\$\$\$$$

After Elle visited Blaze that day, he was so concerned about her safety he made a call to a comrade for a favor. Blaze had his friend, this dude named Race, contact Elle at her crib that night. Race informed her that he had a package for her from Blaze, and instructed her to meet him somewhere.

When Elle picked up the package, it turned out to be a gun. It was a revolver – a .38 Special. Race told her it was clean so she didn't have anything to worry about. He said

Blaze wanted her to carry it for protection, and asked him to show her how to operate it. He gave her a quick lesson on how to load and unload the weapon, and then he took Elle up on the roof of his building to fire it. She let off three shots at the sky. The gun had a kick and was louder than she expected.

Before she left, Race gave her a case for the gun and a box of bullets. He said, "Just be careful, shorty. This a big boy. Whoever it is you beefin' wit', I promise you, they gon' apologize. And if you hit 'em in the right place with this shit, I promise you they gon' die."

Elle just laughed and thanked him.

Race gave her a onceover. He could see why Blaze thought so highly of her. That was his main man but temptation was a bitch. He kept it innocent, and said, "Enjoy your lil' baby cannon, ma. Niggas better duck."

Elle smiled and told him to be safe out there. He nodded and told her the same.

On her way home, Elle grinned the entire way. Blaze was something else. She was awed by his thoughtfulness. That was so attractive. It was totally obvious that he had feelings for her. He really touched her heart with that one.

Chapter 9

When Elle returned to NC, she couldn't stop thinking about Blaze but it was back to business as usual. The truth had finally come out. They found out who the culprit was that tried to break in on them at Jimmy's house that night. It was his brother, Rick. They heard he was limping around with one arm in a sling. Rumor had it that Rick had been shot twice, so that was all the proof they needed.

They hadn't seen Jimmy since he left the house that night. He had set them up so he probably couldn't face them. That was some foul shit he did. They figured they would run into him sooner or later.

Turbo had sent word to them from behind the wall that he had to do a little prison time. He said Jimmy had crossed him for some bread, and he heard he was getting high, so they should stop fucking with him. That part was rather easy, considering the fact that Jimmy just seemed to disappear.

Twyla, Needra, and Elle didn't let that incident stop their flow. They stayed about it and kept their eyes on the prize. The trio was posted up in a hotel on the outskirts of town, and making power moves. Word about their success spread quickly throughout the streets. It spread throughout their family as well. Before they knew it, two of their cousins, O and Gee, got in touch with them.

The boys expressed interest in coming out there to get money with them. The girls told them that wouldn't be a problem but they were living in a cramped hotel room so they needed a little time. When they got a place they would be able to accommodate them comfortably. The boys agreed to give them time, but they said they would be coming

through to check on them soon. They were only about ninety minutes away. The trio told them they were welcome anytime because they were family.

$$$

Elle, Needra, and Twyla decided to take Bilal up on that target practice he suggested. They were determined to never get caught with their pants down again, so one Sunday afternoon they went down to Virginia and met him at his friend's range. They spent hours there practicing with different types of guns. They used handguns, shotguns, and rifles, and ran through boxes of ammunition.

They all got pretty good too. Twyla already had a decent shot, but it got better. And Elle and Needra thought they were baby marksmen by the time they left. Now neither of them was afraid to fire a gun of any size or caliber. In their line of work there was no time for second guessing.

$$$

Twyla yawned and hung up the phone. "Get up, y'all," she yelled. "Bilal just called. He's on his way. We got less than thirty minutes to get ready. Rise and shine, bitches!"

The sleepyheads she was addressing groaned and reluctantly dragged themselves out of bed. It was only four AM, and still black outside. Their day usually started at six. They got up early to catch the morning rush from the working crowd. That morning fix was crucial to some people. More than morning coffee.

Elle got a good stretch, and then sleepily asked, "He comin' here, or we goin' to him?"

Twyla's response to her inquiry was, "We'll see when he gets here. He didn't say." After that, she turned on some music. They started each day with a little prayer and then they listened to their favorite Tupac songs, "Keep Ya' Head Up" and "Dear Mama." That was their morning ritual.

The trio played tag team in the bathroom. They did okay with the shower but bumped heads at the sink and mirror. But by the time Bilal arrived they were all fully dressed, bright-eyed and bushy tailed. It was time to get to work.

Elle, Twyla, and Needra all agreed that their alliance with Bilal was definitely working out better. It really proved to be a smart move. He gave them better prices than Coco and the quality was just as good. More importantly, he offered the convenience of delivery. Bilal was right in Virginia so they could re-up anytime they needed to.

They were now on their third flip dealing with him and it was all good. The fiends were loving the new product. And Bilal was about it. He would drive down and rent a room under one of his aliases, and then set up a laboratory right in the hotel room. He was as professional as they came. And he didn't play that careless shit so he never left residue on anything. He had cleaning supplies of all kinds, and they always sanitized everything he came in contact with - before and after they bagged up.

Elle and Twyla had been sitting there for about fifteen minutes when he called and told them he was in room 311 of the same hotel. Needra had the bubble guts so she was using the bathroom at the time.

Twyla yelled out, "Come on, shitty butt! Time to roll out!"

A minute later, they heard the toilet flush, and then the sound of her washing her hands. The sisters jokingly wrinkled up their noses at their cousin when she walked out.

Needra laughed and gave them the middle finger. "Y'all just mad 'cause I just lost about five pounds!"

The trio laughed together, and headed out of the room. When they got to room 311, Twyla tapped on the door. Bilal let them in and locked the door, and they quickly cleaned up and set up shop.

He opened what they referred to as his doctor's bag and handed out masks and rubber gloves, and the four of them suited up like surgeons in an operating room. The girls watched as he diligently crushed the heroin and cut it with

quinine. Afterwards he put a drop of morphine on that sucker too, which he said was Coco's trick. That put the icing on the cake.

After he was done, it was the trio's job to spoon the dope into hundreds of tiny wax bags, and then fold them and tape them shut. Then they stacked them in bundles of ten and then secured them with rubber bands. Their new bags were white with royal blue stars on them. The word had spread across town that the New York girls with that powerful Chinese Dragon had "Blue Stars" now. Their product was said to have been so good it made you see blue stars.

The girls hurried with bagging up the first few bundles because it was time to hit the streets. The morning was often their busiest time of day. That day it was Elle's turn to go out early. They had a little system working, so they rotated shifts now.

Leaving Twyla and Needra there to assist Bilal, Elle took a cab to the projects. All she took with her was her gun, a book she was reading by Maya Angelou, lip gloss, and ten bundles of dope. When Neej and Twyla were done they were going to scout out another spot on the other side of town, so that day she was on her own. But Elle didn't mind. They were in pursuit of profit.

$$$

When Elle got to Annette's house, she greeted her hostess with a smile and handed her half of her daily stipend for allowing them to use her crib. She always got the other half when they closed up shop at the day's end. But Nette thought she was slick. She usually managed to hit them up for more money here and there throughout the course of the day.

Nette grinned and thanked Elle for the bread, and then she told her Kojak had been there looking for her.

Just then, the doorbell rang. It was Kojak again, reporting for duty. And he looked relieved to see her. Kojak was a slim, brown skinned man of average height and build.

You could tell he had some muscles, but his once athletic stance was now replaced by slightly slumped shoulders. He wore his hair in two cornrows going back and he was clean-shaven, except for this oddly large mustache that completely covered his top lip. And he had an odd scratchy voice to match. Kojak was a funny dude.

After he entered the house, he looked at his watch. In his unique raspy voice, he said, "Good morning, sis! Come on and hit me! I got people lined up and waitin' on me. What I tell y'all 'bout this late shit? I just missed a sale for a ball! We gotta do better, sis, you feel me?"

Elle nodded and handed him two bundles. She didn't protest because he was a hundred percent right.

He looked down at the package like he was unhappy. "Sis, gimme another one."

Elle raised an eyebrow at him. "Jack, I'ma be right here, so when you need more..."

"Come on, sis, I got people lined up down at the park. Nineteen bags ain't gon' be enough. You make me walk all way back up here, and we could lose money. Don't I always come straight?"

He had twenty bags in his hand but they had the understanding that he got one off the top. He was an addict, and couldn't function comfortably until he did his thing.

Elle said, "Yes, you do always come straight. We doin' good, so let's keep it up, bro bro. This here is somethin' new, Jack. So I need some feedback, baby."

He looked like he was flattered that she wanted his opinion. He said he would give her a reading on the new stuff but he wanted to run and collect that money waiting first. Elle didn't argue with that. Business came before pleasure. She gave Kojak another bundle and he hurried out the door.

Elle turned on the radio and tuned into the morning show she had been listening to in the taxi on the way there. She had a seat on the floral upholstery covered sofa, and laughed at the radio hosts making prank calls.

Annette had gone upstairs. She resurfaced a few minutes later fully dressed and ready to go. As classy as she

could, she said, "Honey, I'll be back. I'ma walk up here to the store to get a paper."

"Okay, Nette. I'ma lock the door until you get back."

Nette smiled and pranced out the door trying to look dignified. Elle knew she was going to her buddy's house across the complex to find some ready rock. That money was burning a hole in her pocket. She couldn't wait to spend it. Nette used that same newspaper line every morning, and never once came back with one.

Kojak came back about thirty minutes later. He handed Elle a stack of money, and then excused himself to the lavatory. She counted the bread he gave her, and was satisfied that it was all there.

Kojak came out of the bathroom a few minutes later and gave her the thumbs up sign. Excited, he said, "Goddamn, sis! Whew! We got a *smoker* there! That thang so right, we gon' clean up out there! Before lunchtime I'ma head on over ..."

Mid-conversation, Kojak just started nodding. He caught himself like three times before he went into a real deep one. Elle waited patiently and didn't disturb his grove.

He was back a minute later. The funny thing was he picked up right where he left off. "I'ma head over to Canal Street and get some of that money 'round lunch time. Hit me one more time, sis. Lemme get on back out here. Come on, wit' your pretty black ass. Time is money, and money is time."

Elle shook her head and laughed. Sometimes it was hard to take Jack serious. His raspy voice was just hilarious to her. She went to the stash and gave him three more bundles. After that, comical Kojak took off again. When he got that jet fuel in him, there was no stopping his hustle.

Chapter 10

A few hours later, Nette returned looking all crazy in the face. You could tell she'd been smoking because her eyes were as big as fifty cent pieces. She kept on saying she heard someone at the door. The annoying part was that she kept jumping up and checking out the windows and looking out the peephole.

Elle was getting irritated by Nette's paranoia and pacing so she decided to walk down to the park. She was bored and knew she was sure to see some type of comedy down there. There were always memorable characters in the park's vicinity. She loved to laugh.

Elle had purchased a holster for the gun Blaze gave her, and she'd been carrying it around for protection. She secured it underneath her heather gray Carolina Tar Heels hoodie and left the apartment. Rick had mentioned his plans for retaliation to a few folks, so she was just being on point. Twyla and Needra made sure they were always armed as well.

Elle wasn't afraid of the neighborhood people so she felt comfortable navigating through the projects alone. At that point in the game they knew most of the locals, and had won the admiration of the majority of them. A lot of people treated them nicely, and some were even a little protective of them. That didn't surprise Elle because they got back from folks what they put out - respect and consideration.

There was a mutual respect between most of them on the underground scene. They would warn each other when the police were in the vicinity, so they had each other's backs to a certain extent. There was a decent rapport

amongst them so most folks got along. But there were always exceptions to the rule.

Elle would run into an exception that day. One she'd heard of before. The infamous Freddie Mack. This old-timer named Toby had love for her and her partners because they let him purchase a bag with short money a few times. So Toby had schooled them on the leeches, scammers, and stickup boys in the game. Freddie Mack was a name he kept on mentioning. His advice was to avoid contact with him at all times.

Freddie Mack was a washed up dopefiend with a mean reputation for robbing folks. He supported his habit everyday by strong-arming, scheming, and doing stickups. He combed the streets for dealers he could prey on and lean on for a fix. Freddie was fresh off a three-month prison stay, and terrorizing the north side when he got wind of some good dope on the other side of town that was said to have killed two niggas already. From an addict's perspective, heroin that killed a person was likely the best shit.

Freddie made tracks across town to go find himself a sample of the killer dope, the whole time planning to not spend a penny on it. When he reached the park across from McDuffie Terrace, he asked around to find out who was handling the new shit he heard about. The fiends he asked pointed him to Kojak.

Freddie headed Kojak's way with foul intentions. Kojak saw him approaching and knew drama would follow. Freddie was bad news.

Just as Kojak had expected, Freddie Mack began to make a scene. "Hey, man, that dope you just sold me ain't no good! It done fell, or somethin'! So I'll try another bag, or just gimme my money back!"

Kojak shook his head. He knew the game. Freddie Mack hadn't purchased a damn thing from him. He was simply trying to get a fix for free. Kojak knew about his reputation but he addressed him fearlessly. "Ay, look here, man... No games today. And no freebies. Go 'head on, man."

Freddie stuck out his chest and got up in Kojak's face. "Nigga, I said I'll try another bag, or gimme my fuckin' money back!"

Elle walked up just in time to see the altercation unfold. She didn't know who Freddie was at the time but she could see that he was a problem. She went over and asked Kojak if everything was okay. She was concerned but she also wanted to let onlookers know she wasn't afraid. Kojak worked for her and her partners, so it was their business Freddie was badmouthing. His hollering out how "bad" the dope was would deter people from purchasing it.

Kojak had just told Elle that they had a smoker that day so Freddie was insulting her intelligence. She knew his type. That nigga was looking for a free bag.

Kojak tried to keep the situation under control. He tried talking to Freddie but he stuck to his guns. He affirmed that he hadn't sold him anything. But that bastard kept on yelling out how bad that dope was, and how he was still sick after using it.

People were starting to stare at the commotion so Elle told Kojak to just give that petty asshole a bag so he could get on out of their faces and stop making a scene. That leech had the nerve to say he believed they should give him two for his troubles. Elle looked at him like he was crazy.

She started to tell him off but she was taciturn because she knew that horse was a different type of animal. The monkey on a nigga's back could be a gorilla. A mothafucka would take your life for it. You could be on top of the world, and then six feet under just like that.

There was no need to be verbose so Elle simply suggested he go on about his business. Getting into a shouting match with a fiend was beneath her. "Listen… Please go find somebody else to pull this on, 'cause we don't got nothing else for you. You got a replacement for the imaginary bag you copped, now make sure you don't ever cop from us again. This little game won't work next time. Now go on and enjoy your free fix."

Feeling that he'd been dissed and dismissed, Freddie got offended. No bitch would handle him like that and get

away with it. That was an insult to his character. His hurt pride told him to react. "You must not know who the fuck I am! Bitch, I'm mo'fuckin' Freddie Mack!"

In a flash, he flipped open a switchblade he retrieved from his back pocket and pressed it against Kojak's neck. "I was being nice, but now I want *all* that goddamn dope! Run it right now, or get cut open!"

Elle couldn't believe it. The nigga was trying to rob them with a knife. What part of the game was that? All movement out there ceased as onlookers waited for her and Kojak to react.

She could tell from the look on Kojak's face that he was contemplating making a move. Elle didn't want him to get cut so she intervened. "Okay, Freddie, you got it, bro. Be easy. Go on and give it to him, Jack."

Kojak looked like he really didn't want to. He hesitated for a second, but he dug in his pocket for the last of the bundle he was holding.

Freddie looked down at his hand movement – half in greed and anticipation, and half in precaution. He wanted to make sure Kojak wasn't pulling out a weapon. When he saw the dope, he smirked smugly and assumed it was a done deal. He let his guards down because he did shit like that everyday and just got away with it.

But that day would be different. While Freddie was watching Kojak reach for the dope, Elle reached for her gun. In a split second, she placed the tip of that .38 Special underneath his chin and warned that nigga.

"We tried to be nice, but you tried to turn it up on some gangsta shit. Nigga, do you know who the fuck *I* am? I ain't no bitch, I'm *that bitch*! H-B-I-C, mothafucka! Head bitch in charge! Now drop that fuckin' knife before I *blow your head off.*"

Freddie was pissed but he did as he was told. When he dropped the knife on the ground it made a clanking noise. Then he held up his hands and surrendered.

Kojak looked relieved as hell. He put the dope back in his pocket.

Elle slowly lowered the gun from Freddie's chin. She kept her aim steady and gave that vermin the opportunity to walk away.

Walking backwards the first forty feet, he quick-stepped down the hill. When he got about a hundred feet away, he yelled, "This shit ain't over, bitch! You hear me? I'm Freddie Mack, you whore!" After that he jogged off.

Elle thought about shooting him in his ass, but decided against it. She looked around and then put the gun away. She hated that she had been forced to pull out on that loser. But if she let it slide, mothafuckas would start coming at her team from left and right.

Kojak whistled. "Damn, sis! I'm glad you had that damn .38! If that nigga would'a stuck me, I'da had to kill 'im dead!"

Elle was a little nervous but she grinned. She told Kojak they should head back to Nette's crib. As the two of them walked off, a few people shouted out accolades for the way she'd handled that situation. There were murmurs in the crowd about HBIC, the "organization" she was affiliated with. Someone said, "Those HBIC girls ain't no fuckin' joke! I'd hate to get on they bad side!"

Along the way to Nette's, Elle thanked God for keeping her safe through that mess and contemplated the proper chess move to make about the situation. She had no choice but to take Freddie's threats of retaliation seriously. He said it wasn't over.

$$$

Amongst the onlookers, Elle didn't know that a detective was also watching the ruckus. Betty Benjamin was a veteran detective who'd been on the narcotics task force for fifteen years. She knew all the players in the city's drug scene, from the big timers and suppliers to the lower level hand-to-hand dealers and addicts. And she knew all the faces.

That day she was undercover sitting on a hill in an unmarked car spying on the activity in the park with a pair of

high powered binoculars. This was her biggest method of capturing crooks so far. She was responsible for thousands of arrests – just from seeing folks up to no good with her binoculars. Whenever she saw two people approaching one another, she would zoom in and see exactly what they were up to. Oftentimes she witnessed items exchanged, and it was usually drugs and money. She got a kick out of letting people think they got away, and then running down on them.

That day Betty saw an unfamiliar face. It belonged to an attractive, young, Black woman who was walking through the park. Detective Benjamin stared at her for a second and then moved on. She was busy watching Kojak, a petty thief and heroin addict she had busted for drug possession a few times. She watched as he was approached by another asshole she'd locked up various times, this trouble-making bully by the name of Freddie Mack.

Only when Betty saw the girl walk over and join their conversation did she pay closer attention. Who was she, and what did she have in common with those lowlifes? Betty had a hunch so she decided to keep the girl on her radar.

Just then, she got a call on her radio about a shooting that had just happened across town. The detective started up her vehicle and pulled off just before the attempted robbery happened. She never even saw Freddie pull out the knife.

While en route to the crime scene, Betty kept thinking about that girl for some reason. What was a decent looking young lady like her doing out there in that jungle? She wondered what she and those addicts had to talk about.

$$$

As they were on their way back to Nette's house, Elle thought about the police. She wasn't trying to catch a charge out there. She would be lying if she said that incident didn't shake her up a little. She knew the rules. In the streets, if you pulled a gun on a nigga you better be prepared to use it. That wasn't television, that shit was real. If it came down to it, was she really prepared to blow that man's head off? Was

she ready to take a life?

Elle was deep in thought about it when this dude fell in step beside them. He tapped her on the shoulder, and said, "Baby girl, you handled that shit. Now you gotta get on outta here."

Elle looked over and saw that he was an almond complexioned, friendly faced, chubby guy with dark eyebrows and a slightly receding hairline. He looked like he was in his late twenties, and he had this shrill voice. He talked real fast and country as hell.

The dude continued speaking. "My truck parked 'round the corner. Lemme drive you somewhere safe 'fore one of these snakes call the po'lice on you."

Elle didn't crack a smile but she wasn't rude either. She said, "Thanks, but I'm okay." She wasn't getting in the car with someone she didn't know. He was a complete stranger.

The dude laughed. "I know you don't know me from a can of paint, but trust me, I'm just try'na help. My name Fireball. All you gotta do is ask 'bout me. I'm wealthy as all hell, baby, so I ain't gotta take nothin' from you. I'm just try'na get you the hell on outta Dodge!"

Fireball looked at Kojak, who knew him already. "Tell her, Kojak. Ain't I rich?"

Kojak was honest and nodded his head. He wasn't too fond of Fireball because of his slick mouth, but that nigga's daddy was the richest Black man in town. Their family was loaded.

Fireball kept on. "See there, baby. Lemme give you a ride. Kojak can come too, if that'll make you feel better. I'm a good guy. Err'body love Fireball."

He talked fast and he came on strong. Elle wasn't sure if she liked that about him. But he damn sure had the perfect name. He was a big ball of energy.

Several voices in the park called out "Man down! Man down!" That meant the police were on the scene. That was a warning for everyone doing something illegal to get on point.

Elle looked over and saw a police cruiser rolling through, and her imagination ran wild. She assumed they were coming for her and thought about making a run for it.

Fireball looked at her. "See what I mean? C'mon, girl, let's get the hell outta this damn fryin' pan. It's hot as fish grease out here."

Elle just wanted to get away from those police so she accepted the ride. They nonchalantly walked off towards Fireball's truck. Kojak followed them. He needed a ride to the north side anyway. Elle made a pit stop at Annette's house to pay her the rest of her money for the day, and scoop up the last of the work. After that, they headed on out.

That Fireball was definitely a character. He was one shit-talking mothafucka. It was hard to be in a bad mood around someone so hilarious. He and Kojak argued the whole time they were in the car. It was gut-busting funny. Elle laughed so hard she almost peed on herself.

Fireball kept going in on Kojak's huge bushy mustache. He insulted him about it the whole ride. Kojak was very offended and noticeably uptight. He looked like he wanted to go upside Fireball's head.

Fireball said, "I don't give a damn you get mad! Kojak, you ugly, toothless mothafucka! Man, fuck you!"

Kojak shot him another warning look. He wasn't the arguing type. He rather just fuck a nigga up and call it a day. Besides, his voice was so raspy he couldn't yell loud enough to get his point across. Fireball's high-pitched voice was by far louder.

The next thing they knew, Fireball was yelling at the top of his lungs. "I *hate* that damn mustache! I'ma run by one day and chop that ugly mothafucka off! Ain't seen yo' top lip since 1973. I *hate* that ugly mothafucka! What the fuck is wrong wit' you, man? You done fucked up yo' damn brain doing all them damn drugs and shit!"

Kojak couldn't believe that drug head had the nerve to say that. "Ain't that the pot calling the kettle black! Nigga, you do more drugs than everybody I know put together!"

"Whatevah! But 'least I ain't crazy like yo' funny

lookin' ass. And I ain't ugly as you is neither. You ugly ass, goddamn big mustache, strange ass lookin' mothafucka! I can't *stand* that fuckin' mustache! Cut that damn shit off!"

Kojak was fuming after that. He was too hot to even speak. Somehow he managed to ignore Fireball for the rest of the ride. Elle had to commend him for that because that dude just kept digging and getting on his nerves.

When they got to Kojak's destination on the north side, Fireball apologized. "Jack, man, you know I was just shittin' you. You ain't ugly, man. Shake my hand, man. C'mon, we friends. Shake my hand."

Kojak hesitated but he shook his hand. Fireball talked a lot of shit but that didn't change the fact that he got them up out the projects after that shit with Freddie went down. So that man was alright.

Kojak told Elle he would get up with her later on to square up on the money. After that, he grinned at Fireball. "Yeah okay, we friends. Thanks for the ride, man. You big fat stank mothafucka!" He stuck his dope in his sock and hopped out the car.

Fireball laughed his ass off. He loved when people talked shit back to him.

After Kojak got out, Elle asked, "What I owe you? You want me to get a cab from here?"

"Just gimme two bags of dope. I'll take you anywhere you wanna go."

She hit him with two bags, and they pulled off. At the first stoplight they came to, he tore open the bags and snorted both right in the middle of traffic. Elle just stared at him in shock. That nigga was insane.

Fireball was a lunatic. He snorted dope like it was prescribed medication. And he had the nerve to take out a damn pipe too. He lit it up and started smoking ready rock like it was a cigarette. Elle had never seen anything like it. She couldn't wait to get out of that car.

Chapter 11

Back in New York the following morning, Etta lay in bed tossing and turning. She was just waking up from a nightmare about Twyla and Elle. In the dream, her sisters had been arrested and were facing life sentences. Etta doubted that part was true but just couldn't shake the premonition that something was wrong.

It had always been her duty to protect and look after her younger sisters. They were grown women who were six hundred miles away living the lives they chose, but she couldn't stop now. Etta sat up in bed and made up her mind. It was time to intervene. She was worried sick about Elle and Twyla, and their cousin Needra too. She worried about them so much she was afraid they would turn her head gray early. She was only twenty-five years old.

Etta had kept the secret Elle told her, but she couldn't any longer. Learning that Twyla had been forced to shoot a man trying to break in and rob them had made Etta very uneasy. It had been on her mind since she found out. If her sisters were in that deep, then they were in danger. Etta made up her mind to spill the beans.

A little later on that day, she sat their mother down and prepped her for the news to come. "Lady, I got somethin' to tell you about your two prodigal daughters. You might wanna sit down."

Ellen's first response was, "Are they okay?"

Etta nodded, so she exhaled and sat down. She listened as quietly as she could while Etta told her everything she knew.

Ellen was so flabbergasted by Etta's account of her

sisters' activities she couldn't even respond for a minute. She knew her daughters were doing illegal things they had no business doing, but she was under the impression that they were just selling marijuana. So to learn that they were dealing heroin was pretty sobering. And hearing that they'd been the target of some robber Twyla winded up shooting almost scared her to death. What were her children involved in? Dear Lord, she had to have a talk with them.

After that conversation with Etta, Ellen thanked her oldest girl for keeping it real with her about her sisters. She didn't quite know what to do yet but she went to her room to think. Ellen did some soul searching and knelt down and had a word with God. She prayed aloud for a solution to her daughters' inevitable detriment to themselves.

As she was down on her knees praying, God touched her. The matter was so serious, she thought about telling their father. He was more equipped to handle that particular situation so she needed to have a word with him. They weren't exactly on great terms but she had their children's best interest at heart. They had to do something to stop those crazy girls from destroying themselves. They were playing with fire.

She called Elliot and asked him to stop by. He told her he would be there as soon as possible. He didn't hesitate because he figured it had something to do with the kids. She wouldn't have called him otherwise. Regardless of what had happened between him and Ellen, he still loved his family more than anything in the world. There was nothing he wouldn't do for his wife and kids.

When he got there an hour later, he was forced to admit to himself how good his estranged wife looked. But she looked worried as well. Ellen told him it was the prodigal two again. Elliot just shook his head. Of their four children, Twyla and Elle were the ones who were always into something. Twyla had always been a firecracker, but he was surprised by Elle lately. She was usually the smart one. But now she had followed her sister to the wild side.

Elliot sighed. "What the hell them girls up to now? Where are they now, in Africa, or Sweden somewhere?"

Ellen shook her head wearily. She would just let Etta explain again. "Etta!"

Etta stuck her head out of her bedroom doorway and yelled, "Yes, Lady?" She smiled when she saw her father and made her way down the hall. "Hey Daddy!"

Elliot grinned at his eldest child. Etta was a tall redbone. She took after his mother's side. "Hey there, baby."

Ellen said, "Tell your daddy what you told me about your sisters."

Etta shook her head and sighed. Relieved to have her parents backing her on the matter, she gave her father the rundown.

When she was done, he shook his head. Elle had stopped by to see him the week before, and she told him she and her sister were just dealing a little weed down south. He smoked weed and he knew Elle and Twyla smoked too, so he was no hypocrite. She told him they were trying to stack a little money so they could put their music out, so he knew they had a cause. But he still schooled Elle on the perils and stupidity of petty drug dealing and reminded her what a smart girl she was. Come to find out that joker had lied to him.

When Elliot got the news that Twyla and Elle were out of town dealing horse, he was disappointed but he wasn't really all that surprised. He had grown up in the south watching his mother and all her siblings hustle. His uncle owned a piccolo joint, his aunt had a backwoods juke joint, and his mother sold shots of illegal liquor out the back door of their house when he was a child. So he knew his daughters got that hustling stuff honestly. It was in their blood.

The thing that bothered Elliot was the fact that it was a new day and time now. His daughters had opportunities that his mother and even their own mother didn't have. So it was unnecessary for them to take the chances they did. A Black person could make it without the illegal activity now. Especially young women with educational opportunities like his girls had. They were foolish to believe there was an easy way to the top. Life didn't work that way. There were lots of

consequences associated with that fast money.

Elliot assured his wife that they would try and get those crazy girls back on track. Ellen looked relieved to hear that. As a mother and father, their job was to protect their children and keep them out of harm's way by any means necessary. But their girls had strayed into the belly of the beast. They were living a life they couldn't save them from anymore. All they could do was talk to them and pray they would return from the fool's paradise they had drifted into.

$$$

Coincidently, Twyla and Elle called home that afternoon to find out how their family was doing. To their surprise, both of their parents got on the phone and started lecturing them. Afterwards, they begged them to come home. The girls understood their concern, but at that point they were not even trying to hear that.

They were glad they had praying parents but they had to do what they had to do. They were working to get the money to do something positive – their music. They told their mom and dad this over and over but parents just didn't understand.

$$$

It had been days since that Freddie Mack incident happened but the situation's outcome was still in the air. The streets were talking, and rumor had it that bastard was looking for them. Folks kept telling them he was riding around with a hammer "searching for them HBIC bitches." And they kept warning the girls about how dangerous he was. He was said to have put a few niggas in the dirt for less. So basically, he was a problem.

Before they could react, he robbed Kojak and another worker they had at gunpoint. And he told both men he would be back to terrorize them again. Unwilling to take that lying down, the trio discussed the issue and determined they had to make a move. They were making too much money to let

some dope fiend bully run them out of town. Freddie Mack was running around like a mad dog, so he needed to be put down.

Neither of the girls professed to be murderers but their safety was imperative. There was no way they were just going to live in fear. And there was no point in waiting on him to attack. They had to make a move. Freddie Mack had started it and now they had to finish it. It was kill, or be killed.

As luck would have it, the girls received a visit the following day from their cousins Gee and Olan. Those dudes finally made good on their promise to come check them. It was great to see them too. The five of them all hugged and then sat down and got caught up on everything. The girls gave them a rundown about life out there in the jungle. The money was good but they were surrounded by snakes and leeches.

When Gee and O found out what Freddie did, they were both pretty upset. Elle, Twyla, and Needra were like their sisters so they felt obligated to look out for them. They had been raised real close as children. Their grandmother used to keep all of them together. The boys told their female cousins they needed some manpower and insisted on handling that shit.

Knowing they weren't alone made the girls feel a lot better. Gee and O had their best interest at heart and they weren't crying wolf. They really had the heart to step to that nigga.

After they moved pass the Freddie Mack issue, the boys were honest with them. They were both down on their luck at the time and needed a lifeline. The girls had no choice but to put them on. The dudes wanted to get money, and they were in a position to help them.

That night they sat down and devised a plan, and then they discussed the protocol and positions everyone would play. If everything went the way they predicted, they would all be smiling to the bank. There was enough bread for all of them to eat.

Gee was frank. He wasn't with all that frontline shit. He just wanted some coke he could take back to their hometown and rock out with. He had a lot of clientele out there because selling coke was what he did. So the girls made the decision to delve into the cocaine market too. They figured they may as well go for the gusto. It was just another way to make a profit.

O, on the other hand, said he wanted to stay out there with them. Unlike Gee, he loved the frontline. He said that was his type of environment. He thrived in the jungle because he was a predator himself. He had been pushing dope since he was fourteen.

The next day, the boys went on a mission to find Freddie Mack. Elle rode with them so she could point him out. Around three o'clock that afternoon, they finally spotted him. They had searched the whole city for that worm, and he popped up right there in McArthur Terrace. Thrilled by the opportunity, Gee approached him.

Gee was calm, collect, and inconspicuous in his eyeglasses, gray tee-shirt, and baseball cap. To his advantage, Freddie didn't know who he was. Gee grinned and said, "Freddie, what up? Hey, remember her?" He nodded over at Elle.

Elle was sitting in the car. She smiled at Freddie and blew him a kiss. You should've seen his face when he noticed her. He looked like he saw a bearded midget snowboarding in a pink tutu.

"That girl... that's my family right there," Gee informed him.

Freddie Mack was no coward. He considered himself the baddest nigga around. He poked out his chest in defiance and opened his mouth to talk some shit. But he never got a word out.

O stepped up behind him, and calmly said, "It's bedtime, nigga. Say your prayers." He then fired on him with a sawed off shotgun. BOOM BOOM!!!

After O put holes the size of tennis balls in Freddie's back, he and Gee just walked away like nothing happened.

The fearless young men didn't even wait until that bastard hit the ground.

It was broad daylight but after the shots resonated, there wasn't a soul in sight. That's how fast everybody who'd been standing around got the fuck from around there. But what had just happened, no one would ever forget. HBIC got that nigga Freddie Mack hit up in the street. From that point on, they gained the revere of every nigga within a three hundred mile radius. They had taken out the notorious Freddie Mack, so they were the wrong bitches to fuck with.

Freddie had done a lot of people dirty, so no one was moved to call any authorities on his behalf. Most folks who witnessed his shooting looked at it as a favor.

Chapter 12

Elliot had some business to tend to in North Carolina pertaining to some property he had down there. He needed an excuse to go see about his girls, so that was his opportunity. When he told his wife about his plans to pop up on Twyla and Elle, she was thrilled. She asked him to promise he would bring them home. He reminded her that they were grown but assured her that he would certainly try.

Elliot took a plane to Fayetteville, NC, which was close to their hometown. He had called his brother, Gary, and asked him to pick him up from the airport. Gary had to work so he sent his son, Gary Jr. to get him.

Gary Jr. preferred to go by his nickname Gee. Gee picked Elliot up from the airport about ten minutes late. He apologized to his uncle and blamed it on traffic. Gee knew his uncle liked to smoke a little weed so he told him he had a treat for him. Elliot liked the sound of that. He grinned from ear to ear and told Gee that was why he was his favorite nephew. Gee laughed and passed him a joint.

As they got mellow, the men got to talking along the forty minute drive down the way. Elliot started schooling Gee on life and giving him advice about moving the right way. He knew his nephew was a hustler so he didn't hesitate to give it to him raw. He told him how many niggas he had seen with the same aspirations, and let him know how predictable the dope game was. There were only two ways out – death or prison.

Gee knew his uncle cared. He heard the same things from his father all the time, so he was used to it. His uncle was just funnier because every time he saw him he had a joint in the side of his mouth, and a bible verse or spiritual

proverb on the tip of his tongue. Elliot passed him the joint and asked if he was prepared to forfeit his soul for the love of money.

Gee shook his head. "Look, Unc, I appreciate the advice, and you a hundred percent right. But I ain't ready to leave the game alone just yet. I got a few things I'm try'na do."

Elliot said, "Man, you just as crazy as my daughters. What's wrong with you young people? Elle and Twyla so far gone, their mama scared they might wind up somewhere dead. We scared somebody gon' kill 'em out there, bo'." He shook his head sadly.

Seeing how concerned his uncle was about his cousins, Gee informed him that Elle and Twyla were okay. He told him they were steadily in contact, and admitted they were moving a little weight together.

Elliot didn't like the sound of that part but he was relieved that Gee had recently seen his girls. He asked his nephew if he would take him to where they were so he could see about them.

Elliot was one of his coolest uncles so he couldn't say no to him. Gee promised him they would take that ride in a couple of days. If he wanted to check on his daughters, he had every right to. And it was only right that he take him.

Two days later, they rolled out together. When they got there, O and the girls were all sitting out in the park.

When Elle and Twyla saw their father they thought they saw a ghost. Twyla said, "Oh shit, that's Pop!"

Bug-eyed with surprise, Elle said, "Huh? Daddy?"

Needra was shocked too. She said, "Unc! What you doin' out here?"

O stood up and greeted his uncle with a handshake, surprised as well. "Hey, Uncle E."

Elliot hugged them all, and said, "I come to see about y'all girls. Been hearin' a lot of stuff... Everybody worried 'bout y'all."

"We good," the trio chimed in unison.

He shook his head at his foolish daughters and niece,

and didn't waste any time. "I heard about the money you makin' but lemme ask y'all somethin'. If a man gains the whole world but loses his soul, then what has he gained?"

The girls looked around at each other. They knew a sermon was coming. Their father was right but they wanted him to understand their motives.

Twyla said, "Pop, this is just temporary, trust me. So you ain't even gotta preach."

"Girl, I'm not preachin', I'm *teachin'*. There's a big difference between the two."

Each of them nodded, acknowledging the fact that he was right.

Elle said, "Daddy, we just try'na get up the money to put our music out and do our video. Ain't nobody try'na be no kingpins or nothing. So it ain't like *that*."

Elliot grabbed his head in frustration. They just didn't get it. "Elle, don't you understand? Twyla, Needra, do you? O? God ain't gonna bless y'all and let you make it like that! You're selling your souls, darling. The bible say "No weapons formed shall prosper." You know what that shit y'all pushin' do to people? It's a weapon because it destroys people's lives. Destroys innocent little babies! Y'all workin' for Satan! And you messin' with somethin' that'll get you locked up for the rest of ya' lives! Is you retarded? Or psychologically impaired? *Somethin'* wrong wit' y'all. Damn, y'all girls *wanna* go to jail!"

All of their heads were hung low from Pop's verbal lashing. They were all substantially more God-fearing than they were afraid of the law, so the spiritual warnings hit home the most. Especially after they had just killed Freddie Mack. It had just been days now, so it was really on their conscious.

Elliot saw how dumb they were looking so he just shook his head. "Boy, Ellen's kids are crazy!"

Elle and Twyla just looked at each other when he said that. Every time they did something their father disapproved of, they became just their mother's children.

Elliot continued. "I don't know where y'all get off, because I ain't *never* sold no drugs. Me or your mama. I

rather lose everything I have than to work for Satan. Y'all girls movin' through life too fast, and too stupid. You gotta be wise and wait on God for your blessings. You gotta be like Job! Job waited on the Lord 'til the flesh fell from his bones! You got to wait on God! Messin' with Satan will destroy you!"

Elliot prayed that his words were having some type of effect on those crazy kids. He knew they heard him. He just hoped and prayed they would listen.

In their hearts, they all knew Elliot was right. They knew what they were doing was wrong but that fast money had them in a vise. They told him they would be getting out of the game soon, but they all knew that was easier said than done.

Elliot looked around and addressed his daughters, his niece, and his nephews. "Listen here, lemme tell y'all one thing. It's easier for a camel to get through the eye of a needle than a rich man to get into heaven. Quit chasin' that fast money. Y'all know better. God looks out for babies and fools, and y'all are neither. You know better, so your luck is gonna run out. Just remember what I told you."

$$$

Pringles sat alone in her apartment frowning at her ratty old furniture in distaste. She kept on playing back her conversation with Elle, and was so heated she wanted to scream. Those bitches were on top again. Every time she thought she was passing them, they did something to make her accomplishments seem pale in comparison. Frustrated, she hollered at the top of her lungs. "Aaaaaahhhhhhhhh!!!!!"

She jumped up and punched the wall. That dumb move prompted another scream, this one in excruciating pain. She shook it off and wondered how those bitches Elle and Twyla always managed to outshine her. As she sat on the floor nursing her scarred knuckles, she contemplated a scenario that wouldn't just rain, but piss on their parade.

It had been a month now, and Elle never called her.

They were getting it and they wouldn't put her on. Those bitches didn't want to see her eat. She was starting to take it real personal.

Chapter 13

A few weeks rolled by, and everything was going smoothly. One evening Twyla, Elle, and Needra were sitting down having dinner at Shoney's. After they attacked the salad bar, they talked about the possibility of going home for a few days. Since Bilal had been supplying them, their trips to New York had been few and far between.

All of the girls missed New York, so a trip there was definitely due. They hadn't had the opportunity to all go home together yet, so they wanted to go floss a little bit. They had bags of brand new clothes with tags still on them, and didn't have anywhere to wear them. They hung out sometimes but down there was nothing like their city. The social scene was dry. There were so many dudes on drugs, they were afraid to give one a shot.

The trio agreed that a trip up top was definitely in order. Excited, they planned it for the upcoming weekend and came up with their itinerary. When they got up there, Elle and Twyla needed to search for a photographer for their promo pictures. And of course there would be family time and fun time with the kids, a shopping spree, and then they had to get up with their homegirls. Sunday night they would hit The Tunnel, which was this new and happening nightclub in Manhattan where all the celebrities partied. Elle also planned to find time to visit Blaze.

Now that plans were made, they needed to make sure their business would be taken care of during their absence. If they all left together there would be no one there to oversee things. Their cousin O had proved to be trustworthy so the girls decided to leave things in his hands while they went to

New York. O was a soldier. He had showed up ready and willing to help them, and he had their best interest at heart. It felt good knowing they had someone they could trust.

When he was delegated the responsibility of holding shit down for a few days, O said he was honored and promised to stay on top of business. The girls figured he was the last person they had to worry about snaking them, so they left him with product and instructions, and headed home.

When the trio arrived in New York they were loaded. Before they left NC, they had hand counted over a hundred thousand dollars. $104,628 to be exact. They took $60,000 off the top and divvied it up so they each had twenty grand to do as they pleased with. The rest they would invest in cocaine. Gee was pushing that weight hard, so backing him had proved to be a wise and lucrative decision. Prices had just dropped so they planned to cop heavy. They had notified Coco already, so plans were in the works.

To Elle, Twyla, and Needra's surprise, each of them had mail waiting on them from the United States Department of Immigration and Naturalization. The letters said that the authorities were conducting an investigation that was triggered by a drastic increase in marriages between young women in the New York City area and young men in Chittagong, Bangladesh. They said they suspected that the marriages were fraudulent and would take it upon themselves to annul them unless they made a formal dispute. They had the opportunity to respond within a given timeframe with a long list of proof that was listed on the back of the letter.

Those letters scared the girls out of any intentions they had to try and stay married. They would never see the other half of that money now. Immigration was on to that scam so there would be no green cards issued. The jig was up.

With the exception of receiving those letters, the girls were having a great time at home. Their second day there they all went shopping on Fifth Avenue. Needra, the tightest one as usual, stuck to a budget but Elle splurged with her sister. Twyla didn't care about price tags. She just threw shit

on the counter. They spent so much money it was incredible. They were balling out of control. They spent over $7,000 apiece on clothes and shoes, and then around $3,000 more on handbags.

The girls had earned over a quarter million dollars since they had been out of town. But the truth was none of them had any real money saved. Elle knew the reason was because they were all shopaholics. They sent a lot of money orders home as well, but they steadily blew money splurging on expensive designer labels and things. They were being completely financially irresponsible but stunting felt so good. They were young and living for the moment.

The one time Elle suggested that they slow down on their spending, Twyla said, "Look, Elle, I ain't no regular bitch. And neither are you, booboo. If you wanna be in charge you gotta look the part. HBIC is a lifestyle, baby sis."

$$$

Sunday came, and it was party time. The trio broke out their best outfits from the batch they bought. The goal was to shine at The Tunnel that night.

Draped in Dior, Gucci, and Armani, Elle, Twyla, and Needra made their grand entrance into the Hip-hop Mecca just after midnight. The Tunnel was where all the who's who and elite from the streets and industry rubbed elbows. The celebs that were present mixed with the crowd like regular people. Amongst others, that night Puff Daddy, Biggie Smalls, Busta Rhymes, Ice-T, and supermodel Naomi Campbell were in the building.

The girls were at the bar purchasing a bottle of Moët when they heard the DJ send a shout-out to Tupac, who he said was also in the building. Elle looked at Twyla and Needra, and they all broke out in huge grins. They loved Tupac fanatically. "Keep Ya' Head Up" was their theme song in the mornings.

Hoping they would run into him that night, the girls bought another bottle on ice and began to dance. They were

classy and sassy in their sexy upscale European getup so they blended right in with the A-Listers.

Needra had her legs out, and kept tugging at her hem like she could make it longer. After they got her to relax and stop fidgeting, they had a great time. They got especially hype when Biggie Smalls' new hit "Unbelievable" came on. The deejay kept mixing and bringing back their favorite part.

"Live from Bedford-Stuyvesant – the livest one - representing BK to the fullest. Live from Bedford-Stuyvesant – the livest one - representing BK to the fullest."

Twyla, Needra, and Elle pumped their fists in the air and shook their asses. That record was a tribute to their Brooklyn neighborhood so they had to represent. They were getting down. They partied so hard they were the livest chicks in there that night for real. The way they were popping bottles, mothafuckas recognized. They were getting stares of envy and admiration from chicks and dudes.

At the end of the night, just minutes before the club was about to close, the girls headed to the coat check section to get their jackets. They each got a few numbers that night. And they met some dudes they had agreed to go have breakfast with.

When the sexy trio walked in coat check, standing there with no bodyguard or entourage whatsoever was their favorite rapper of all time, Tupac Shakur himself. With the exception of the excited groupie who was writing down her phone number for him, he was all by himself.

Twyla was never shy but drinking so much made her extra bold that night. She walked right over and interrupted the girl's moment. "You givin' him your number for real? Pac don't want your groupie ass, trick!"

The prissy girl saw that she was outnumbered so she didn't respond. She just handed Tupac the number and told him she'd be looking forward to his call. Then she sashayed away like she was cute.

Pac just looked amused when Twyla came over and spazzed on that chick. When she ran her off he didn't even protest. He laughed, and asked, "Where y'all from?"

Twyla said, "We from Brooklyn, and *we love you* with all our hearts, baby."

"Yes! But not on no groupie shit," Needra chimed in.

"Yeah, on some real *respect* shit, boo," added Elle. "Real talk."

Pac grinned. He had the warmest, friendliest eyes. "Thanks, ladies. I love y'all too. I knew y'all was from Brooklyn. Y'all girls got some fire in y'all."

Just then, this dude walked up and asked Pac if he was ready to go. The club was closing and people were about to bum rush the coat check line. Elle Needra, and Twyla wanted to beat the rush so they each gave Tupac a big hug and let him know how much they loved and appreciated his music.

His eyes were wisdom-filled beyond his years. He looked at each of them appreciatively and thanked them. Tupac was so humble and genuine. That was a real dude. He smiled and winked at them, and he and his buddy walked off.

As they waited to get their jackets, Needra was like, "Y'all think we should've let him know y'all sing?"

Twyla said, "Nah, it wasn't the time or place."

"Word," said Elle. "Everybody come at him like that. He probably just came out to party, and shit."

Twyla nodded. "You gotta let a nigga breath. We gon' see him again, but at the top!"

"Word," Elle and Needra said in unison. The tipsy threesome laughed and hit five.

$$$

After the trio left the club they changed their mind about those breakfast plans. Needra felt nauseous from drinking too much champagne so she was ready to go home. Twyla decided to call it a night too. She admitted she had backslid with her baby daddy again since they had been up there. Now she wanted to go see what Rome was up to. She wanted to make sure he saw her in that outfit before the night was over. She laughed when Elle said he would be the one to

take it off her too.

Elle wasn't mad at her girls, but unlike those two party-poopers, going home was the last thing on her mind. She was feeling naughty and in the mood to stay out all night.

Earlier that night she met this dark-skinned cutie named Talib. She saw him outside in his car, which he had left the club early enough to get out of parking so he could floss in. He was pushing a brand new, dark blue Lexus GS. The car had shiny expensive rims on it, so the brother was turning heads. The bitches out there were on it but Talib was acting all nonchalant. He seemed like a laidback type of cat.

He noticed Elle from the club and winked at her. He was getting a lot of attention from the broads out there, so the fact that he acknowledged her was a huge compliment. He recognized. That was a plus for him. He was also riding solo that night, which was another plus to Elle. He rolled the window down and summoned her over.

She walked over to holler at him. He was a cool dude with a nice smile. Elle was a sucker for a smile. After they kicked it for a minute, she decided to slide off with him. He looked good and smelled good as hell. She wasn't usually the one night-stand type but she hadn't had sex in so long, she just wanted to get her jollies off. She was in New York, the only place she had a shot. And there was something empowering about having her own money. She didn't feel like a hoe or a groupie about the sex she was contemplating. She was a made bitch who was just out for a good time.

She winked at her girls and told them she would see them later. Her partners gave her knowing glances and told her to be careful. They made her promise to use protection and be sure to let them know she was alright. Needra and Twyla both thought about intercepting, but Elle was grown so they settled for jotting down homeboy's license plate number.

Elle hadn't had sex since she was with Jimmy. It had been a while so she was looking forward to getting worn out. It seemed like she was in good company so she stayed on point, but she let her guards down a little bit. She and her

newfound friend rode through the city laughing and conversing. He was from Uptown so they headed that way.

He was honest along the way and told Elle he had a little situation in the form of a baby momma who happened to reside with him. He said they had a son he wanted to be there for. Elle respected that. She joked that she was just coming out of a marriage so she wasn't looking for any commitments. He was totally okay with that.

That night she and Talib winded up at a breakfast spot Uptown that he spoke very highly of. The food there was as good as he guaranteed her it would be. They got to know each other a little more over their meal, and then decided to get a room.

He happened to smoke weed too, so they puffed an el to relax and get in the mood. Before long, Elle was bent over sweating and clawing the sheets. Talib fucked her like he was trying to make her fall in love with him. He had that dangerous dick. She was yelling out his name.

He was a satisfying lover who undoubtedly left a big smile on her face. The sex they had was nasty, sweet, and safe. At one point he tried to slide in her raw, but she shut that down immediately. He was cool with her "no glove, no love" policy, so their night went pretty smooth. After he hit it from the back, the front, and the side, they climaxed together and lay there sweaty and entangled.

Elle was soaking wet. When he withdrew his penis from her love canal it made a suctioning sound. She reached down to make sure the rubber was still intact. It was. Both completely spent, they fell asleep in each other's arms.

Elle called herself just closing her eyes for a few seconds but she didn't wake up until about thirty minutes later. She glimpsed at the clock and realized it was after 5:00 AM. Talib was still laid out. He was snoring lightly. Elle had to urinate so she hurried to the toilet.

After she used the bathroom, she decided to take a quick shower. Careful not to wet her hair, she washed away the secretions of evidence from her lustful affair. She used the little personal sized bar of soap the hotel provided to

shower with, and then the lotion to moisturize. When she was done, she left the bathroom to find her clothes.

Talib was still snoring. Elle smiled to herself and turned on the light so she could find her undies. She decided to put on her bra, but put her panties in her purse: Now that she had showered, she didn't feel like putting on the same ones.

Elle didn't see her underwear on the floor so she assumed they were lost in the bedcovers. She looked closely at the bed in search of them. She found her bra and panties, as well as an unwelcome surprise that almost sent her vomiting. Talib lay snoring with his penis resting flaccid on the side of his thigh. He was still wearing the rubber, which was filled with what appeared to be semen and blood.

Elle was appalled. His dick was bleeding! There was blood coming out of his fucking dick! She literally gagged and choked back vomit.

"It's all my fault," she told herself. She had no business being there with him in the first place. That's what she got for chasing some damn dick. She should've just bought a toy or something. That's what the fuck she got.

Elle had a quick word with God in her head. *"God, please let me be okay. Don't let this affect my health. Please, dear God."*

A part of her wanted to wake Talib up and demand answers. She wanted to yell, *"Nigga, what the fuck is wrong with you? Why the hell is blood coming out of your damn dick?"*

But Elle wasn't sure how'd he'd react to that. He might jump up and punch her in the face, or something. She wasn't in the mood for a shiner. Anxious to put some distance between them, she quickly got dressed as quietly as she could. She left him sleeping peacefully and exited the room quietly. She closed the door behind her, careful not to slam it.

Elle had some homegirls who would've gone through that nigga's pockets before they left, but she wasn't living like that. She might run into him again, though she certainly hoped not.

She rode the elevator downstairs and flagged a taxi outside. She was relieved to get the hell out of there. Her night turned out to be a big disappointment, but she was glad she had crept out of there before the sun came up. The night had been crazy enough. The last thing she needed to end it with was the walk of shame.

In the back of the taxi, Elle discarded Talib's number from her mental rolodex. She couldn't believe what happened. You couldn't even make something like that up. She couldn't wait to see Twyla. She had to tell somebody.

About forty minutes later, she stood in her sister's kitchen whispering about her ordeal. Rome was in Twyla's bedroom sleeping, so Elle kept her voice down. That wasn't really the kind of story she wanted to share.

Elle hissed, "Sis, lemme tell you! This nigga dick was bleeding!"

Twyla made a face. "Uggghhhh! Why, it had a cut on it?"

"No, there was blood comin' out of the shit! We just finished fucking, and it was inside the condom when he came! I almost fuckin' threw up! That shit is so disgusting! Oh my God, I'm going to the doctor!" Elle had the heebie jeebies.

"Ooh, I can imagine how you feel. Calm down, sis. The rubber broke?"

"No! Thank God! I'd probably be calling you from jail because I would've killed that mothafucka!"

"If the condom didn't pop, then you alright, girl. Don't worry. But ewwww… gross! I know you ain't fuckin' with that nigga no more."

"Hell fuckin' no! I'm scared to death! I don't ever wanna see that bastard again!"

"I don't blame you. Elle, something gotta be wrong with him for that to happen. He might have some horrible type of STD, or even cancer, or something. There could be something wrong with his prostate, and shit. Damn, he was a dime too."

"I *know*, sis. But I'm so grossed out by that shit. Damn it! I'm going to the doctor tomorrow."

Twyla yawned so Elle told her to go on back to bed. She was tired too so she went in the kids' room to lay down. They were down the block with Etta as usual.

Before Elle closed her eyes she said another prayer and made a vow of celibacy. She decided she was locking it up now. No more sex with random niggas. Waiting on Blaze to come home didn't seem like such a bad idea now.

Chapter 14

The girls had a lovely vacation in New York. Their six day stay was great. The best part of it all was that Twyla got to spend some time with her kids. Elle had visited Blaze, and her doctor visit turned out okay too.

While they were in New York they did everything they had planned, and also made an impromptu decision to get matching tramp stamps. They had all gone to a tattoo parlor and gotten "HBIC" on the back of their left shoulders. The letters were sitting on top of a gun, and bordered with roses. The guns and roses concept was their idea, but the tattoo artist had done a great job jazzing the artwork up.

Against their family's wishes, the trio returned down south. They copped that weight from Coco and got it back down there safe, so they figured it was all uphill. When they got back they were under the impression that O had everything under control. They didn't think they would have anything to worry about, but they couldn't have been more wrong.

They were very disappointed because their money was shorter than a half-priced hoe's skirt. O barely had two thirds of what they usually averaged on a weekend. They'd been gone for almost a week, so he should've had at least three times as much. The trio knew something was up.

The notion was heartbreaking, so no one wanted to believe it, but each of them wondered if O was stealing. He claimed shit had been moving slow because the batch of shit they left him was weak.

Later that day they spoke with Kojak, who told them a different story. He said O was lying about the product

being weak, and the sales decline as well. He also said O had
been a real asshole while they were away. Kojak looked
pretty pissed about whatever had happened between them.

The girls had to face it. Their cousin was guilty of
treason. He was family so they couldn't hurt him, but they
would switch up the way they moved with him. They took
that one on the chin and voted to demote O to a lookout until
further notice. He could no longer be trusted.

It hurt to accept the bullshit he did, so they told
themselves that O had just skimmed off the top the first
opportunity he got because he was young and ambitious. He
wanted to be on their level. They even blamed themselves
for leaving things in his hands. The temptation had
overwhelmed him. The girls agreed to never leave their
business unattended again. At least one of them would be
standing watch at all times.

The trio tried to let that money issue slide, but they
found out the streets were whispering things. Some horrible
things they didn't want to believe. O was said to have been
telling folks that he was the new boss, and things were going
to change. They had given him the benefit of a doubt, but
after those negative reports came back to them, the girls had
no choice but to have a word with their unruly cousin.

Lately O had been staying with some chick he was
screwing. They'd told him they wanted to have a meeting, so
now the four of them sat in their hotel suite opposite each
other.

When they asked him what the deal was, he just gave
them short answers and shrugged nonchalantly. He had
adopted this arrogant little attitude, and it was really
annoying. There was blatant deceit and disrespect in his tone.
The nigga was handling them like they were wasting his
time.

The girls were silent for a short period while they
evaluated the situation. O was just sitting there like he was
done talking, so it was completely quiet. You could've heard
a pin drop in there.

Almost overnight, their cousin had changed. And the
trio was really baffled by this. The cold, distant stranger

sitting before them was nothing like the seemingly humble and eager young man they left in charge just days before. Was all that smiley faced shit he gave them fake? Had he just pretended to be an alliance? The girls just weren't sure. The only thing that was clear was the fact that the little nigga was feeling himself. They had to nip that in the bud immediately, or there could be a problem.

O had pissed everyone off, but Twyla broke first. "Nigga, what the fuck is wrong wit' you? Is there some type of problem? You been on some bullshit ever since we been back. And where the fuck is the rest of our fuckin' money? All the workers said they turned in the usual to you, so we know yo' ass did some foul shit."

Stone faced, O just shrugged again. "Believe what you wanna believe."

The girls just looked at each other. Each of them felt the sting from that slap in the face. He wasn't even trying to defend himself. It seemed like he didn't give a rat's ass what they thought. They had been patient with O but he kept on pushing buttons. He was really trying them.

Twyla stood up and started pacing. She scoffed, "I believe you took that money 'cause we family, and you know we ain't gon' kill yo' ass! You try'na take advantage of this family shit, but don't sleep, nigga!"

Elle made a face and nodded in agreement. "Look, O, you straight disrespectin' us. Don't think shit sweet 'cause we bitches. Mothafucka, this is business, so you better give up some answers! We brought you out here, so don't *ever* try to play us. We all yo' ass got. We family, and we been try'na keep it on the up and up. But you start this sideways shit, and there'll be some consequences."

O laughed snidely at Elle's words. "Like *what*? What *consequences*?"

Needra was fuming too. She answered the question before Elle could. "Nigga, like we cut you the *fuck* off! Don't bite the hands that feed you!"

O screwed up his face. "Cut me *off*? Man, y'all think y'all queens, and shit. I ain't try'na work for y'all no way!

Fuck *all* y'all!"

Twyla barked, "Nigga, you wasn't saying that shit when you was begging us to put yo' ass on!"

He shrugged. "Word, you right, Big Cuz. But I don't need y'all for nothing else."

Elle cocked her head to the side and screw-faced him. "So what you sayin'?"

O's ego was puffed-up as hell. He stuck out his chest, and said, "Take it how you wanna take it, cuz."

Twyla got fed up and cussed that bastard out. "You little piece of dumb gutter shit! You gon' need us again, trust and believe. You ain't got nobody out here, fool!"

O hopped up and slapped his chest like he was tough. "I don't need *no* mo'fuckin' body! I'ma take over these fuckin' streets all alone! And anybody who get in my way gon' get *laid down*!"

Elle just shook her head. O was still the little wannabe who had followed Knight to Baltimore with pipe dreams. "You stupid nigga, this ain't television! You ain't Scarface!"

He angrily pounded his chest again. "I'm the *new* Scarface! The deadlier version! Who the fuck is *you*? None of y'all ain't shit! Got niggas callin' y'all HBIC! Head bitches in charge of *who*? Y'all bitches ain't in charge of *me*!"

Twyla nodded at him and chuckled for a few seconds. "Oh, so is that what this is about? You wanna be HBIC? Huh, you *bitch ass nigga*? This nigga wanna be the *head bitch in charge*. Wow!"

Upset by the truth dagger she hurled at him, O responded with the most disrespectful and inappropriate thing he could think of. "Fuck you, bitch! Suck my dick!"

That foul comment just lingered in the air for a second while the girls each had a "no he didn't" moment. Then the bull came out of Twyla. She yelled, "You little disrespectful faggot, I'ma fuck you up," and ran into O like a tornado. She was throwing some powerful punches; jabs, uppercuts, haymakers, and the whole nine. Twyla was a firecracker.

She hit hard like a man so O got pissed off and started fighting back. After that, Elle and Needra jumped in too. Twyla was holding her own but they weren't going to just stand there and let her fight a dude. Men were naturally stronger.

Before they knew it, they were all fighting like hell. O was wilding in there but he was no match for his three crazed cousins. They were all girls who fought like dudes. The four of them exchanged some serious heavyweight punches and continued scrapping until they were out of breath and panting.

Elle and Needra tried to subdue O by holding his arms. Twyla was still angry at him so she kept hitting him. He couldn't block her punches while they were holding him, so he got fed up.

Unable to take it anymore, O reached in the back of his waist and pulled out. He pointed his gun at Twyla, and growled, "Hit me one more fuckin' time, and I'ma pop yo' ass!"

Everybody just stopped and got quiet for a second. Things were getting carried away. Elle and Needra both said, "O, chill!"

Twyla didn't display any fear because she didn't believe he would shoot her. She had helped raise that little prick. She looked at O like he was crazy. "Nigga, you won't bust that little toy ass blickie! I'll shove that shit up yo ass!"

O was livid that she had spoken to him that way. He bit his lip angrily and snarled, "I'm tellin' you, bitch, I'll put you in a body bag!" He cocked the gun and pointed it at her face.

Elle said, "O, chill, 'fore that shit go off! Don't point that shit at my sister like that! Put that damn gun away!"

Twyla was insanely bold. She kept on talking shit. "Go on and use it, nigga! Because if I make it to my .45 over there, I'ma give you a whole new asshole!"

Needra was quiet but she tiptoed over to her purse to get her heat. She cocked it and aimed at O to get his attention, and then she tried reasoning with him. "Look, O,

we all family so ain't no need for all this. Please put that gun down. *Please*."

O didn't respond at first. He just kept screw-facing Twyla with his firearm trained on her.

Needra pleaded with him. "O, I'm *begging* you. We cousins. Please don't make me shoot you!"

Elle stood there praying they would all calm down. Their grandmother was probably turning over in her grave about them carrying on that way. That didn't make any sense. And they were just going at it over money. It was really the root of all evil. They were in there about to kill each other.

Elle said, "Y'all cut it out! Please! Grandma probably crying tears in heaven right now! Stop it!"

She got through to O with those words. He snapped out of it and lowered his weapon. Relieved, Needra lowered hers as well.

O didn't say another word to them. He just put his gun away and walked out, slamming the door behind him.

$$$

The girls called Gee later that day and spoke to him about Olan's behavior. Gee wasn't even that surprised. He told them the last time he had seen O, he was talking all tough and crazy. He said he thought he was Nino Brown, and shit.

Gee said he didn't want to be affiliated with O when he crashed and burned, and made it clear that his views were different. He wasn't on that power tripping shit. He would rather maintain alliances.

That night the trio passed around a blunt and had a discussion about their wayward cousin. It was ironic how he had come down there to "protect them." He had convinced them that they needed people they could trust, and now they couldn't trust him. O's problem was that he was greedy, and wanted mothafuckas to be afraid of him. He would rather be feared than loved.

It broke the girls' hearts but they predicted that O's thought process was going to get him taken out the game. They just prayed they wouldn't have to be the ones to do it.

Chapter 15

A few weeks went by, and things didn't get any better. They only got worse. O was completely out of control. Now he was on some cutthroat shit. He was competing with them by selling his own shit right underneath their noses. The trio felt especially disrespected because they had put him on.

Someone told them he said "fuck them bitches, I'm out for self." Another person said he told them he didn't fuck with HBIC anymore, and had bragged about having better product and prices than theirs. Talking shit about them was one thing, but badmouthing their dope was a whole new violation. He was trying to take food out of their mouths. O's "family pass" was running out fast.

That dude had turned into a real snake. He was really digging to get a reaction from them. Anything he could do to ruffle their feathers, he did. He even robbed two of their workers. Unmasked!

That was the straw that broke the camel's back. The girls couldn't take that one lightly. They had a meeting to discuss O's fate. They faced a particularly tough dilemma because he was family. They shared the same blood but he had to be dealt with. To not react was to display weakness. O needed to be spanked.

Needra got so fed up with the situation, she said, "Maybe we just need to go on and take this nigga out."

Twyla nodded in agreement. "Hell yeah! We the ones who put him *in* the game out here, so we *should* take that bitch ass nigga out. I can't take that mothafucka no more! He gotta go!"

As usual, Elle was the voice of reason. She shook her head, and said, "As great as that may sound, let's not forget - this fat fuck is our first cousin. We can't just kill him, and then send him home for the family to bury him. He's our aunt's child. That's our fathers' *sister*. Come on, y'all."

"So what *you* got in mind, Elle?"

Elle didn't respond because she didn't have a solution. A part of her agreed with her partners because O was really a pain in the ass. He was interfering with their cash flow with all the bullshit he was doing. But that bastard was family.

Then it came to her. She said, "We ain't gotta do nothing, y'all."

Her partners looked at her like she had three heads, so Elle explained her reasoning. "Y'all, that dumb mothafucka O is out here *wide open*. He's being all careless, and shit, try'na out-hustle us, so it's just a matter of time before he gon' fuck his self up." She nodded her head for reinforcement. "Watch."

Elle made sense so it was hard for the other two thirds to dispute what she said. But Twyla and Needra weren't completely convinced. They didn't want to slay their own flesh and blood but he was behaving like he had a death wish. They couldn't allow him to mess up what they had going.

The girls all looked around at each other. They needed to make a decision before their rebellious cousin did any more damage. Their next move was crucial.

Needra said, "But what's next? That nigga done pulled out on us! What we gon' do, wait until he hurts one of *us*? That nigga don't give a fuck about *nobody*! To get this money, he'll throw us under a bus *and* in front of a bullet! The way I see it, O is a threat to our safety. We gon' have to kill this mothafucka. Y'all might as well accept it. We don't got no choice."

Faced with the truth, Elle was forced to grasp reality. They had to react. They'd been backed into a corner. "So who we gon' get to handle this," she asked.

Twyla looked at her, and said, "We gon' do this shit ourselves. That way we can keep it a secret. I know *we* would never tell on each other, but who else can we trust like that?"

"Nobody," Elle and Needra said in unison.

"Exactly! Now let's come up with a plan. Put your thinking caps on, bitches. We gotta do this shit right so it don't come back and bite us in our asses."

$$$

The following day the trio got up early. They had devised what they considered a master plan. All they had to do now was complete their mission.

It was so early it was still black outside. The girls were all dressed in dark colors and incognito in a hooptie they had borrowed from this money hungry but cool smoking chick named Jackie. It was a big old rusty black Cadillac that belonged to her mother. The car had seen better days but would serve the purpose they had in mind just fine.

Twyla was driving as usual, and Needra rode shotgun. She was literally holding one in her lap too. It was a 12-gauge shotgun with a pistol grip. They had purchased it the day before, right over the counter. The plan was to use it to blast a hole in O's chest. They had decided to do a drive-by on him in a car nobody recognized. Needra would be the designated shooter.

Elle sat in the back seat in complete silence. The guilt from the atrocity they were conspiring to commit was overwhelming. It was haunting her before they even did the do. Her conscious was gnawing away at her soul. She couldn't believe what they had planned. They were on their way to kill their brother. O was their blood.

For the tenth time since they pulled off, Elle started to protest, but decided to keep her mouth shut. The other two thirds thought it was best, and the majority ruled. She closed her eyes briefly and said another silent prayer. She had a feeling she wasn't the only one in the car who kept doing

that. They all knew better. The Ten Commandments had been drilled in their heads as children. *Thou shall not kill.*

Elle reflected over the past months and years back to a time and place when they were younger. It was all so simple then. But the innocence of yesteryear was long gone. The money had managed to rip their beautiful family bond to shreds. Shit had gotten real ugly. Their hearts had been so hardened by the game they were ready to take each other's lives.

Elle kept hearing her father's voice. *"Y'all working for Satan..."* Pop was right. Look what the devil had them about to do. It was reprehensible.

She reminisced back to when she and Olan were just sixteen and fifteen years old. When he had fled Baltimore seeking solace from her ex, Knight, he had trusted her with his life, and then cried to her like a frightened child. She had been there to comfort him and pray with him.

Twyla and Needra had looked out for O a lot too. They all had their whole lives. Now they were ready to administer his death. What had become of them?

Silent tears rolled down Elle's face and clouded her vision. Inside her head, she screamed, *"Turn the car around! Let's call it off!"* She just couldn't bring herself to voice this. She looked at her partners in the front. They appeared melancholy as well. They probably didn't want to do it anymore than she did.

Elle heard her father's voice again. *"The bible say "No weapons formed shall prosper."* They had formed a lynch mob for their cousin. What good would come of that?

In the front, Twyla and Needra were going over the last minute details of their plan. Their strategy involved posing as potential customers and luring O to the car.

Twyla said, "Needra, I'ma pull up and roll the window down a little bit. Just disguise your voice and holler *'who got that good boy?'* I guarantee you his thirsty ass gon' come running to the car try'na get the sale."

Needra took it from there. "Yup, and when he step up, I'ma just blast that nigga in the chest. Close range. Then

you just pull off. Nobody will ever guess it was us."

Elle noted that Needra was pretty calm for a would-be assassin. And so was her sister. She was in the car with some cold bitches. They were in too deep.

Elle looked at the street sign and realized they were only about two minutes away from their target. She was moved to try reasoning with her partners one last time. "Listen, y'all, I'm having second thoughts."

Needra said, "Elle, actually you're having third thoughts. I thought we talked about this."

"It just don't feel right, Neej! His blood will be on our hands forever."

"Would you rather ours be on his? He pulled out on us, and did everything else he could think of to initiate this war! Now it's our move!"

"Okay, so he pulled out on us. Y'all know we grew up seeing that shit all the time in our family. We thought our fathers and uncles were fuckin' cowboys when we were little! They pulled out on each other lots of times, but they never killed each other."

Needra said, "Elle, you dead ass right. But when this type of money is at stake, it's a whole different ballgame. I got a feeling O is gon' try to knock us off. What else is it gon' come to? We can't just accept that nigga robbing us, and shit!"

Twyla knew Elle had a soft heart. She said, "Baby sis, I understand how you feel, but we gotta do what we gotta do."

"Whatever you say, sis. Just know that it's gonna really be a task trying to live with that. O is our cousin. Don't think we gon' just be able to forget about this shit." As an afterthought, Elle added, "And he also killed that nigga Freddie Mack for us."

Needra said, "And we thanked him for that, and then gave him the opportunity of a lifetime. And he blew it! O started this shit, we ain't the bad guys! Fuck that, when we turn this corner, it's going down! You ready, Twyla?"

"It's now or never, Needra."

Elle realized there was nothing else she could say, so she prayed for God to forgive them.

They sat at a red light waiting to turn the corner, and Needra got the weapon in position. The light changed and Twyla hit the gas. They drove towards the dope strip with clear intent. It was time to kill.

The girls spotted O as soon as they rolled up. Just as they figured, he was up and out early to catch the morning rush. That part didn't surprise them. But the three of them were astonished by the rest of the scene they were met with.

There were four police cars out there with their lights flashing. O was surrounded by pigs that were in the process of placing him under arrest. They got there just in time to see them place the cuffs on him. The trio's mouths hung open in surprise.

Elle remembered they had that 12-gauge in the car, so she said, "Wow. Just keep on driving, sis. Keep it steady, don't speed up."

Needra carefully put the shotty under her seat, and Twyla kept her cool and drove right pass the police. She kept going until they were back on the freeway safely en route to their hotel.

They would later learn that O had been arrested for making a sale to an undercover cop. Elle didn't know about her sisters, but she was grateful to God. O's getting locked up had blocked them from doing something they would've regretted for the rest of their lives. That was Divine Intervention at its finest. If O had known how he'd literally just dodged a bullet, he would have thanked God too.

Elle was in pretty high spirits about the change of plans, until Twyla voiced concern over something that was on her mind. She said, "What if that nigga O starts running his mouth and snitch on us? How we know he ain't gon' start talking?"

Elle and Needra didn't respond, but the possibility had crossed their minds as well. They weren't on good terms, and O had already proved that he was out for self. What assurance did they have that he wouldn't give them up

to save himself?

To be continued…

Coming Soon From Synergy Publications...

HBIC - Head Bitch In Charge
Volume II
"Hell on Heels"

"Another Day...Another Dollar"
A series of "A Dollar Outta Fifteen Cent" Novellas

By Caroline McGill

For Info...

Email the author at CarolineMcGill160@msn.com

Or call (718) 930-8818

Join Caroline McGill on ...

Facebook at facebook.com/caroline.mcgill.142

Twitter at twitter.com/CAROLINEMCGILL

A snippet from…

A Dollar Outta Fifteen Cent
Part 5

"A Little Bit of Change"

The EMTs arrived on the scene and quickly whisked Cas away from the chaotic scene at he and Laila's destroyed wedding reception. Sirens blaring, they sped towards the hospital. Inside the ambulance, Cas was in and out of consciousness. He kept on forgetting where he was. He wasn't sure if the paramedics gave him something or he was dying.

Cas kept hearing Jay and his mother's voices in the distance. They were telling him to hold on. He wanted to but it was getting harder and harder to keep his eyes open. He was slipping into darkness. And it was getting harder to breathe. Cas was gasping for air.

Before he knew it, he drifted into a deep slumber. The next thing he knew he was floating. A flash of light appeared and then his new wife, Laila, was there. They were standing on opposite sides of a huge field of full of pretty colorful flowers. They were calling each other's names but couldn't seem to get across the field to touch each other. The closer they moved towards each other, the further apart they winded up. It seemed like the field was growing wider and wider. It was really weird.

Suddenly the flowers in the field began to wilt and die all around them. The dew drops on the petals turned crimson red and the sky turned dark gray. Then Cas realized that Laila was wearing a blood stained dress and she was crying her heart out. She turned and ran away from him. Cas

went after her but she just disappeared like she had evaporated into thin air.

He stopped short because he saw a rainbow in the distance. It was surrounded by the bluest sky he'd ever seen. There was something about it that beckoned him towards it. Drawn to its beauty, he smiled at it welcomingly. Cas wondered if that was heaven. It was breathtaking. Serenity at its peak.

Inside the ambulance right by Cas' side, Jay and Ms. B sat watching every move the paramedics made and praying nonstop for his wellbeing. Both were terrified and desperately holding on to their faith. Their prayers were identical. God had to spare Cas' life.

Ms. B had tears streaming down her face. She was holding her son's hand and going down memory lane. Caseem was her only child. Flashbacks of his childhood ran through her mind vividly like a full color slideshow. She pictured the day he was born. And then his first birthday and his first steps. His first fall off his first bike, his first day at school, his first girlfriend, and his first car. The first time he went to prison, when his first child was born … Lord, reminiscing was painful. She had been a single mother almost his whole life so Cas was all she had.

She squeezed his hand and prayed he would make it. "Come on, Caseem, I need you to pull through, baby," she emotionally told her unconscious son. She was a mother in tears trying to will him to fight to live. Cas had always been a fighter. "Your mama needs you, baby boy. Come on, you all I got."

Listening to his wounded comrade's mother's anxious pleas, Jay's heart was broken also. He sat there having flashbacks of his own. He saw him and Cas slap boxing and wrestling as nine year-old kids. That was his ace. His number one crimie. He had to make it. Jay was so worried he kept asking the paramedics for an update every three seconds. He was willing to let a lot of things go in life but Cas was not one of them. That dude was a part of him.

He was the brother he never had. Life without him was unimaginable.

He looked at Cas and saw that his eyes were closed. That scared him even more. "*Please* God," Jay prayed aloud, "Bring my man through. Only You got the power to do so, so *please God.*"

Just then, one of those funny machines they had hooked up to Casino started beeping and blinking. The paramedics moved quickly to aid him. They were speaking in medical jargon that Jay and Ms. B didn't comprehend but they got out of the way so they could do their jobs.

Hearts racing, Casino's best man and his mother were both on the verge of cardiac arrest waiting for the outcome. They tried to be optimistic but they knew whatever just happened couldn't have been good. Exasperated, they squeezed hands and sat there helpless and praying for Cas' survival. He had to make it. Their family needed him. All of them did.

Meanwhile, Cas was literally having an out of body experience. His soul ascended from his dying body and he stood there looking down at himself laying there while the paramedics fussed over him. They were doing everything they could to save him.

"What the fuck ...? Yo, what's going on," Cas mumbled to himself. He didn't like the sight of him laying there lifeless. It frightened him to say the least. He prayed he was dreaming and tried not to panic. Damn, he wondered what happened. Whatever it was, it looked bad. He tried to tell his mother and Jay that he was okay but they couldn't seem to hear him or see him.

He looked down at his attire and realized he was wearing a custom tailored black suit with no blood on it. He ran his hand over his chest. He looked okay and felt fine. Casino wondered if he was bugging. Confused, his soul moved on.

The next thing he knew, he was looking down on a luxury car that was speeding down the highway. He could see the vehicle's occupants' faces as clear as day. He

zoomed in on the one that belonged to his new bride first. Laila was sitting in the backseat in tears. Portia was sitting beside her and comforting her. Wise was driving and Fatima was riding in the passenger seat. Everybody looked real upset. Their eyes were all swollen and red. Cas yelled to them that he was fine but no one could hear him there either. That was starting to bother him.

Casino's wandering soul moved on. He had to find his children. Suddenly he was looking down on his son. Jahseim was with his grandmother, Mama Mitchell. She was hugging him and telling him everything was going to be okay. She had all of the children with her. There was his baby Skye, Wise's daughter Falynn, and Jay and Portia's little girls, Jazz and Trixie. They all looked teary eyed too.

Cas was baffled until he saw his stepdaughter, Macy. She was knelt on the floor crying over what looked like a body that was covered by a tablecloth or something. Jayquan and her grandmother, Mama Atkins, were hovering over her. Cas noticed that Macy's grandmother was also weeping. Lil' Jay was comforting both of them like a gentleman.

Casino realized then what had happened. Everything came back to him with a jolt. He and Laila had just gotten married and then he'd been shot by her crazy ex-husband. He was usually armed but that nigga Khalil caught him slipping on his wedding day. The bullet he took to the chest had punctured his right lung.

Cas guessed that sheet covered body on the floor was Khalil. He looked over on the other side of the table at the spot where he laid shot and bleeding waiting on the paramedics. There was a small pool of blood on the floor. That had to belong to him.

The events leading up to the shooting began to replay in his head.

The wedding had turned out lovely. He and Laila had both been happy because it had been a success. They had tied the knot. Afterwards, they all headed to the reception, where Laila resurfaced in another bad ass dress that was equally stunning compared to her wedding gown, but a little

more revealing. They had all eaten and then Jay had
proposed a toast to him and Laila's future. It was just about
time for their last dance. Right after that was when that lame
Khalil showed up and serenaded them with bullets. Cas
remembered quickly moving to cover Laila, who was sitting
on his lap at the time. He took a slug to the chest in the
process.

He looked down at poor Mama Atkins. The weeping
woman had lost her son because of that nonsense. Just
because that dude couldn't move on. That didn't make any
sense.

Cas looked down at his body in the back of that
ambulance. He wasn't breathing but they were working hard
trying to revive him. Jay was sitting by him holding his
mother, who was crying just like Mama Atkins. Would she
lose her son because of that nonsense as well?

At that moment Cas had an unwelcomed epiphany.
Wow, was he fucking dead? Panic set in as he grasped his
situation. He realized exactly how afraid he was, and blurted
out, "Oh shit!" He was starting to feel defeated. Lord, he
wasn't ready to go. He had a lot to do and a lot of people
depending on him. He had kids who needed him. His mother
and Laila did too.

Cas knew it was time for a change. Just hours before
he was shot, he had promised God that he was turning over a
new leaf. And he meant what he had said. He was sorry
about killing Jay's trifling baby mother Ysatis for him, and
all the other dirt he had done as well. But could his
repentance be a little bit too late? God had to give him
another chance…

"A Dollar Outta Fifteen Cent

Part 5

A Little Bit of Change"

Fall, 2012

Synergy ✚ Publications

www.SynergyPublications.com

Books You Can't Put Down!!

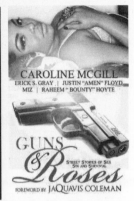

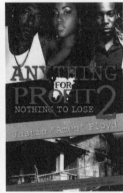

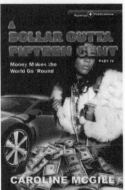

Available wherever books are sold!

Thoughts About the Book

Order Form
Synergy Publications
P.O. Box 210-987 Brooklyn, NY 11221
www.SynergyPublications.com

_____ A Dollar Outta Fifteen Cent	$14.95
_____ A Dollar Outta Fifteen Cent II: Money Talks… Bullsh*t Walks	$14.95
_____ A Dollar Outta Fifteen Cent III: Mo' Money… Mo' Problems	$14.95
_____ A Dollar Outta Fifteen Cent IV: Money Makes the World Go 'Round	$14.95
_____ Sex as a Weapon	$14.95
_____ Guns & Roses: *Street Stories of Sex, Sin, and Survival*	$14.95